THE GHOST ON THE BEACH

Scarlett Dunn Books

Historical Novels

Promises Kept

Finding Promise

Last Promise

Christmas at Dove Creek

Whispering Pines

Return to Whispering Pines

Christmas in Whispering Pines

Christmas Novella - Christmas Road

Mystery Novels

Murder on the Bluegrass Bourbon Train

Masquerade and Murder at Bourbon Ball

The Ghost on the Beach

THE GHOST ON THE BEACH

WHO KILLED ELEANOR MARLOWE?

SCARLETT DUNN

The Ghost On The Beach

Lone Dove Publishing

For more information about this author please visit: www.scarlettdunn.com

Cover Design by Elizabeth Mackey
Interior Design by Creative Publishing Book Design

eBook: ISBN: 978-1-7331796-7-6
Paperback ISBN: 978-1-7331796-6-9

To Morgan—the greatest person I know (but I haven't met Bigfoot). Because of you, the days are sunnier, the stars are brighter, and love is never-ending.

To Michael—you'll never realize what an inspiration you are to so many. We never know where our paths will lead but are forever grateful to those who help light the way.

CHAPTER ONE

Who Killed Eleanor Marlowe?

Who killed me?

And why?

I had no enemies. But that can't be true. Someone hated me enough to kill me.

Every night, I walk alone on this quiet stretch of beach, asking the same questions over and over. Still, I have no answers. This nagging feeling persists, telling me that I should remember—something. At times, I think the answers lurk in the dark recesses of my mind, teasing me—haunting me.

What was the killer's motive? Why do people kill? Could it have been a random act? Maybe some deranged person just wanted to kill—someone—anyone, and I was in the wrong place at the wrong time. I didn't see anyone commit a criminal act. I didn't owe anyone money. I've never been into drugs. I had no spouse—no one who would collect a large sum of money upon my death. I was a normal person with a normal life.

Will I ever know the answers?

Like the lips of a sensuous lover, the gentle breeze caresses my skin. Do I feel the sensation, or is it just a memory? I don't know.

Either way, it's a sad reminder that I will never have the one thing I wanted most—that one great love—someone to grow old with, to hold at night—feel the warmth of their skin beneath my fingers, to say I love you as I look into their eyes—to fall asleep in their arms.

I want to feel someone's heartbeat. I can't feel my own.

I'm here, but I'm not.

Before my death, I walked on the beach at this time of night when the sky and horizon merged into nothingness—the moon casting its silvery reflection on the water like a pathway leading straight to heaven. This beach was always my refuge. I could solve any problem as I walked.

Now, I can't solve the one thing I need to know—I must know. Who killed me?

This beach is now my prison.

I was never lonely here.

I'm lonely now.

I must be dreaming.

I can't be dead.

Moving was almost as bad as getting shot. At least, it was one of the top five things that Steele Harper dreaded the most. Tilting the dolly loaded with his refrigerator, Steele pushed it down the ramp of the U-Haul. He narrated said list in descending order to his two buddies who were helping him move. "*Being shot—moving—talking about my feelings—answering dumbass questions—shopping with a woman.*" Silently, he amended his list. Moving should move into the third or fourth spot since today it wasn't a dreaded chore, thanks to his new home—his little slice of heaven right on the beach. He vowed this would be his last move. *They will cart my dead, rotting carcass off in a box from this place. This is home. Forever.*

Three years prior, Steele inherited the property from his grandfather, and he'd rented it during the vacation seasons until he was prepared to make a career change. The small modern bungalow-style home was tucked away in a secluded area on Siesta Key Beach. Fortunately, Steele enjoyed remodeling, and he'd spent every free hour working on the interior for months before he scheduled his moving date. He'd removed walls, painted the remaining walls, and completely renovated the kitchen and master bedroom. Improving the exterior was next on his agenda. The bungalow wasn't a showplace like the newer McMansions doting the coastline, but he didn't have a mortgage.

The property was less than a quarter of an acre, with lush, tropical vegetation shielding one side of the house. Sand, six palm trees, and a dilapidated sand fence separated him from the neighboring bungalow. The neighbor's house was similar in size, but the exterior had been updated, and Steele was curious to see what changes they'd made to the interior.

"Hey, Steele, where do you want this table?" Tom yelled from the doorway.

"Hang on. I'm coming," Steele pushed the refrigerator in place and peeked around the corner to see Morgan and Tom maneuvering the massive live edge table through the doorway. He pointed to the dining area. "It goes under the chandelier. You girls need any help?"

"Help? From you? I don't know how you even made this thing; you're so weak," Tom replied.

Steele flexed his biceps. "They don't call me the man of steel for no reason."

Morgan and Tom laughed as they situated the table in the designated spot.

Steele pulled three beers from the cooler sitting on the kitchen counter. "Time for a break."

Tom caught the beer sailing through the air and popped the top. "This is a nice-looking table."

"Yeah, nice and heavy. Do you have one piece of furniture that doesn't weigh five hundred pounds?" Morgan asked, snagging the can Steele tossed him.

Chuckling, Steele said, "I want pieces that will last my lifetime."

Tom looked around the room. "Every piece you've made looks great in here. Just so you know, I'm putting in my order for a coffee table in exchange for my free labor. I like that live edge look."

Steele grinned at him. "That's a fair trade. I appreciate your help."

"I like what you've done with the place. Removing those walls makes the place appear ten times larger," Morgan said.

"Replacing those old sliding doors with the bi-fold doors made the biggest difference. I got the idea from the house next door."

"Yeah, that place looks great. Have you been inside yet?" Tom asked.

"No. I've seen a woman over there a few times, but I haven't had a chance to meet her." Of course, that wasn't exactly true. Each time he'd caught a glimpse of the woman walking from the beach, he was wearing sawdust from head to toe. He didn't want to look like a bum when he met a beautiful woman—assuming she was beautiful.

"Is she older . . . young . . . married . . . attractive?" Tom asked.

Steele grinned at him. "What? You think you're a detective or something?"

"This is information you need to know about your neighbors. I mean, you don't want a crazy living next door."

"Some private eye you are, Steele. I can't believe you haven't checked her out," Morgan teased.

Steele narrowed his eyes at Morgan. "I prefer private investigator."

CHAPTER TWO

Brownies?

Steele walked over to the window that faced his neighbor. The woman they were discussing was walking from the beach, wearing a big floppy hat and a long, flowing pink bathing suit cover-up. Every time he'd seen her, she was wearing a hat. Just once, he'd like to see her face. He watched her, observing the way she moved—leisurely as if she didn't have a care in the world. He turned to Morgan and Tom and said, "There she is now."

Morgan and Tom exchanged a look, and like two high school boys fighting to be first in the cafeteria line to grab the last slice of pizza, they raced to the window.

Steele laughed at them. "Too late. She just walked inside."

Tom elbowed Steele in the ribs. "You did that on purpose so we couldn't see her."

"I bet she's a looker, and he doesn't want any competition," Morgan said.

"Why don't we invite her over when we order pizza?" Tom suggested.

Morgan snorted. "What woman in her right mind would come over here with three men she doesn't know to eat pizza and drink beer?"

Steele nodded his agreement. "Good point. I think I'll wait until I get the place finished before I invite the neighbors over."

Tom laughed. "Let me know if you want me to check her out."

Steele was curious about his neighbor. He hadn't seen any men around, leading him to believe she was single. "Did you forget I'm a private investigator? I can check her out."

"Admit it, Steele; you miss working with us," Morgan said.

"Not on your life. I don't miss the aggravation of the hierarchy in the police department. I'm not politically correct." He did miss the camaraderie with his friends, but it was a small price to pay for his independence. He could see his friends on the weekends. Now, he called the shots and worked on cases that interested him. His preference was finding missing people. Most of the time, the work was rewarding, and it was a bonus that he'd made more money in the last year than he had in the prior five years. "You two should turn in your badge and work with me. I'm turning down business right now because I don't have the time to do justice to all the cases."

"I'm tempted, Steele. To be honest, I wish I had left the force when you did," Morgan said.

Tom nodded. "Yeah. Keep your offer open for a while."

Crushing his beer can, Steele said, "Let me know when you're ready to leave Miami. Now, finish your beers, and let's get this over with so we can order dinner. I'm starving."

"You're always hungry," Tom said.

Morgan gulped his beer and slapped Steele on the back. "You need a woman to get your mind off of food."

"Until you find one, you can always talk about your feelings with us," Tom joked.

"Yeah, I can't believe that was number three on your list, Steele. I would rather get shot than *talk about my feelings*. That's number one on my hit parade," Morgan said.

"Does that pizza place have brownies?" Steele asked, his mind remaining on food.

Morgan grinned at him. "I think they have some kind of large chocolate chip cookie. I'll ask when I place our order."

Thirty minutes later, Morgan was carrying the last chair through the door when he heard a car in the driveway. "The pizza guy is pulling up."

Grabbing his wallet from the counter, Steele headed outside. After paying for the three extra-large, all-meat pizzas, Steele noticed a small basket by the front door. He called out to the pizza guy, "Did you leave this basket here?"

The delivery man shook his head. "No, that was there when I walked up."

Balancing the pizzas in one hand, Steele picked up the basket and carried it inside.

Morgan and Tom had beers waiting on the table, along with some paper plates and napkins. They tore open the pizza boxes as soon as Steele dropped them on the counter.

Steele set the basket on the table. "This was by the front door." He removed the red and white checkered cloth napkin covering the contents of the basket. "Well, I can't believe it! It's brownies." Grabbing one brownie, he shoved it in his mouth. "They're still warm." After he swallowed, he said, "That's the best brownie I've ever had."

"Where did they come from? Are you sure you should eat that?" Tom asked.

Steele grinned at him. "Too late now."

Morgan pointed to the basket. "There's a note."

Steele grabbed the card and read, "Welcome to the neighborhood."

"It has to be from the woman next door since that's your closest neighbor," Tom said as he pulled out a huge slice of pizza.

"I didn't hear anyone at the door," Steele replied.

"Maybe she didn't want to interrupt us. We should've invited her over for pizza. But now you have a reason to go next door and thank her in person," Morgan said.

Tom chewed his mouthful of pizza, then said, "She's probably an older woman if she's baking. Probably has grandkids."

Morgan shrugged. "Who cares? Those brownies look delicious."

"Wonder how she knew you wanted brownies, Steele? You sure you haven't met her?" Tom asked.

"No, I haven't met her. It's just a coincidence."

Morgan and Tom exchanged a look.

Reading their thoughts, Steele said, "Yeah, I know. There are no coincidences."

CHAPTER THREE

Reflecting Time

2:00 a.m.

Steele saw the time reflected on his bedroom ceiling in large orange numbers, thanks to the housewarming gift from Morgan and Tom. They told him he wouldn't have to fumble for his watch or his phone to see the time in the middle of the night. Hell, he didn't even have to turn his head. It was the perfect gift from two detectives who shared the same problem—waking at odd hours and rehashing cases they couldn't solve. While Steele didn't like his sleep being interrupted, he often did his best thinking when the world was quiet. No distractions. But he was tired tonight, and he didn't want to think. Turning over, he covered his head with his pillow and closed his eyes. Within seconds, his eyes snapped open again, and he flopped on his back. *Damn.*

2:02 a.m.

He closed his eyes. Nope. Not happening.

He got out of bed, pulled on his boxers, and headed to the kitchen.

Since Morgan and Tom were occupying the two additional bedrooms, he didn't want to turn on the television and disturb them.

He opened his refrigerator, pulled out a bottle of water, walked to his new bi-fold glass doors, and pulled them open. He decided he'd sit on the patio and listen to the ocean. *This should be relaxing*. He plopped down on a lounge chair, opened his water, and took a gulp. He glanced at his neighbor's house and saw light filtering through the blinds from what he assumed was the master bedroom. While he'd been remodeling his house, he'd sit on the patio each night, and the same light was always on at her house. He was still looking at the window when the silhouette of a woman appeared. The thought crossed his mind that she might be afflicted with similar sleeping problems. When the woman moved away from the window, Steele's gaze shifted to the beach. The sound of waves gently lapping at the shore relaxed him. It was a great place to think.

One of his cases was keeping him awake tonight. *Amy Carson*. Amy was twelve years old but small for her age. On a beautiful, sunny day, she rode her bike to an ice cream shop in a local strip mall. Her bright pink bicycle was found later that afternoon behind the mall. No one remembered seeing the petite blond girl who was wearing a pink blouse dotted with white hearts, pink shorts, and pink tennis shoes. That was a year ago, and Amy hadn't been seen since. The police had no leads, and the case was cold, which meant it received little attention.

Amy's parents hired him last month to look into the case. The grieving mother told him that pink was her daughter's favorite color. Steele kept a picture of Amy in his wallet. He didn't have to pull it out to remember every detail of her delicate little face; bright blue eyes, a bow mouth, and a pointed chin. A lovely child.

Steele recognized the signs of another case becoming personal. He'd never understood how anyone could harm a child, and he couldn't prevent cases like Amy's from turning into an obsession. Her case was particularly difficult for him. Someone whisked this child away in a well-traveled area, and he had no clues and no leads. He didn't know what he was going to do next, but he wouldn't quit—that word wasn't in his vocabulary.

"Can't sleep, huh?" Morgan asked as he plopped down in a chair next to Steele.

"Yeah, but on the bright side, I saw the time on the ceiling."

Morgan chuckled. "I have the same clock, and I love it."

"I was thinking about Amy Carson's case. I don't have one lead."

"That one is a real puzzle. This is one of those cases that will drive you crazy."

"That's the truth. I'd like to know how a little girl can get kidnapped in broad daylight from a place with a lot of foot traffic and no one sees a thing."

Morgan leaned forward, bracing his elbows on his knees, and sighed. "You know, Steele, a year is a long time. I don't have to tell you those cases generally don't have happy endings."

"Yeah, I know. For once, I'd like to find that happy ending. I can't imagine being a parent and going through something like that. I don't know how they do it."

"There was no divorce? No irate spouse?"

"No. They're a happy couple. Been married for twenty-something years. By all accounts, they are salt-of-the-earth people. Can't find one negative thing about either one."

"And no one saw anything? Nothing reported at the time?"

"I talked to the detective who handled the case and read all of the notes. Nothing. One officer told me that he thought a woman called around the same time Amy was taken and reported something suspicious happened in the mall involving a little girl, but there's no paperwork to back that up. Nothing to go on."

"What's your next move?"

Steele shook his head. "I have no idea."

CHAPTER FOUR

Rock, Paper, Scissors

Just after dawn, Eleanor Marlowe watched her new neighbor swimming in the ocean. His long, strong strokes made the exercise appear effortless as he glided through the water. For weeks she'd observed him coming and going as he was renovating his home. Considering his muscular physique, she wondered if construction was his profession.

She thought it would be a welcome change to have a permanent neighbor instead of vacationers who were only there for one or two weeks. She wouldn't miss the loud music, or the people partying until the wee hours of the morning, not to mention picking up the beer bottles left in the sand. Even if she didn't meet her new neighbor, it would be nice to have someone she could wave to on occasion. She couldn't explain it, but just having a full-time resident next door was somehow—comforting.

Steele showered off outside, and he caught a whiff of bacon frying. At first, he thought it might be coming from his neighbor's house, but when he walked inside, he saw Tom standing at his new gas range. Morgan was sitting at the counter, nursing a cup of coffee.

Steele grabbed the coffee pot and filled a cup. "That bacon smells good."

"Steele, I didn't think you liked to cook," Tom said.

"I don't. Why?"

"The way you outfitted this kitchen, one would think you were a professional chef."

"One of these days, I might find a woman who likes to cook, and I'll marry her," Steele joked. He reached for the last brownie in the basket.

"Hey, split that with me," Morgan said.

"Don't spoil your breakfast. I'm cooking bacon and eggs," Tom told them.

"Yes, mom." Steele broke off a quarter of the brownie and handed it to Morgan.

Morgan looked at the small offering and frowned. "You ate seven out of twelve already."

"Yeah. But I'm the only one who worked off calories this morning." He shoved the remaining three-quarters of the brownie in his mouth.

After cooking a dozen eggs and twenty-four slices of bacon, Tom loaded the three plates and placed them on the counter.

While they ate, Tom said, "After you two went to bed last night, I saw a few people walking on the beach after midnight."

"I've seen a woman walking late at night several times," Steele said. "But Morgan and I were sitting on the patio after 2:00 a.m., and there wasn't a soul out there."

"After I finish eating, I'll take the basket back to your neighbor, and thank her for you, Steele. I'll let you two know what she looks like," Tom said.

"No way. I'm going over there. Everyone knows women like me the best," Morgan replied.

"She's my neighbor, and I'm taking the basket back," Steele said.

Tom shook his head. "It was my idea, and I'm going."

Dropping his fork onto the plate, Morgan looked at them and said, "Let's settle this right now. Rock, paper, scissors."

Steele's fork clanked to the counter. "Rock, paper, scissors, it is."

Tom dusted off his hands like he was preparing to arm wrestle. "Let's go."

Morgan laughed as Steele and Tom moaned about losing. "You guys never learn." He gulped the remainder of his coffee and stood. "I gotta go brush my teeth and comb my hair. This is gonna be fun."

"How does he beat us every time?" Tom grumbled.

Steele shrugged. "The luck of the Irish, I guess."

Tom frowned. "Is he Irish?"

Morgan tossed the empty basket on the kitchen counter. "She's not home."

Tom laughed. "Serves you right since it was my idea in the first place."

Steele glanced out the window. "I saw her on the porch just before you walked over there."

"I knocked several times and heard music, but no one answered. The doors were open and I peeked inside."

"She was probably afraid you were a Peeping Tom. Maybe you should have shaved before you left," Tom teased, then added, "I wonder why they call it a Peeping Tom. Why not a Peeping George or a Peeping Morgan?"

Laughing, Steele said, "Good question."

"Anyway, Morgan, you do resemble that serial killer we arrested a few years ago," Tom said.

Morgan scratched his two-day-old beard. "There is that. Her place is beautiful. I bet a designer charged her a pretty penny. You know, light colors and all soft and cozy looking. A woman definitely lives there."

Tom rolled his eyes. "Yeah, we've already established that fact, Sherlock Holmes."

"I bet she's not married. I didn't see any guy stuff."

"When you meet her, Steele, you should tell her she shouldn't leave her doors open if she's not there. By the way, what's her name?" Tom asked.

"I have no idea."

CHAPTER FIVE
Poleaxed

Later that afternoon, after Morgan and Tom left, Steele started to grab a beer from his refrigerator when he noticed the basket on the counter. *Why not?* Forgetting the beer, he decided to take a quick shower and put on some clothes that weren't decorated with paint.

Dressed and ready to leave, he ran back into his bathroom and sprayed on a little cologne. He always received compliments from women when he wore Mont Blanc. Returning to the kitchen, he snagged the basket off the counter and walked out the door.

Nearing his neighbor's house, he heard music through the open bi-fold doors. He jumped up on the patio and tapped on the glass. Within seconds, the woman he'd seen at a distance was walking toward him. It was the first time he'd been close enough to see her features. She took his breath away. His imagination hadn't done her justice. She was a vision—long, pale blond hair, large grey eyes, and a heart-stopping smile that made him forget the reason he was at her door.

She hesitated a moment, waiting for him to speak. When he didn't say anything, she said, "Hello. Did you like the brownies?"

Steele stared at her for a few seconds before he realized she'd spoken to him. "Huh?"

Pointing to the basket, she repeated, "Did you like the brownies?"

His brain finally clicked in, and he held the empty basket out to her. "No, they were terrible."

Her eyes widened.

He grinned. "They were delicious. Thank you so much."

She smiled back at him. "I'm Eleanor Marlowe."

Steele nodded. "Steele Harper."

"Have you finished remodeling? I've seen you working on the place for several weeks."

"The inside is finished, but I have a lot to do on the exterior." Steele managed to take his eyes off her long enough to glance at the interior of her home. Morgan was right; the place was the definition of cozy. An oversized white sofa with huge cushions in pale colors and light wood floors lent to its coastal charm. "I like what you've done with your place."

Eleanor stepped aside and said, "Would you like to come in and look around?"

Steele touched the bi-fold doors as he walked inside. "I liked your doors so much that I put them in my place."

She flashed him that mega-watt smile again. "I noticed. I got the idea from a home remodeling show and fell in love with them. The room feels so much larger when they're open, and the breeze is wonderful."

"I considered visiting you before to see your place so I could steal more ideas."

"I wouldn't mind. Let me show you the kitchen."

"How long have you lived here?"

"A long time."

Steele followed her through the room. Like his place, the open floor plan allowed him to see the entire area. When they reached the kitchen, Steele could hardly believe his eyes. "I renovated my kitchen, and it's almost identical to yours. I have the same marble countertop."

"Really? What a coincidence."

Coincidence. There was that word again. "Speaking of coincidences, how did you know I love brownies?"

She shrugged her shoulders. "Most men do. Anytime I gave a dinner party, I would have several desserts, and if I had a plate of homemade brownies, they were always devoured first."

Steele couldn't stop staring at her. "I ate most of them at one time."

"Your friends didn't have any?"

"We fought over them."

She smiled again. "I guess you won."

"Yeah, I love brownies."

They stood with their eyes locked for a few moments.

She glanced away first and said, "Let me finish showing you around."

Steele told himself to get control. He felt like he'd been poleaxed. He was acting like a teenager on his first date.

They finished touring the house, and he asked, "Do you like to walk on the beach?" *Stupid question, idiot. She's always going for a walk on the beach.*

"Yes, it's my favorite thing to do."

"Why don't we take a walk down the beach? When we come back, I'll show you my place if you would like to see it."

"Sounds wonderful."

On a good day, Steele wasn't great at small talk, but he made an effort with her. He wanted to get to know her better. They walked the beach for an hour before they returned to his bungalow.

"It is very similar to my place." Eleanor pointed to his dining table. "Did you make that?"

"Yes."

"It's beautiful. You're very talented."

"Thank you." He didn't want her to leave, so he asked, "Would you like a drink?"

"No, thank you."

Great. Now, what do I do? Steele casually walked outside and invited her to sit for a while. He asked her questions, but he was careful not to sound like he was holding an interrogation—a common complaint from prior relationships. "Do you work?"

"I used to be a clothing designer."

"No longer?"

She shook her head from side to side. "What do you do? I thought you might be in construction."

Steele chuckled. "No, I'm a private investigator."

CHAPTER SIX

The Yum Yum Shoppe

"Mr. Harper, I told you everything I remembered the last time we spoke. The police interviewed me the day it happened, and my memory was fresher then. I don't remember seeing Amy that day. Believe me, I wish I had seen something. My daughter and Amy were friends and classmates. I would do anything to help find her. Amy was in here frequently, and I can tell you she liked lots of sprinkles on her ice cream, but I don't think that information will help you find her." Mr. Simpson, the owner of the Yum Yum Ice Cream Shoppe hesitated when his emotions overwhelmed him. Tears were in his eyes when he continued, "My daughter is still not over Amy's disappearance. To this day, she won't go outside alone, and she won't let my wife out of her sight at home. It's affected all of the kids in school. I'm glad you're looking into her case. I thought the police forgot all about her."

Leaning on the counter, Steele said, "Call me Steele. I know you want to help, and I'm sorry about your daughter. I'm just going over the case one more time, hoping someone will remember some small detail—something that may not even seem significant. If you don't mind, go over that day again for me."

Mr. Simpson nodded and walked around the counter. "Sure, I understand." He pointed to a small table with two ice cream parlor chairs. "Have a seat."

Pulling out one of the vintage iron chairs with a twisted heart back and a soft pink cushion, Steele was reminded of Amy's favorite color.

Mr. Simpson sat down, took a deep breath, and said, "It happened on a particularly busy weekend. I think it was five days before Valentine's Day." He hesitated and looked outside as he tried to recall that day. He glanced back up at Steele and continued, "Every store in the mall was having a sale. You know that exclusive women's store, two doors down, *Infinities*?"

Steele nodded, and he said, "They were having a big sale on jewelry, and the whole parking lot was full from the time we opened until we closed. I'd never seen as much traffic in the mall, and we'd been in this location for ten years. We were swamped all day; people were lining up on the sidewalk, waiting to get in. I remember I even ran out of vanilla ice cream, and my delivery guy didn't make it that day."

Steele knew Amy's disappearance happened before Valentine's Day, but he didn't remember reading any information about the additional traffic in the mall that day. Being on the coast in Florida, there were always many vacationers. And before a holiday, there were countless visitors to the city. The way he saw it, that meant more criminals had a target-rich environment available to them. "Who delivers your ice cream?"

After Steele wrote down the information, he opened a leather portfolio he was carrying and pulled out a poster. "Would you mind if I put this in your window?"

Mr. Simpson took the poster and saw Amy's picture, along with a reward of five thousand dollars offered for any information leading to an arrest. "Of course. Leave some extras with me. I will personally see to it that every business in the mall places one in their window." Mr. Simpson stared at the poster for a minute, cleared his throat, and said, "Listen, if you want to print more of these posters offering a ten-thousand-dollar reward, I will ask the shop owners to contribute. We all have kids Amy's age, and it could happen to any of our girls."

"Thank you, that's very generous. I'll have the posters printed tonight and bring them back in the morning."

Steele stood to leave, then remembered one last question. "One of the officers remembered a woman called the station saying she saw something odd involving a young girl around the same time Amy disappeared. You wouldn't happen to know anything about that, would you?"

"No, I'm sorry. I never heard about that. Didn't the cops get her name?"

Steele shook his head. "I'm afraid not."

Spending the remainder of the afternoon questioning the other shop owners, Steele decided to drive to the back of the mall and look around. He parked his car behind one of the stores and walked to the large field beyond the unloading areas where Amy's bicycle was found. The only prints on the bike belonged to Amy. The detectives who had worked the case combed the entire field looking for evidence but came up empty-handed. He didn't expect to find anything a year later, but he wanted to look around.

He stood there for several minutes, observing the traffic flow behind the shops. He made a note of the store owners who parked in the spaces behind their shops. Thinking about what Mr. Simpson said, he also wrote down the names of the delivery trucks.

Turning in every direction, he saw some condos about three hundred yards from the back of the mall. Some of the condos had balconies that offered a bird's eye view of the parking lot. Nothing in the case notes mentioned interviews with the individuals living in those condos.

What do I have to lose except a little time? I have nothing else to go on.

CHAPTER SEVEN

Butt Ugly

Steele was pouring over his notes late that night when his cell phone rang. Yawning, he answered.

"Keeping you awake, Cinderella?"

Chuckling, Steele said, "Long day, Morgan. How's Miami?"

"Hot. What's happening your way?"

Shoving his notes aside, Steele leaned back in his chair. "Just going over some case notes."

"Un-huh." Morgan knew by his friend's frustrated tone which case he was working on. "Anything new?"

Steele pinched the bridge of his nose. "I spent the day interviewing the shop owners again and occupants of the condos behind the mall. Nothing."

"Sorry." Morgan hesitated, then said, "On a lighter note—had any more brownies?"

"No, but I did meet her?"

"And? Butt ugly?"

"Far from it. She's the most beautiful woman I've ever seen in my life."

"How many beers did you have?"

"Not one."

"Tell me about her."

Steele spent the next few minutes discussing Eleanor Marlowe.

"Maybe Tom and I can meet her the next time we visit. What does she do?"

Steele thought for a moment, then said, "She said she *was* a clothing designer. She didn't say what she does now."

"I guess she's single?"

"I didn't ask, but she wasn't wearing a ring."

"I think you're outta practice, friend."

"You could be right about that. But I don't want a woman to feel like I'm grilling her. I try to wait for them to tell me what they want me to know."

They discussed some of the cases Morgan was working on, and when they hung up, Steele stood, stretched, and walked outside. For a moment, he considered walking down to the beach, but he decided he was too tired, so he sat on one of the lounge chairs. Once again, his thoughts drifted to Amy Carson.

He was so lost in his thoughts that he jumped when a dog barked. The shoreline was visible under the full moon, and Steele spotted the barking dog, playfully jumping around someone walking beside him. At first, he thought the person walked like Eleanor, but they were further down the beach, and he couldn't be sure. After watching them for a few seconds, his gaze drifted to the calm ocean. Tonight, the water looked like glass with the moon reflecting on the surface. When his gaze traveled down the beach again, both woman and dog were gone. He assumed they lived in one of the houses further down the beach.

Glancing over at Eleanor's house, he saw the light shining from the bedroom window. He briefly thought about visiting, but one look at his watch told him it was too late.

Maybe tomorrow.

Just as Steele decided it was time for a shower and bed, the dog he'd seen earlier sprinted up the beach. The big black Labrador made a sharp turn toward Steele's house as if Steele had a neon sign in the window saying *I'm awake, come visit me.* The dog leaped onto the patio, jumped on Steele, bracing his front paws on his thighs, and started licking his face.

Laughing, Steele said, "Haven't you played enough tonight?" He felt for a collar as the dog continued giving him his free facial. *No collar.* "I can't take you home if I don't know where you belong. Do you have a name?"

The Lab sat on his rear and looked up at Steele with his big dark eyes. His tongue was lolling to one side.

"Are you thirsty?"

Steele grinned as the dog's tail thumped on the wooden deck. "I'll get you some water." Steele walked inside, and the Lab followed him to the kitchen. Once Steele got a good look at him, he noted he was, in fact, a *he.* He was clean, had a nice shiny coat, and appeared well-cared for. "You're a handsome dog." Steele filled a bowl from his bottled water and placed it on the floor in front of him.

The dog lapped it up quickly, and Steele said, "Take it slow, buddy. I don't want you to get sick."

When the water was gone, Steele said, "Are you hungry too?"

The dog sat back down, tail thumping again.

Steele had grilled a New York strip for dinner, so he grabbed the remaining uneaten half from the refrigerator, and cut it into bite-size pieces. Once he placed the plate in front of the Lab, it took him all three seconds to polish it off.

"Okay, until I find out where you belong, you can stay here tonight."

Tail wagging, the dog followed Steele to the bedroom.

Pulling out a large, fluffy rug from his bathroom, Steele placed it near his bed and motioned for the dog. "You can sleep here tonight."

The dog hopped on the rug and circled three times before he plopped down.

Smiling at his ritual, Steele said, "I can't just call you dog, so until I find your owner, I'm gonna call you Bear. You look like a black bear to me."

Bear barked.

CHAPTER EIGHT

A Clean Sweep

Early the next morning, Steele walked to the beach with Bear beside him. He was planning an early morning swim, but Bear had other ideas. The Lab snagged a branch on the way to the shore and dropped it at Steele's bare feet. Steele chuckled as Bear bounced around, waiting for him to play. He didn't have the heart to disappoint the hopeful-looking dog, so he tossed the stick into the water and watched as Bear jumped in without hesitation. Within seconds the stick was lying at Steel's feet to be thrown again.

Nearly an hour later, Steele's shoulder was burning, but Bear didn't show signs of slowing down. When Bear came bounding back with the stick clutched between his teeth the last time, Steele held onto it. "Sorry, buddy, but I can't throw it anymore." Steele knew his usual morning swim was out since that would require moving his shoulder. "Let's jog for a little while, and maybe we'll see your owner." They passed a few early morning beachcombers as they ran, and Steele thought someone might recognize Bear or vice versa. No luck. And Bear didn't appear to have an interest in any of the homes along the beach.

When they returned home, the pair showered and toweled off outside. They walked into the house, and Steele said, "We'll have some breakfast, and then I'll take you next door to see if Eleanor knows you or your owner. How's that sound?" Opening the refrigerator, Steele looked at the few options inside. "I hope you like scrambled eggs and toast. That's all I have since someone ate my steak last night."

Bear looked up at him with his dark eyes and whimpered.

"I wish I could keep you, but I bet your owner is out looking for you right now." Steele thought if he didn't find his owner today, he'd have to stop at the grocery on the way home and buy some dog food. He had to admit he had mixed feelings about finding Bear's owner. *He's a great companion.*

As they approached Eleanor's place, a woman walked from the house and turned to lock the door.

"Good morning," Steele said.

Not realizing someone was behind her, the woman jumped at the sound of his voice. She turned to face Steele with her hand on her heart. "Oh, my, you gave me a fright. I didn't hear you. Good morning." She started to walk past them but stopped and said, "No one is there. I just cleaned the place and locked up. Can I help you with something?"

Steele noticed a label on her shirt, *A Clean Sweep*. "Do you know if Miss Marlowe will be home soon?"

The woman shook her head. "I'm sorry, I don't know who that is. No one lives here. I clean the place every week."

Noting the basket of cleaning supplies the woman was carrying, Steele said, "I've seen a woman here several times."

"Maybe she's a real estate agent. The company I work for does a lot of business with real estate companies. We clean houses that are for sale and rental properties."

Puzzled, Steele glanced toward the house and then back at the woman. "How long have you been cleaning this place?"

"About a year. As far as I know, it has never been rented. The place is never dirty or messy—all I do is vacuum and dust every week. Most places I clean are a total disaster after the vacationers leave."

"Do you usually work in this area?" Steele asked.

"Yes, every day."

Pointing to Bear, who was sitting patiently by his side, Steele asked, "Have you ever seen this dog before? I'm looking for his owner."

"I've often seen him on the beach, but I've never seen him with anyone in particular. Usually, it's the vacationers who feed and play with him." She smiled at Bear. "He seems like a good dog."

"He's a great dog." Steele reached for his wallet and pulled out his business card. "If you hear of anyone missing a dog, please give me a call."

The woman nodded. "Sure thing."

"Have a good day." Steele turned to walk back to his home. He didn't know what to make of that odd encounter. Perhaps the woman was mistaken. Perhaps Eleanor chose to leave when someone came to clean. Steele glanced down to say something to Bear, but Bear wasn't beside him. He turned to see the Lab was sitting on his haunches, staring at Eleanor's home. "What are you looking at, Bear?"

Bear barked.

Steele walked back to Bear and looked at the house again, but he didn't see anything unusual. "She's not home, buddy. That's a puzzle I'll have to solve later. Right now, let's go to a few houses to see if we can find your owner. If we don't have any luck, I'll have some posters printed with your picture on them when I pick up Amy's posters this morning."

He glanced down at Bear, who was looking at him as if he understood what he was saying. *He looks like he's smiling at me.* Pulling his phone from his front pocket, Steele turned on the camera, held it a few feet from Bear's face, and clicked. "Good boy."

CHAPTER NINE

A Broken Heart

"Let's get a bowl out for your food, Bear." Opening the bag of dog food, Steele poured two cups into the bowl before he chopped up one of the four hamburgers he'd bought at a drive-thru. He looked down at Bear and grinned at the drool dripping from the corners of his mouth. "I told you I was going to give you one of the burgers." After adding the burger to the dog food, he placed the bowl on the floor in front of Bear. Instead of gobbling the food, Bear cocked his head at him and whined.

"Why aren't you eating?" Steele asked as he picked up a French fry.

Bear jumped up and tried to snag the fry before it landed in Steele's mouth.

"Oh, you want some fries to top it off. Your own version of a Happy Meal?"

Bear nudged his leg.

"Okay, I get it. They're good." He dumped a few fries on top of the bowl, and Bear dug in.

While Bear ate, Steele leaned against the counter, eating his fast food burgers and talking. "Sorry we didn't find your owner today, but those posters will probably do the trick. After we finish dinner, we'll go see if Eleanor's home. I bet she's seen you before."

Mentioning Eleanor made Steele think about the encounter with the maid earlier that morning. Now that he had time to think about his conversation, it was obvious that the woman was mistaken. He'd seen Eleanor next door several times, and a light was always on in the evening. Eleanor certainly didn't look like a squatter. *Looks are often deceiving*. He'd been so stunned by her beauty that he was lucky to string two words together the first night he met her. If she was home tonight, he'd try to find out more about her.

He glanced at Bear and said, "I hope she's not a criminal, Bear. That would break my heart."

"Hi, Steele."

Steele's first thought when Eleanor opened the door was that his mind hadn't been playing tricks on him. She was gorgeous and looked even better tonight in her long, pale pink silky dress. Before he spoke, Bear nearly knocked him down, trying to jump on her.

"Bear!" Steele latched onto the new red collar he'd purchased earlier and tried to pull him away.

"It's okay. We're old friends." She stroked Bear's fur and added, "He a good dog. I didn't know his name was Bear."

"That's what I've been calling him. He wasn't wearing tags, and I've been looking for his owner. Would you happen to know where he lives?"

"No, I'm sorry. All our encounters have been on the beach, and he's always alone. Would you like to come inside?" Eleanor asked.

Steele smiled and glanced down at Bear. "He might mess something up, and I know your maid service was here earlier."

Eleanor leaned over and rubbed Bear's ears. "He can't hurt anything."

As soon as they walked inside, both Steele and Bear sniffed the air.

"Something smells good. I hope we didn't interrupt your dinner."

"I just pulled some brownies with caramel and sea salt out of the oven. Would you like one?"

Steele's mouth was already watering. "I'd love one if it's not too much trouble."

"No trouble at all. I was going to bring them to you to try. Consider yourself my guinea pig since I've never made these before."

"I'll be your guinea pig any day." Steele and Bear followed her to the kitchen.

Eleanor pointed to the counter. "Please have a seat. Would you like milk with your brownie?"

"Yes, thank you." When she opened the refrigerator, Steele saw some items on the shelves. It wasn't full, but there was more food than he had in his refrigerator. The pan of brownies was on the counter, and Steele saw his opportunity to snoop right in front of her. "Eleanor, if you point me in the right direction, I'll get the glass while you cut the brownies."

She pointed to the cabinet beside the sink. "My friends call me Ellie."

"Are you having some, Ellie?"

"Not right now."

"Where are your plates?"

"The next cabinet."

Opening the next cabinet, Steele saw each shelf was filled with china.

Ellie cut off a huge chunk of brownie and placed it on a plate. After Steele poured the milk, he sat at the counter next to her.

Savoring his first bite, he said, "I didn't think anything could be better than your last brownies, but these might be."

Ellie sat in the chair next to him. "I saw the recipe on a cooking show and thought they looked good." Eleanor reached down to pet Bear, and Steele noticed the gold bracelet on her arm. It had heart-shaped links, and a large puffed half-heart dangled from the end. He saw the large heart was broken in half. He thought it could be one of those pieces where one person kept one half of the heart and gave the other half to their significant other. "That's a beautiful bracelet."

"Thank you."

"Do you mind if I have a closer look? My friend is looking for something to buy his girlfriend for Valentine's Day."

Eleanor extended her arm, and Steele took the puffed heart between his fingers. The jagged edge of the heart told him it was broken and not made that way. "Your heart is broken."

CHAPTER TEN

Raising the Short Hairs

"If you find the missing half of your heart, I think it can be repaired," Steele said.

Ellie continued to stare at the bracelet with a quizzical look on her face. "I don't remember breaking it."

"That heart is solid gold, so it would have taken a heck of a whack to break it."

Unclasping the bracelet, Ellie handed it to Steele and said, "Do you think it can be repaired?"

Steele noticed the heart links were solid gold as well, and the bracelet was heavier than he expected. On closer inspection, he could see that the large puffed heart charm was not as thick in the center where it had broken. "It looks like it was made with two halves and soldered together in the middle of the heart." He held it up for her to see. "It's thinner in the center, and that's probably the reason it broke there if you hit it on something. It could be repaired, but the other half of the heart would have to be made." He clasped the bracelet back on her arm.

Ellie's eyes widened. "I think your right. It had a zigzag line down the center."

Steele wondered if someone significant had given it to her as a gift. "Even with the broken heart, it's still a beautiful bracelet. Where did you get it?"

Shaking her head, Ellie said, "I don't remember."

Steele didn't think a woman would forget where she got such a costly gift or the person who gave it to her. "It would be difficult to forget someone who gave you such an expensive gift."

They stared at each other for a few moments, and Ellie said, "I can't remember where I got it."

He didn't want to question her word about the bracelet. *But I am.* At that moment, Bear nudged his hand, allowing him time to think of another topic to discuss. "Bear and I came over this morning, and we ran into the cleaning lady. She made the most interesting comment."

Ellie arched her brow at him. "Really? What was that?"

"She said no one lived here."

Ellie gave him a puzzled look, then shrugged. "Well, it's a large cleaning service, and they probably send over someone new each week. I'm never here when they come."

Steele remembered the woman told him she cleaned the house each week. The woman must have been mistaken because Ellie certainly didn't seem to be the least bit rattled by the woman's comment. Yet, Steele felt something was not quite right. Though the cabinets were full, and the refrigerator had food, the counters were too neat. There wasn't one dirty dish in the sink, and there wasn't the usual kitchen paraphernalia on the counters. While he was an admitted neat freak, even his kitchen wasn't as orderly as Ellie's.

"If you don't mind, I'd like to use your facilities."

"Of course," Ellie replied.

As he walked to the bathroom, Steele heard her talking to Bear, so he decided to make a quick detour to the master bedroom. Part of him felt guilty for snooping, but the detective part of him said something was raising his short hair. He liked Ellie, and he told himself that was the reason he was prying. He didn't want to date a criminal. *Date? Where did that come from? I just met her. But I like her, and Bear likes her too.*

Ellie's bedroom was a replica of her kitchen, everything in perfect order, not a knickknack to be seen. He opened the door to the walk-in closet. It was stuffed with dresses, skirts, slacks, blouses, shoes, handbags, everything to outfit twenty women—a typical woman's closet. He didn't know what he expected, but he breathed a sigh of relief, thinking that a person trespassing on the property wouldn't bring so many clothes. He glanced at some of the labels to check the size. All of the dresses were size six. He turned to walk out of the closet but stopped suddenly. He realized all of the labels were the same. He pulled out another dress and looked at the tags inside the neckline—*Eleanor Marlowe Designs.*

CHAPTER ELEVEN

Houdini

On his way back to the kitchen, Steele told himself he shouldn't be so suspicious. But the cleaning lady specifically said she cleaned this house each week.

"Tell me about the cleaning service," Steele said when he sat at the counter. "I was thinking about calling one to clean my home, but I worry about theft. Have you ever had any problems?"

Ellie shook her head. "No, never."

"Have you used them a long time?"

"I can't remember how long they've been coming here."

Steele thought that was an odd response. "And you've never met the women who do the cleaning?"

Ellie stared, not at him, but something past him. She looked to be in deep thought. Moments later, her gaze met his, and she said, "No, I can't remember meeting anyone. I don't even remember hiring them."

Steele had many questions, but sensing a change in her mood, he decided his best course of action was to back off. "I think Bear needs to get some energy out before bedtime. Would you like to go for a walk on the beach with us? It's a nice night, and there's a full moon."

"Not tonight. If you don't mind, I'll take a rain check."

"What do you think, Bear? Was it just me, or did we get the brush off?" Steele asked as they walked along the shoreline.

Bear emitted a sound between a low growl and a whimper.

Steele held his hands in the air. "Don't look at me. I was trying to be nice. I thought she liked walking on the beach." He realized Ellie's demeanor had changed when he asked her about the cleaning service. She had a far-away look in her eyes as if she was trying to remember something significant. After that, she was less talkative, and Steele could tell that her mind was elsewhere. That little voice was telling him that Ellie acted like a woman with something to hide. "Maybe she just has a memory problem, Bear. Early onset dementia, or something like that."

Bear nudged his leg.

"But she likes you, Bear. I could tell she didn't want you to leave. And she did give *me* the whole pan of brownies to take home. I think that means she might like me a little."

They stopped walking, and Steele stared at the moon. "She might be hiding something, Bear. I hope it's not a boyfriend or a husband. I like her. It's a plus that she makes great brownies. Too bad you can't have any." He glanced at his watch and rubbed Bear's ears. "I think it's time to take a shower and go to bed."

One minute Steele was sleeping soundly, and the next minute his eyes snapped open. He thought he heard someone call his name. Though his eyes were adjusting to the dark, he thought he saw something—or someone dressed in white at the foot of his bed. In one swift motion, he grabbed his pistol from the nightstand, sat up, and aimed his weapon. But no one was there. Swiping his hand over his face, he glanced around the room. Empty. *I must have been dreaming.* The orange numbers reflected on the ceiling told him it was only 11:30 p.m. He hadn't been asleep long. He looked to see if Bear was sleeping, but his new plush sofa bed was empty. "Bear," he called out.

Hearing no response, he crawled out of bed and walked to the kitchen. No Bear. He checked every room in the house, but Bear was not there.

He was positive he closed and locked the patio doors before he went to bed, but he thought he'd double-check. When he reached the glass doors, he looked out and saw Bear on the beach, walking beside someone dressed in white. Steele could tell by the person's stride that it was Ellie. He started to open the door, but he found it locked. Running his fingers through his hair in confusion, he thought he might be dreaming. He shook his head and walked to the kitchen to grab a bottle of water.

After a long swig, he said aloud, "Nope. I'm not dreaming." Spotting the pan of brownies on the counter, he removed one and walked back to the patio doors.

He stood there munching his brownie as he watched Ellie and Bear stop and stare at the moon. *How in the heck did Bear get outside? Maybe I should call him Houdini.* He replayed their nightly routine in his mind. He locked the patio doors, turned out the lights, and walked to the bedroom. *I watched Bear do his three-circle ritual before he settled on his bed. Then it was lights out.*

He cracked the patio door so Bear could get in and went back to bed.

CHAPTER TWELVE

The Psychic Hotline

Steele returned home from his early morning swim, and Bear was still sleeping. After he threw some bacon in a pan and it started to sizzle, Bear finally managed to amble into the kitchen. He greeted Steele by nudging his leg before he plopped down on the cushion in the corner by the table.

"Late night, Houdini?"

Bear yawned.

"You can thank me later for leaving the door open for you last night. I didn't think you could walk through walls."

Bear looked up at him and sniffed the air.

"But I'd like to know how you got out in the first place. I know I closed and locked those doors."

No response.

Steele cracked six eggs in a bowl and started scrambling. "I guess you and Ellie had a late-night stroll. Lucky for you, I have a lot of phone calls to make this morning, so you can go back to sleep after breakfast and catch your forty winks." He stopped whisking the eggs and stared down at Bear. "Why don't you give me some suggestions as to how I can make headway with Ellie? You don't seem to have a problem impressing the gals."

Spending two hours non-stop on the phone wasn't Steele's idea of a good time, but it was a necessary part of his job. After his last call, he tossed the phone on his desk and glanced at Bear, who was stretched out on the sofa in his office. He was just about to ask him if he wanted to go for a walk when his cell phone rang.

Seeing it was Morgan, he answered, "Hey, Morg."

"How's it going?"

"Good. What's happening there?"

"Tom and I were discussing your case this morning over breakfast."

Steele didn't need to ask which case—Amy Carson. "Yeah?"

"We know you've investigated all of the friends and relatives of the Carsons, and at this point, we all agree that it was probably a stranger abduction."

"Right."

"It's been so long since she was abducted that we thought you might be interested in talking to that psychic we know to see if she can help. You remember we told you about Mae Rogers, don't you? Tom and I worked with her on a couple of cases."

"I do remember, Morgan." Steele leaned back in his chair and ran his fingers through his hair. "I admit that I'm running out of ideas. And I would like to give the Carsons some . . . I hate the word closure. I don't think there is ever any closure when you lose someone you love. But I would like to give them some answers. I don't know how they keep going, not knowing what happened and why."

"Other police departments around the country have asked for Mae's help, and she's proven to be very useful. Her track record is impressive. If she doesn't think she can assist, she tells you upfront.

I don't pretend to understand how she knows certain things, but she does."

"I remember you and Tom fought against bringing her in on your case at first," Steele replied.

"That's a fact. We were skeptical as hell, but we were wrong. I might not broadcast that we used a psychic, but I don't know if we would've solved the case without her."

Steele exhaled loudly. "At this point, she may be my best and *last* hope. I've not had a bite on that reward yet."

"You want me to call Mae, or do you want her number? She doesn't live too far from you."

Steele picked up his pen. "Give me her number."

After Morgan gave him the psychic's phone number, he said, "You want some company this weekend, or is your datebook full? Tom and I have the weekend off."

"Come anytime you want. Maybe I should schedule the psychic when you two are here. She already knows you, and that might be more comfortable for her."

"Yeah, that's a good idea. By the way, she's a good-looking woman—and single."

"Did either one of you make a move on her?" Steele asked.

"It crossed my mind. But think about it, Steele. She would know everything you did before you did it. That's kind of scary."

Steele laughed. "I've known women like that, and they weren't even psychic."

Chuckling, Morgan said, "There is that."

CHAPTER THIRTEEN

Clairvoyant

"You haven't mentioned your neighbor once, and we've been here," Tom glanced down at his watch, then smiled at Steele, "all of twenty minutes."

Steele shook his head. "Bear has made more headway with her than I have."

Morgan laughed. "I can understand that, he's one handsome dog."

"Haven't you invited her out to dinner yet?" Tom asked.

"I've been busy the last few days and haven't had time. I'm whipped by the time I get home, but Bear has more energy. Somehow he's found a way to open doors, and I've seen him walking the beach with Ellie around midnight."

Tom ruffled Bear's fur. "Smart dog."

"I take it Bear's owner hasn't turned up?" Morgan asked.

"No, I've placed posters up and down the beach, but no one has called."

"He seems to like it here with you," Tom said.

"Truthfully, I hope no one calls. I enjoy having him here." Steele looked at his watch. "We've got to take off. We're meeting Mae down the beach at the Oyster Bar for lunch." He tapped Bear on the head, "Come on, Houdini, you get to go with us. We're eating outside."

Lunch ended, and Steele said, "Mae, Morgan told me that you'd need some of Amy's personal items, so I picked up a few things from her parents. If you want to go back to my place with us, I can give them to you today. My house is just down the beach."

"Why don't you cancel anything else you have going on today and spend the day with us? We're grilling out later, and since Tom's cooking, we guarantee you'll have a good dinner," Morgan said.

Steele could tell that Morgan was attracted to Mae, and it was understandable. She was a petite strawberry blonde, and she was intelligent. Judging by the way Mae looked at Morgan, Steele thought the attraction was mutual.

Mae smiled at him. "I'd love to. This was my only meeting today, so I'm free for the remainder of the day."

Walking back to Steele's home, he asked Mae what she saw when she touched items owned by the victims.

"I guess the best way I can describe what happens is I see a vision of the life-changing event. I have seen what the victim is seeing in the present moment. At times, the visions are vague, and it can be extremely frustrating. Normally, I sense if the person is alive." She looked up at Steele. "Does that make sense?"

"Yes, it does. I don't know if I would have called you if Morgan and Tom didn't convince me of your abilities. I don't have to tell you that they are big fans."

Mae laughed. "They weren't always. I think the successful resolution of their case was what finally convinced them. But I don't want to mislead you. There are times that I can't help."

Steele appreciated her honesty. "We'll hope for the best."

Bear ran ahead and snagged a branch for Steele to throw. Steele played the game as they walked, and suddenly Bear didn't return for another toss. Steele saw him running down the beach, but before he lost sight of him, Bear stopped beside a woman. "There's Ellie."

"Where?" Morgan said.

Steele pointed down the beach. "She's standing beside Bear."

"I don't see her," Tom said.

"What? She's right next to Bear. Do you need glasses? It's not that far."

"The blonde woman?" Mae asked.

"Yeah, that's her."

"I don't see anyone," Morgan said.

Steele and Mae exchanged a puzzled look, and Steele said, "You guys are spending too much time indoors, or you're getting old. They're walking toward my house."

When they reached Steele's house, they found Bear waiting for them by the patio doors.

"Where did Ellie go?" Steele asked Bear.

"Why don't you go to her house and ask her if she wants to have dinner with us tonight?" Morgan asked.

Steele slapped him on the back. "Good idea, I'll do that."

Mae sat on the porch step beside Bear and rubbed his ears. "Bear likes his name."

The men stopped talking and stared at Mae.

Arching her brows at Steele, she said, "You did give him that name, didn't you?"

"Ah . . . yeah."

"He doesn't have an owner. And he wants to stay here with you," Mae added.

Steele tried to recall if they'd discussed Bear at lunch. They hadn't. He'd had that conversation with Morgan and Tom before they left for lunch.

"How did you know Steele wasn't his owner?" Morgan asked.

"Bear just told me."

CHAPTER FOURTEEN

Is This a Dream?

Stunned by what Mae said, Steele, Morgan, and Tom just looked at each other.

Steele's first thought was that Morgan and Tom were playing a joke on him. He looked at them and frowned. "Very funny, guys."

"What do you mean?" Tom asked.

"Which one of you told Mae about Bear?"

Morgan said, "This is the first time Mae and I have seen each other in months. You were there the entire time at lunch. We didn't discuss how you found Bear."

"The last time I saw Mae was when we worked on our case," Tom added.

Mae smiled at Steele. "I know this is difficult for you to believe, but Bear just told me. I understood what he was thinking when I touched him." She continued to rub Bear's ears and added, "He didn't like the vet you took him to see."

"You took him to a vet?" Tom asked.

"Yeah, I wanted to see if he had a chip. I agree with Bear; I didn't like her either." Steele hadn't told Morgan or Tom he'd taken Bear to a vet. *How did Mae know? Maybe Morgan was right—she did have special powers.* He looked at Mae and asked, "No one owns him?"

"Someone dumped him as a puppy."

"I'd like to meet the jackasses who would do that to an animal," Morgan said.

Steele and Tom nodded their agreement.

Steele couldn't believe he was talking to someone who had just read his dog's mind, and everyone was acting as though it was normal. He needed a moment to think about this conversation. He stood and said, "I'm going to Ellie's and invite her to dinner." He looked Bear in the eyes and asked, "Do you want to go with me?"

Bear jumped up and walked downs the steps beside him.

Morgan watched Steele and Bear walk toward Ellie's. He understood Steele's hesitation to believe in Mae's talents. He'd been there. "Mae, you remember how long it took us to accept your abilities. Steele will probably take longer."

"Yeah, he's a bit more skeptical than we were," Tom added.

"So I see. If I can help him with his case, I think he'll become a believer."

"Think I'll go make some margaritas. We're going to need them" Tom said and walked inside.

Within minutes, Steele and Bear returned to the patio. "She wasn't home."

"We'll keep an eye out for her. Maybe she'll get back before dinner," Morgan said.

Tom heard their conversation as he walked through the door carrying a tray filled with margaritas. "She doesn't know what she's missing."

Later that night, Mae told them it was time for her to leave. "Thank you for a lovely dinner."

Morgan said, "I'll walk you back to your car."

"I forgot you left it at the Oyster Bar," Steele said. "Morg, one of us can walk down to get it if Mae's too tired."

Morgan gave Steele the evil eye.

Steele realized his mistake, so he turned to Tom and said, "Tom, you look like you could use some exercise. Why don't we walk down to get Mae's car?"

Not paying attention to the plan unfolding, Tom said, "I'll drive you down."

Steele rolled his eyes.

"What?" Tom asked.

Mae smiled at them. "I'm not tired, and after that wonderful meal, I'm sure I need to work off some calories."

Steele winked at Morgan.

An hour later, Steele, Tom, and Bear were sitting on the patio when Morgan returned to the house, smiling from ear to ear.

Tom smacked him on the back. "Judging by that shit-eating grin on your face, I guess things went well with Mae.

"Yeah. We're having dinner tomorrow night."

"You better not let her touch you, or she'll know what's on your mind. Or keep your thoughts clean and not X-rated," Steele teased.

"You can laugh if you want, but that does concern me. What if she *can* read my mind?"

"Think only pure, innocent thoughts," Tom advised.

Steele chuckled. "Yeah, don't let her know what you're *really* thinking."

Once again, Steele woke up suddenly and glanced at the ceiling. *11:53 p.m.* He'd only been in bed for thirty minutes. He checked to see if Bear was in his bed. He wasn't. He tossed his sheet aside, jumped out of bed, and headed to the patio doors. As he expected, Bear was on the beach with Ellie. Instead of going back to bed, he headed back to his bedroom and pulled on a pair of shorts.

When he reached the shore, he stood beside them and stared at the moonlight glowing on the water. "I think my dog likes you better."

Ellie didn't respond, and she continued to stare at the ocean. Bear turned to him, nudged his leg, and Steele leaned over and ruffled his fur. "You have to tell me how you're getting out. I know I locked those doors tonight." He thought it odd that Ellie didn't say a word. Just as he was about to ask her if she knew how Bear got out, she turned around.

Steele thought she was going to walk back to the house, but then he saw blood covering the front of her white dress. He stumbled backward as he stared at the gaping hole in her stomach. "What the . . .?" His brain couldn't process what he was seeing. *How is she standing?* For a moment, he thought he might be dreaming—wished he was dreaming. But he wasn't. Eve was seriously injured and bleeding profusely. He had to act. He pressed his hand to her stomach, trying to staunch the bleeding. "Ellie, lie down! I need to stop the bleeding."

"Steele, you can't help me."

"What? Lie down!" As he continued to apply pressure to her wound, he reached into his pocket for his cell phone. His pocket was empty. *I left it on his nightstand. Morgan and Tom won't hear me if I yell for them.* He looked at his hand and saw blood flowing freely over his fingers. He wasn't staunching the bleeding, and the wound was life-threatening. "Ellie, I need to get you to a hospital. Who did this to you?"

"I don't know. Maybe you can find out."

Steele looked up and down the beach, but it was deserted. He leaned over to pick her up to carry her to the house.

Ellie disappeared.

CHAPTER FIFTEEN

Truth is Stranger Than Fiction

Ellie disappeared from Steele's arms. Doing a three-sixty, he saw no one on the beach other than Bear, who was also turning in circles. Steele looked down at his hands in disbelief at the blood dripping from his fingers. She was there, and it wasn't a dream.

"Bear, where is she?"

Together, they ran toward Ellie's house. The house was dark, and only one light lit the outside porch. Steele banged on the patio door. "Ellie! Ellie!"

He checked to see if the door was locked. It was. He ran to the front of the house to check that door. Locked. Glancing down at Bear, who seemed equally frantic, he debated breaking into Ellie's house. *How could she be here if she was bleeding on the beach? What's going on?*

Once again, he ran to Ellie's back porch and smacked the glass so hard he was surprised it didn't break. He waited two seconds, then ran back to his house, and into Morgan's bedroom. "Morgan! Wake up." He hurried to Tom's bedroom and woke him.

Morgan ran into Tom's room behind Steele. "What's wrong, Steele?"

"It's Ellie! She's been . . . stabbed . . . shot . . . I don't know." Steele started pacing the room. "I went to her house, but it's locked . . . I don't know . . . I don't know . . ."

Tom and Morgan exchanged a worried look.

"Calm down, Steele. Sit on the bed and start from the beginning," Morgan said.

Tom ran to the kitchen, poured a shot of bourbon, and carried it back to the bedroom. He put it in Steele's hand and said, "Drink this."

Steele swallowed the bourbon and took a deep breath. His eyes darted from Morgan to Tom. He ran his fingers through his hair. "This is going to sound nuts." After he released a deep breath, he said, "I woke up not long after I went to sleep, and I noticed Bear wasn't on his bed. He wasn't anywhere in the house, so I looked out the patio doors and saw him with Ellie on the beach. I walked down there, and when Ellie turned toward me, she was bleeding profusely from a wound in her stomach. I tried to stop the bleeding . . . so much blood . . ." he hesitated and looked at his hands. There was no blood. He turned his hands over and over. "No blood," he mumbled. He glanced down at Bear. "There was blood, wasn't there, Bear?"

Morgan and Tom exchanged another glance, and then Morgan said, "Steele, I think you were having a nightmare."

Steele shook his head. "No, I wasn't dreaming. It was real."

He repeated the story.

"If you weren't dreaming, and you tried to stop the bleeding, you would have blood on you. Where's the blood?" Tom asked.

Examining his hands, Steele shook his head from side to side. "I don't know."

"You went to her house, and no one answered?" Morgan asked.

"Yeah. I knocked on both doors."

Tom pulled on his shorts. "I'll go over there and see if she's there."

Morgan and Steele walked to the kitchen to wait on Tom. Steele sat at the counter, and Morgan poured them both a shot.

"You know, Steele, after what Mae said tonight, it wouldn't be surprising if you had a weird dream. I know when I first saw her talents, I had strange dreams for weeks. It's perfectly understandable."

Swirling the bourbon in the glass, Steele said, "I wasn't dreaming." He tossed back his second shot.

Tom walked into the house. "She's not home."

"Where did she go? She's wounded," Steele said.

Morgan put his hand on Steele's shoulder. "Steele, you said you picked her up, and she disappeared. Don't you think it's possible you were having a dream or a nightmare?"

Steele felt like saying, *ask Bear*, but he knew that would sound even crazier. The old saying, *truth is stranger than fiction*, played in his mind. "I wasn't dreaming." His gaze slid from Morgan to Tom. "You guys know me, and you know I would tell you if I thought I was dreaming. I'm not crazy, and I wasn't dreaming."

Tom poured himself a shot, walked to the patio door, and stared at the shoreline. The moon had disappeared behind a cloud, but he thought he saw someone dressed in white walking down the beach. When the cloud moved on, and the moon shone brightly again, no one was there. He walked back to the kitchen and said, "Okay. Let me get my flashlight. We'll break into her house and see if she's there. Maybe we can figure out what's going on."

CHAPTER SIXTEEN

Breaking and Entering

Morgan grabbed a small pouch from his duffle bag and carried it to Ellie's house. Reaching the door, Tom braced his shoulder against it and pushed hard.

"Stand aside. We don't have to break it down." Morgan pulled a small tool from his pouch. "Thankfully, I still know how to pick a lock. And we don't need a B & E on our record."

Five seconds later, the three men were inside Ellie's home.

Steele called out, "Ellie!"

After turning on a light, they checked the floor to see if there were any signs of blood. The place was spotless.

They split up, and Steele walked to the master bedroom and flipped on the light. The bed hadn't been slept in, and nothing was out of place. He walked into the bathroom and looked around. Like every other room, it was sparkling clean. None of the usual creams, potions, or make-up lined the counter. Ellie wore make-up. He'd noticed.

They met back in the kitchen, and Morgan said, "This place is beautiful, but it looks like no one lives here. It's too neat."

"Yeah, I was thinking the same thing," Tom said.

"Was it this orderly when you were here before?" Morgan asked.

Steele knew they were thinking that someone could have cleaned the place after committing a crime. "Yes, it's the cleanest place I've ever seen." He sat down at the counter where he'd sat with Ellie.

Morgan and Tom looked at each other, both unable to explain what was happening to their friend.

In the ensuing silence, the refrigerator's icemaker dropped some ice, and it sounded like a bomb exploding.

They jumped.

Morgan looked up and said, "I don't understand any of this."

"Steele, maybe it was the tequila. That crap makes people do some stupid stuff," Tom said.

"Not only that, but you've been putting in long hours on the Carson case, and you said you haven't been sleeping," Morgan added.

"I only had one margarita, and you both know that I've drank a hell of a lot more. I've always had trouble sleeping, but I've never walked in my sleep. This was no dream."

Morgan shoved his flashlight in his back pocket and slapped Steele on the back. "We should get out of here. What if she comes home, and we're sitting in her kitchen? That might not go over too well."

"Why don't we walk down to the beach and look around?" Tom suggested.

Steele pushed away from the counter, and when he stood, he felt something under his shoe. He leaned over and picked up Ellie's gold heart bracelet. "This is Ellie's. She was wearing it the last time I saw her."

"You mean when she was bleeding on the beach?" Morgan asked.

Steele tried to remember if he'd noticed the bracelet on her arm tonight. He hadn't. He was busy trying to keep her alive. "No . . . I don't know. But she was wearing it when I came over here before."

"Let's go," Morgan said.

Steele laid the bracelet on the counter, and the men left the same way they came in and locked the door.

Once Bear saw the men walking back to the beach, he ran ahead of them. He stopped at the spot where he last saw Ellie.

Pointing to Bear, Steele said, "Bear is standing where I saw Ellie."

When they flashed their lights on the sand they saw two fresh sets of footprints and Bear's paw prints headed to the beach. Bear's prints and another set of footprints returned to Ellie's house. Those footprints belonged to Steele.

But they didn't see blood or a body—nothing to indicate anything nefarious had happened on the beach that night.

Morgan pointed to Bear, who was sniffing the sand. "He acts like he's on a scent."

As the three moved closer to the shore, Steele directed the beam of his flashlight on the area where Bear had his nose buried in the sand. "Bear and I saw the same thing. I'm *not* going crazy here. And I didn't have too much to drink."

"Okay. Then I'm going to call Mae. She seems to be able to communicate with Bear in some way . . . I guess it's called telepathy. Let's see if Bear can tell her what happened here and where Ellie went," Morgan said.

Tom exhaled loudly. "Oh, geez. You can't call her at this time of night. She'll think we're all nuts or drunk."

"Tom's right. We'll call her in the morning," Steele said. "I need to make sense of this."

Tom shook his head in agreement. "Yeah, and I'd like to know if I need to put one of my two best friends in the nuthouse."

CHAPTER SEVENTEEN

Meaner Than a Junkyard Dog

"Mae can't get here until this evening. She's the keynote speaker at some psychic convention in Miami," Morgan said when he walked back to the patio where Tom was sitting drinking a cup of coffee.

Tom laughed, and coffee dribbled onto his shirt. "What? A psychic convention?"

Taking a seat, Morgan grinned. "I know. Sounds like fun, huh?"

"Why do they bother with a convention? They should already know what the speakers are going to say."

Morgan couldn't help but laugh with him.

Tom leaned over and looked inside the house. "Steele's in the shower. What do you think is going on?"

"I think Steele saw something. I guess he could've been sleep-walking, but he's so adamant that he wasn't." He looked Tom in the eyes. "We've been friends a long time. I believe him. He definitely experienced something weird."

Tom sighed. "Yeah. Me, too. Whatever he saw rattled him. That's a fact. I've seen him in circumstances where he was meaner than a junkyard dog, so whatever happened shook him up. It doesn't make a hell of a lot of sense, but we need to find out what's going on."

Steele's hair was still wet when he joined them on the patio. Turning to look at Ellie's house, he said, "Seen anyone at Ellie's?"

"I haven't seen anyone since I've been sitting out here," Tom replied.

Morgan told Steele about his conversation with Mae. "She'll be here around 7:00 p.m."

"I guess there's nothing we can do but wait for her," Steele replied.

Mae arrived promptly at 7:00 p.m. and after listening to Steele's story, she said, "I assume you want me to see if Bear can tell me what happened."

Slouching back in his chair, Steele said, "I'd like Morgan and Tom to know I'm not going off the deep end. And if that means having you talk to Bear to confirm what we saw, then yes, that's what I want."

Morgan leaned over and gripped Steele's shoulder. "We don't think you're going off the deep end, Steele. But we need to figure this out."

Bear plopped down beside Steele's feet, and Mae sat on the floor beside him. She didn't utter a sound as she stroked his fur, then closed her eyes.

The men remained silent, watching Mae's interaction with Bear. Steele noticed Bear had also closed his eyes. He wondered what it was like to be able to read an animal's thoughts. It would certainly make life easier if an animal was lost or ill.

Suddenly, Mae opened her eyes and stared at him. "Bear has seen her many times on the beach."

"Did he see her injury?" Steele asked.

"Every night."

Morgan and Tom exchanged a wide-eyed glance. Before they had a chance to ask what she meant, Mae asked, "Can we go to Ellie's house?"

"Yes. If Ellie's not there—well, I don't know how she could be if she's . . . if she's . . ." Morgan's gaze slid to Steele's, and said, "We can say we are doing a wellness check if someone comes by."

"Good thought," Tom said.

"Let me get my tools," Morgan said.

Tom stood and said, "I'll get the flashlights."

"No lights are on, but the patio doors are open," Steele said as he grasped Bear's collar to keep him from running inside.

Reaching the patio, Steele called Ellie's name. No response. "Mae, you stay here with Bear."

The men walked through the house, and again, no one was there. Morgan told Mae and Bear to come inside.

"Do you think I could look around?" Mae asked.

"We're prepared with a cover story, so you might as well," Morgan replied.

"I'll show you the master bedroom," Steele said.

When they reached the room, Mae looked at all the surfaces, but she didn't see one personal item she could hold. There were no photographs, no bottles of perfume, no jewelry or mementos on the dresser.

Opening the closet door, Mae found something she could touch. There was a wide selection of expensive clothing, which Steele said belonged to Ellie. "Steele, can you point out something you've seen her wear recently?"

Walking inside the closet, Steele pointed to a dress Ellie was wearing the first night he met her. Mae ran her hand over the dress and grasped the cloth tightly as she closed her eyes.

Quietly, Steele waited.

He didn't have long to wait until Mae's eyes snapped open.

"She's dead."

CHAPTER EIGHTEEN

Dead Dead

"Steele!" Morgan shouted from the kitchen.

Running from Ellie's bedroom, Steele found Morgan and Tom standing in the kitchen. "What's wrong?"

"You put Ellie's bracelet on the counter when we left last night, right?" Morgan asked.

Steele tapped the counter. "It was right there."

"It's gone," Tom said.

"The patio doors were open when we arrived. She came home, or someone else was here," Steele said.

Mae was standing in the doorway, listening to their conversation. "Steele, we need to talk about this."

Morgan and Tom's eyes slid from Steele to Mae.

"Talk about what? What's going on?" Tom asked.

Mae looked at Steele, and said, "I think we need to sit down for this conversation."

They all pulled out chairs and sat at the counter.

"What do you want to say?" Steele asked.

Mae took a deep breath and said, "Ellie's dead."

The men exchanged a glance, and Tom asked, "You mean she's playing dead, or she's *really* dead dead?"

"I'm afraid I mean she's dead dead. And she was deceased before last night," Mae responded.

Steele leaned forward, bracing his arms on the counter. "Mae, how can she be dead?" He tapped the marble surface. "I've sat at this counter with her. We've talked. She removed her bracelet and handed it to me. It had a broken heart. We walked the beach with Bear. We've had drinks together." Steele thought about that statement. He'd had a drink, but he remembered Ellie had declined.

"Have you ever communicated with people who have passed before?" Mae asked.

Steele looked at her as if he thought she'd lost her last marble. "Of course not." He turned to Morgan and Tom and said, "You saw her the last time you were here."

Both men shook their heads from side to side.

"Not really. Remember, she'd already walked into the house by the time you told us she was there," Tom replied.

"Oh, yeah."

"Mae, if she's dead, why has Steele seen her in the daytime, and she looked normal?" Morgan stared at Steele. "She did look normal, didn't she? You didn't mention she had a hole in her when we talked on the phone, and you told me about meeting her."

"She was as normal as you are. She said she'd been a designer, and that she loved walking on the beach . . . ," Steele tried to recall everything they'd discussed. He realized he hadn't learned much about her.

"Did you say she was a designer?" Mae asked.

Steele nodded. "I think she said she didn't do that anymore, or at least, that was the impression I got."

Mae left the kitchen and returned a few minutes later, holding the dress she'd touched earlier. "The label in this dress says *Eleanor Marlowe*. Do you know who that is?"

"Yeah, that's Ellie," Steele said.

Mae's eyes bounced from Steele to Morgan and Tom. "Haven't you guys ever heard of her?"

The men shook their heads back and forth.

"Should we recognize that name?" Morgan asked.

"She was a well-known designer," Mae told them.

"She didn't mention she was famous," Steele said.

"She designed clothing for movie stars and other prominent people," Mae said.

"Sorry, I've never heard of her, but I'm not into fashion," Tom said.

"You don't have to be into fashion to know that Eleanor Marlowe was killed last year. It was in the headlines for weeks," Mae told them.

Steele stared at Mae in disbelief. "That was her?" He remembered the story of Ellie's murder was on the nightly news for days. "That happened around Valentine's Day, didn't it?"

"Yes, it did." Morgan had already pulled out his cell phone to find some information. He held up a picture of Eleanor Marlowe.

"That's her," Steele said.

"You're right, Steele. She is one beautiful woman." Morgan held the screen for Tom to see.

Tom leaned back in his chair. "Wow! Who killed her?"

"They've never found her killer. She was well-respected in her industry, and she had many friends. They couldn't find a motive or a suspect for her murder," Mae replied.

"That's a real shame," Morgan said.

Mae pointed to the ocean. "She was killed on this beach."

CHAPTER NINETEEN

Ghosts, Spirits, Apparitions

"I need a stiff drink," Tom said.

They walked back to Steele's house, and while Morgan and Mae waited on the deck, Steele and Tom went inside. Steele grabbed a bone for Bear, and Tom poured two fingers of bourbon for everyone.

They carried their drinks to the deck and sat with Morgan and Mae. Sipping their bourbon in silence, they were lost in their thoughts, trying to make sense of what Mae told them.

Finally, Morgan asked, "Mae, what do you remember hearing about her murder?"

"I remember reading that it was late at night, and she was walking on the beach. Several people came forward and told police they had seen her that night. She was alone."

Morgan pulled out his cell phone again and started reading about Eleanor Marlowe's murder. "You're right, Mae. According to the coroner, she died around midnight. She was shot at close range."

Tom turned to Mae and asked, "Have you seen cases like this before? I mean, have you seen people who were dead, but they weren't moving on—or seeing the light—or whatever the hell is supposed to happen after death?"

"Yes. A few times. Each time, the person was murdered and their murder was never solved."

"Are you saying that dead people hang around to find out what happened to them?" Steele asked.

Mae nodded. "That's been my experience with the ones I've seen. They can't find peace, and they are unable to move on. They seem to think their death was premature or it was a mistake. They need to know why it happened to them."

"What happened to those ghosts?"

"I was called to help solve their murders."

"Did you?"

"Yes."

"Did they *move on*?" Tom asked.

"Well, the people no longer saw them. I didn't see them either," Mae replied.

Tom glanced at the shore to see if he saw anyone walking on the beach. "Do they *have* to move on, or can they stay here forever?"

"That's a question I can't answer," Mae replied.

Steele stared at Mae. "I'm not psychic. Why did I see her?"

"I don't know. Do you think you could have met her before? In the cases I've seen, usually the people who see . . . spirits have a connection with them."

Morgan stopped reading and clicked off his phone. "You mean *ghosts*."

Shrugging, Mae said, "Ghosts, spirits, apparitions . . . there are many names for these lost souls."

"I've never met Ellie before now," Steele said.

"And you first saw her walking on the beach?" Mae asked.

Steele nodded. "Then, one night, I saw Bear with her. When they walked further down the beach, I thought she must live in one of the other homes, and Bear belonged to her. But later that night, Bear came to my house."

Tom pointed to Ellie's house. "Someone is living there."

"I've not seen anyone else there, Tom." Steele recalled the encounter with the cleaning lady, and said, "Wait a minute. I saw the lady who cleans the house once a week. She told me that no one had lived there for a year. I just thought she was mistaken."

"Considering what you've told me about Ellie, I think she is more *advanced* than most spirits. I think she may have powers that I haven't encountered before."

"You mean like the ability to walk through walls? I know I've locked the doors at night, but somehow Bear gets out and walks the beach with her," Steele said.

Mae nodded. "It's possible. She seems to have unique abilities. In the cases I mentioned, the spirits are in the same condition as they were at the time of their murders. You've seen Ellie as a normal person—no wounds—like she wasn't deceased."

Morgan groaned. "You mean you saw the ghosts with bullet holes, blood, and everything? That kind of thing?"

"Yes. One man I saw was said to have hung himself, and his spirit still had the noose around his neck until we found the person who had staged the scene. He didn't hang himself."

Closing his eyes, Morgan shook his head and said, "I wouldn't want to be in your brain, Mae."

Tom rolled his eyes. "We are sounding crazier and crazier. I hope to hell no one is recording this conversation."

"Last night . . . before she disappeared, I asked Ellie who did this to her, and she said, '*maybe you can find out*,'" Steele said.

"Tomorrow morning, I'll call a detective I know in the local police department. See what I can find out about her murder and the investigation," Morgan said.

Steele didn't know what he thought Mae would tell him, but he didn't want to believe Ellie was dead. He made a silent vow that he would find out who murdered her. The problem was, he didn't want her to move on.

CHAPTER TWENTY

What Was Your First Clue?

"Weren't you going to dinner with Mae tonight?" Steele asked Morgan.

"Yes, but we decided we'd go the next time I'm here. We want to stay here tonight and see if Ellie walks the beach."

"All this talk about spirits and ghosts has made me hungry," Tom said. "I'm ordering some food. Chinese anyone?"

While they were eating their dinner on the deck, they saw a light come on in Ellie's bedroom.

Tom swallowed a bite of his pot sticker and said, "If I didn't see that with my own eyes, I wouldn't believe it."

"I see it, and I'm still having a hard time believing it," Morgan added.

"Steele, do you think you should go over and talk to Ellie alone?" Mae said.

Steele stuck his chopsticks in the carton of food and set it on the table. "I don't know what to say to her. I've never talked to a ghost."

Morgan chuckled. "It seems that's what you've been doing since you met her."

"I guess that's true enough. I still can't wrap my brain around this."

"I think you've handled this situation well. Much better than most," Mae said. "There is one thing I haven't mentioned."

"That sounds ominous," Morgan said.

"No, not ominous, but it's something Steele should know. I've met some psychics who have seen spirits who do not realize that they're deceased. I've never personally encountered that situation."

"How could they not know they're dead if they have a hole in their body?" Tom asked.

"I can't explain it, but they are so confused that they can't remember anything, so they can't face the truth. I've been told that sometimes these spirits become very angry when you tell them that they're dead," Mae responded.

Steele saw another light from the deck area at Ellie's house. "Ellie did seem to have trouble remembering some things when I asked her questions. I asked her where she got her gold bracelet, and she said she couldn't remember. I thought most women would remember if someone gave them such an expensive gift. Do you think that means she doesn't know she's dead?"

"She probably can't remember. I would broach the subject of her death carefully," Mae replied.

"Why don't you give her a call and see if she wants to come over?" Tom asked.

"I don't know her number."

Morgan said, "Boy, you are slipping. I can't believe you didn't ask for her number?"

Steele shook his head. "I hadn't thought about this before, but I've never seen her with a cell phone."

Tom laughed. "Maybe that should have been your first clue that she was dead. How many people do you see without a cell phone glued to their ass today?"

"I'm curious to know if we'll be able to see her or if Steele is the only one who can," Mae said.

"Bear sees her," Steele said as he stood.

As if on cue, Bear stood, and Steele said, "Let's go, buddy. I know she'll want to see you."

CHAPTER TWENTY-ONE

The Kiss

Ellie smiled when she saw Steele and Bear standing on her deck. "Hi, Steele." She leaned down and kissed Bear on his head. "How's my favorite beach partner?"

Steele saw the heart bracelet dangling on her wrist. He couldn't help but notice how beautiful she looked in her blue blouse and shorts. She seemed so vibrant and . . . alive. *Is it possible I'm just having a long, crazy nightmare? Or am I just going crazy?*

Ellie looked up at Steele and said, "Are you okay? You look tired."

"I'm fine. We've had a busy day."

"Come in, or would you prefer to sit on the deck?"

Steele knew everyone next door would be watching if they sat on the deck, so he said, "Let's go inside."

They sat on the sofa, and Ellie asked if she could get Steele something to drink, but he declined.

"I came by earlier, but you weren't home."

"I must have been on the beach." She tapped the sofa next to her leg, and Bear climbed up beside her as if he'd done it a thousand times. He laid down with his head in her lap.

Steele watched her for a moment, thinking she looked so beautiful sitting there with Bear. She looked normal. He told himself nothing about this situation was *normal.* "Ellie, can you tell me what happened last night?"

Ellie turned her wide gray eyes on him. "What about last night? What do you mean?"

"When I saw you on the beach. What happened to you?"

Cocking her head to one side, she gave Steele a puzzled look. "I didn't see you on the beach last night."

Steele felt out of his element. He didn't know how to tell her that she might be a ghost. *How am I supposed to say—you're dead?* He thought he would ease his way into that conversation. "Ellie, do you think you have difficulty remembering some things?"

Ellie looked out toward the ocean, and Steele could see her lips start to quiver. After a few moments, she nodded and said softly, "I can't figure out why that's happening to me." When she looked at him, a single tear dropped over her cheek. "Maybe there's something wrong with me."

Bear raised his head and licked her face. Wanting to comfort her like Bear, Steele reached over and clasped her hand. "It's going to be okay." Clutching her hand, he noticed how soft and warm it was. "Can you remember the last time you had someone in your house other than me?"

She tried to smile as another tear trailed over her cheek. "What about Bear?"

Steel chuckled. "Excluding Bear."

She looked away again. "I can't remember the last time someone was here. You've been the only person to talk to me in a long time. Most people ignore me—it's like they don't even see or hear me when

I'm talking to them." She hesitated, then added, "But there have been times when I walk on the beach late at night, and I see a few people who speak. They say . . . they tell me . . . that I'm a spirit."

Steele breathed a sigh of relief. *She knows. I guess she just can't face it.* "What do you think when they say that to you?"

"I think they're wrong, and I don't understand why they say that to me. If it's true, why am I here and not . . . I don't know . . . in heaven or somewhere else. I don't want to be a spirit. I want to live my life."

"Does it make you angry when those people tell you that?"

"Not really. It confuses me."

Lacing his fingers through hers, Steele said, "I think those people who see you could be right, Ellie."

More tears flowed, and she swiped them away with the back of her hand. "How do you know?"

"I'm not positive, but I saw you on the beach last night, and you had . . . well, let's just say you didn't look like you do now."

"What do you mean?"

Steele didn't think he should overload her with details at the moment. She looked so fragile that he didn't know what would happen if he told her how she appeared to him last night. "I'll explain later. Right now, I came over to tell you that I have a psychic at my house with two of my friends who are detectives in Miami. The psychic helped them solve murders in the past, so they trust her, and she is helping me on a case. I've told them about you, and Mae, the psychic, told me she has helped spirits in your situation before. Why don't you come over to my house and we can talk to her? Maybe we can make sense of this."

She was quiet for several minutes, but he waited for her to decide what she wanted to do.

Finally, she said, "Steele, would you do me a favor?"

"Anything."

"Would you kiss me?"

His expression must have told her he was caught by surprise at her question because she quickly added, "I want to know if I can feel it. I don't think I've been kissed in . . . a long time."

After he got over the shock of her request, he said, "You don't have to ask me twice." He slid closer to her, cupped her face in his hands, and kissed her. It was a gentle kiss at first, but it quickly turned passionate when she wrapped her arms around his neck. Desire welled inside of him and he had to force his lips from hers.

She opened her eyes and said, "Wow."

Steele stared at her, trying to collect his wits. *Wow was right. That was a life-changing kiss.*

Standing, Steele took her hand in his again. "Come on, let's go to my house and we'll see if we can figure this out. I'm not going to let you get away from me without a fight."

Reaching his back deck, Steele found everyone waiting for him. "Ellie, this is Mae Rogers."

Mae stood and hugged her. "It's nice to meet you, Ellie."

Steele pointed to Morgan and Tom. "This is Morgan and Tom. They are my detective friends from Miami."

Morgan looked at Steele and laughed. "All right, enough kidding around. Didn't Ellie want to come over?"

"Are you losing your touch, buddy?" Tom asked.

Steele and Mae exchanged a glance.

Steele said, "This is Ellie."

"What are you talking about?" Morgan asked.

Ellie gripped Steele's hand. "They really can't see me."

Steele's gaze slid to Morgan, then Tom. "You two aren't messing with me, are you?"

Morgan shook his head at him. "Stop joking around, Steele. The joke's over."

"He's not joking, Morgan." Mae pointed to the chair where Ellie was sitting. "Ellie is sitting in that chair."

Morgan and Tom stared open-mouth at the chair. Bear was sitting beside the chair with his head suspended about six inches from the cushion.

"Does Bear have his head on her lap?" Morgan asked.

"Yes, he does," Steele replied.

Morgan and Tom couldn't believe what they were seeing. They saw Bear's fur moving as if someone was stroking his head.

"I guess I didn't think it was possible," Morgan said.

"Tell me about it," Steele replied.

CHAPTER TWENTY-TWO

Covered in Blood

Everyone was silent for a moment, then Steele said, "Mae, Ellie doesn't remember what happened to her. She's seen other people on the beach who have told her she's a spirit."

Mae sat beside Ellie and smiled. "I've met several people like you, Ellie. I know it can be difficult to come to terms with what has happened to you."

"Do you know why can't I remember?"

"I'm not sure I know the answer to that question. It may be because it was such a frightening experience, and it's too painful to remember. I think the reason differs for everyone."

Steele could hear what was said, but Tom and Morgan could only hear Mae's side of the conversation.

Ellie gave Mae a pleading look. "Steele said you're a psychic. Can you tell me what happened?"

Steele said, "Ellie, we know what happened to you, but we don't know why it happened." He reached over and clasped her hand. "Are you sure you want to know?"

"Yes, I do. I've been confused for such a long time."

Steele stood and said, "I'll be right back."

Returning with his laptop, he typed in Ellie's name. He clicked on a newspaper article from a year ago that covered her murder. After he moved Bear's head from her lap, he replaced it with the laptop. "Read this."

Ellie finished reading the story and looked up at Steele. "A year ago, I was murdered on this beach."

Steele took the laptop from her, closed it, and set it aside. "Yes. And you can't remember anything that happened that night?"

Shaking her head from side to side, she said, "I don't know why anyone would murder me."

Bear laid his head on her lap again, and Ellie rubbed his ears. "Is that the reason I walk the beach at night? Am I trying to remember?"

"It could be." Mae hesitated, then said, "From what Steele told me, I think you have unique skills."

"What do you mean?"

"Everyone I've met in your situation is confined to one area. You seem to have the ability to move about freely; you're not confined to one place. And Steele said your wardrobe changes. How do you do that?"

Ellie shrugged. "I just *think* about what I want to wear, and it appears. But I'm not good at some things. There are times when I want to go to a store, and I end up in the wrong place."

Mae chuckled. "Still, what you can do is remarkable. I've never heard of anyone else with your abilities."

"Your case was never solved, Ellie. I want to try to find out who did this to you," Steele said.

"Tom and I want to help," Morgan said.

"Ellie, if you don't mind, I'd like for all of us to go to the beach with you tonight. Is that okay with you?"

"Yes."

"Did you always walk the beach late at night before your murder?" Mae asked.

"I think so."

It was a chilly evening, and Steele gave Ellie one of his jackets to wear to the beach. Mae told Ellie to stick with her nightly routine. They walked the shoreline with Ellie for nearly an hour. Just before midnight, and without explanation, Ellie turned around and started walking back toward her home.

Morgan and Tom didn't know why they turned around, so Steele started to explain when he saw Ellie walk through Morgan.

"What's going on? I felt like something just moved me," Morgan asked.

Steele said, "Ellie just turned around."

Tom frowned. "She walked through me, didn't she?"

Steele nodded.

Reaching the stretch of beach in front of her home, Ellie stopped and turned to stare at the ocean. Suddenly, her shorts, blouse, and Steele's jacket were lying on the shore. Steele thought she would be nude, but she wasn't. Her clothing had been replaced by a long, flowing white dress that was swirling around her legs from the ocean breeze.

Mae and Steele looked at each other, and Steele said, "Ellie . . ."

Ellie turned around to look at him, and just like the night before, the front of her dress was covered in blood.

"I see her!" Morgan exclaimed.

"So do I," Tom said.

Steele reached for her, but his hand grasped air. "Ellie!"

She disappeared.

CHAPTER TWENTY-THREE

Pink Teddy Bear

When Ellie disappeared, Steele, Mae, Morgan, Tom, and Bear ran to Ellie's home. They searched every room, but she wasn't there. Once they returned to Steele's house, they sat on the deck and waited to see if she would reappear.

"Mae, why do you think Morgan and Tom could see her for a second before she disappeared?" Steele asked.

Mae shrugged. "I can't explain that. But when I touched her hand, I saw her on the night she was murdered—what she was doing—what she was wearing—everything. She was standing just as she was tonight, looking out at the ocean, and then she turned around to walk back to her home. A man was behind her, holding a gun. I didn't see his face, and I don't think he said anything before . . . before he shot her."

"Did she know the man?" Steele asked.

"I'm not sure."

"I'm thankful Tom and I saw her for a moment tonight. At least we know we're not having a group mental breakdown," Morgan said.

Tom nodded his agreement. "I'm just happy to know I'm not going crazy."

Morgan leaned forward, braced his elbows on his knees, and looked at Steele. "We have to get back to Miami, and we'll try to find out what we can about the investigation from our friends in the department here. What else can we do?"

"I'll start my investigation in the morning. Maybe you two can come back next weekend, and we can compare notes," Steele replied.

"Steele, since we're going to the mall in the morning, I'd like to come back here afterward and talk to Ellie if she has reappeared," Mae said.

"Of course. I think she already trusts you. Hopefully, I'll uncover some useful information that may help her to remember some things." Steele couldn't bring himself to tell them that he didn't want Ellie to disappear forever. He didn't want her to *move on*. How could he explain his feelings to them when he didn't understand them? Since meeting Ellie, she was his first thought in the morning and his last thought at night. He couldn't shake the feeling that she was supposed to be in his life—permanently.

Mae held Amy's pink teddy bear in her hand as she and Steele walked toward the Yum Yum Ice Cream Shoppe.

Suddenly, she stopped walking and turned toward the busy parking lot. "Someone is watching Amy." She pointed to a row of cars near the ice cream shop. "He's sitting in a car in that area."

Steele was tempted to ask questions, but he remained silent, not wanting to interrupt her visions.

"It's a nice, expensive car . . . shiny black . . . but I can't see him." Clutching the stuffed bear to her chest, Mae turned and continued walking.

Reaching the ice cream shop, they walked inside, and Steele said hello to the owner, Mr. Simpson.

"Would you like something, Mae?"

"Yes, I want one scoop of vanilla in a waffle cone with extra sprinkles."

Steele gave Mr. Simpson their order, and as Mr. Simpson scooped the vanilla ice cream and started to add the sprinkles, he glanced up at Steele and said, "This is what Amy Carson always ordered. How did you know? I don't remember telling you that."

Steele turned around and looked at Mae, who was now seated at one of the tables and appeared to be in deep concentration, oblivious to their conversation. He glanced back at Mr. Simpson and said, "I didn't know." Inclining his head in Mae's direction, he added, "This is her order. The chocolate is for me."

Mr. Simpson looked at the woman sitting at the table. "That's where Amy always sat."

Steele had doubts about a psychic helping him on a case, but it was becoming more difficult for him to remain skeptical. There was no way Mae knew what Amy ordered or where she sat in the shop. She couldn't know because he didn't know.

Taking a seat across from Mae, Steele stared at Amy's pink teddy bear sitting on the table. He noticed the cute little stuffed bear was holding a red heart in his mouth.

CHAPTER TWENTY-FOUR

Someone is Watching

"Mae, do you always eat vanilla ice cream with extra sprinkles?" Steele asked.

Mae glanced at the cone she was holding and shook her head. "Never. I don't know why I ordered it."

Inclining his head toward Mr. Simpson, Steele said, "The owner of the shop just told me that was what Amy always ordered. He also said you were sitting where Amy always sat."

Mae nodded slightly. "I'm connecting with her."

Steele sat back and licked his chocolate ice cream, waiting for her to say more.

Mae picked up the bear again and held it against her chest. "Whoever was in that car watched her the entire time she was in here."

"But you can't see him?"

"No, it's more of a . . . feeling I get. It's hard to explain, but it's like I'm an observer of what is happening around Amy, but at the same time, I can feel what she was feeling."

Steele glanced outside at the parking lot. *Could she have seen a man watching her from his car?* "What was she feeling?"

"She was thinking about the cards she'd bought to give her friends at school on Valentine's Day. She liked one particular young man . . . and she was hoping she received a card from him." Mae stared into Steele's eyes and answered his unasked question, "She wasn't aware that someone was watching her."

It unnerved Steele the way Mae could read what he was thinking. He'd never met anyone with her unusual abilities. "Why don't we walk to the back of the mall, and I'll show you where they found Amy's bike."

They left the ice cream shop and walked down the sidewalk. As they neared the last store, Mae pointed to a bike stand. "She locked her bike there and walked to the ice cream shop."

They walked toward the bike stand, and Mae stopped in front of the window of *Infinities.* "Amy stopped and looked in the window. She was looking at . . . something with hearts."

Stepping up to the window, Steele stared at the display advertising Valentine's Day. The small pink and red heart pillows held expensive heart bracelets, necklaces, and rings. "Amy's mother said she loved hearts." He started to walk away, but a heart bracelet caught his eye. It was exactly like the one Ellie wore. "That's the bracelet Ellie wears."

"I noticed it last night." Mae moved closer to the window and said, "They hide the price, but it's quite expensive."

"It's a heavy piece, and all of the hearts are solid gold. She couldn't remember where she got it."

"Maybe she bought it here. It's an exclusive women's shop. Why don't we go in and see if they carry Ellie's clothing line? I don't know if her business continued after her death."

Steele hadn't thought of that possibility, but he did need to find out more about her life, including her previous business. He needed to know everything about her. "Good idea."

Once inside the shop, Mae guided Steele to the area where they displayed the expensive dresses. A saleswoman approached, and Mae asked, "Do you carry Eleanor Marlowe designs?"

The woman's eyes lit up. "Why, yes, we do. Follow me." She led them to the designer section and said, "We have a nice selection. If you see something you like, just let me know. My name is Georgia."

"Thank you, Georgia. I'm surprised her clothing is still available in stores since she was killed last year."

The saleswoman's expression changed. "How sad was that! I guess someone took over her company." She started to walk away, then turned back to them and said, "We also have some of her jewelry designs."

Mae and Steele exchanged a glance. "I didn't know she designed jewelry."

"She'd just started her jewelry line before her death. Her pieces are gorgeous."

Steele and Mae hurried to the jewelry department, and Mae asked the salesman to see the gold heart bracelet.

"You have wonderful taste. That's an Eleanor Marlowe design," the man said as he lifted the piece from a locked display case.

"I was admiring this in your window," Mae said.

The man smiled at her. "This bracelet draws many customers inside. It's quite expensive, but the quality is exquisite and worth every penny."

Mae handed the bracelet to Steele. As he examined the piece, he saw a little gold heart tag with the initials *EM* engraved. That piece was missing from Ellie's bracelet. "What is the price?"

"This one is 18k gold, and the price is ten thousand."

CHAPTER TWENTY-FIVE

Lost the Connection

Steele and Mae left *Infinities,* and she said, "That car . . . it's a black Lexus . . . and he pulled to the curb. I think he . . . "

When she stopped speaking, Steele could see she was in a trance-like state. He gripped her elbow, urging her away from the door. A woman passed them on the sidewalk and bumped into Mae. She lost her grip on the teddy bear, and it tumbled to the sidewalk.

Steele picked up the Bear and handed it to her. But he saw that she no longer had that far-away look in her eyes.

"I lost my connection, but the man who was watching Amy pulled to the curb in front of this store."

Mae had given him more information than he expected. "Let's go to the field behind the mall." Once they were behind the mall, Steele led the way to the location where Amy's bike had been found.

Mae walked around the grassy area in silence for several minutes. She looked up at Steele and said, "I only feel fear. I can't see what she is seeing now."

"Do you know if the Lexus followed her back here?"

Mae closed her eyes momentarily, and when she opened them, she shook her head from side to side. "I don't know. I need to rest my mind."

Steele was new to this psychic stuff, but he imagined seeing what other people saw could be exhausting, particularly in situations involving children. "We can go back to my house, and you can rest or go to the beach if you prefer. I appreciate the time you've given me, and you're welcome to stay as long as you want. I'll be making phone calls all afternoon, so you'll have the place to yourself."

"Thanks, Steele. I planned on staying for a couple of days. It all depends if I can connect with Amy and be helpful with the case.

"If you have the time, I'd like your help with Ellie's case too."

Mae smiled. "I want to help, and I have the time. I have a lot to learn about Ellie's abilities."

"I'm going to find out what happened to her business and why her home wasn't sold."

Mae said, "I hadn't thought about that, but it is unusual. Maybe the person who inherited her estate couldn't bear to sell it."

Steele was determined to find out everything about Ellie's life and her death.

When they reached Steele's house, Mae decided to sit at the beach with Bear. Steele took a cup of coffee to his office and started making calls. His first call was to Mr. Simpson at the Yum Yum Shoppe. Mr. Simpson said he'd never noticed a man sitting in a black Lexus near his shop.

"I know you're busy inside your shop, but if you happen to see a man in a black Lexus watching young girls in your shop, or if you see anything unusual, give me a call."

After a few more calls, Steele reviewed his notes on Amy's case. He realized he didn't see anything to indicate that Amy had a cell phone. *What girl Amy's age didn't have a cell phone?* His next call was to Amy's parents. As expected, Amy's mother confirmed she did have a cell phone, and the police didn't find it. Mrs. Carson gave him the number and said the phone case was pink with white hearts.

"Did you disconnect the number?" Steele asked.

"No, but the police said the phone was probably destroyed. I guess we thought if we closed the account, it would make it seem so . . . final . . . like we would lose our only connection to her."

Hearing the emotion in her voice, Steele swallowed hard and said softly, "I understand."

When he ended the call, he thought about the cell phone. He envisioned a scenario where the perpetrator found Amy's phone, tossed it, or destroyed it. Anything was possible. He thought about what Mae said earlier—*she'd lost connection—Mrs. Carson didn't want to lose connection with her daughter.*

He thought about the conversation he'd had with Morgan and Tom about Ellie's cell phone. He didn't know if her cell phone was important, but he was still curious. He'd gleaned helpful information from cell phones in the past. He added another note to his list of questions—*what happened to Ellie's cell phone?*

CHAPTER TWENTY-SIX

Beam Me Up, Scotty

Having spent three hours on the phone, Steele was encouraged by the information he'd learned about Ellie's business and who'd inherited her estate. He had a lot to think about, so he decided to get out of the house for a while and move around. He thought better on his feet. He decided he would go back to the mall. He found Mae at the beach and gave her a house key, and Bear left with him.

Steele parked behind the mall, and when they left the car, he said, "Bear, we're looking for a pink cell phone," They walked to the field where Steele thought he would start his search for Amy's phone. He knew it wasn't likely that he would find the phone, but he might get lucky.

Detectives knew they needed to think like a criminal. If Amy was frightened and had the time and the presence of mind to call 911, the perp might have panicked and destroyed her phone. Of course, the kidnapper would've been in a hurry to get out of the area, so it would be more expedient for him to toss the phone. By the time the cops found the phone, if they did, the perp would be long gone—with Amy.

After searching the field for an hour and coming up empty-handed, Steele and Bear drove home. On the way home, he stopped and grabbed three sandwiches, hoping Ellie would be home so she could join them.

Mae was in the kitchen when Steele returned. "I brought lunch, and I thought I would walk over and see if Ellie's there and invite her to join us."

"Great. I'll make some iced tea."

Steele reached Ellie's home and he shouted through the open patio doors, "Ellie!" He didn't hear anything, so he walked inside and called out again, "Ellie, are you here?"

Still no response.

He walked toward the kitchen and suddenly came to a halt when he saw something . . . what he didn't know . . . it looked like some sort of image flickering in and out. He reached for the pistol he had clipped to his belt. The image flashed again. *What the hell? I feel like I'm in a Star Trek movie. Beam me up, Scotty.*

After a few more flickers, a human form began to take shape, and Ellie appeared dressed in a long aqua-blue dress.

She smiled at him. "Steele, what are you doing here?"

Steele blinked and blinked again.

"Steele?" Her eyes drifted to the pistol in his hand. "What's wrong?"

Steele returned the pistol to his holster. "Nothing. I thought I heard something when I walked in." She looked so . . . solid, and Steele reached out and touched her arm. It was soft and warm. "Ah . . . I came to invite you over for lunch."

"I'm not hungry, but I'd like to talk to you."

"Mae is still at my house. Do you want to talk in front of her?"

"Yes, I think she can help me."

On the way to his house, Steele asked, "Where were you when I walked into your house?"

"I was at a store and felt I had a reason to go home. Why do you ask?"

He didn't answer her question but asked another one, "Do you know how you return to your home when you are somewhere else?"

She gave him a puzzled look. "I think about home, and then I'm there. I don't understand how it happens."

Steele didn't understand it, either. He still couldn't believe what he saw.

They lunched on the patio, but Ellie didn't eat or drink anything.

As Steele ate two sandwiches, he discussed what he'd found out about Ellie's estate. "I discovered that your uncle, John Marlowe inherited your estate."

"Yes, he's my father's brother. The only family I had left. I saw him—not long ago, but he didn't talk to me, so I guess that means he didn't see me."

"Where does he live?"

"Palm Beach."

"He inherited your company?"

"Yes. He's an excellent businessman and gave me great advice when I started my business. I couldn't have done it without him."

"Do you mind if I talk to him?" Steele asked.

"Not at all. Maybe I could go with you, and you could tell him that you see me and talk to me."

Steele glanced at Mae, and she arched her brows at him.

Oh yeah, that would be just great.

CHAPTER TWENTY-SEVEN

Hearts Hearts Hearts

"Ellie, do you know what happened to your cell phone?" Steele asked.

Leaning back in her chair, Ellie said, "No, I don't."

"When was the last time you saw it?"

Growing quiet, Ellie tried to remember the last time she'd made a call. "I can't remember, but I always had it with me before . . . well, you know."

"Would you look around for it in your house? It might provide some useful information."

"Of course."

Steele could tell Ellie became frustrated when she couldn't remember something, so he changed the subject. "Why don't you tell me about your business?"

"Many in my profession told me I was a fool not to move my business to New York or California, but I didn't want to leave Florida." She looked out at the ocean. "I love it here, and this is where I was always inspired. I guess you could say I preferred a more laid-back lifestyle."

They discussed Ellie's business until Steele felt he understood the design industry. He was impressed with Ellie's business knowledge and that she didn't cave to the pressure to work somewhere else. She lived her dream on her terms. He could relate. That was the reason he became a private investigator. He wanted to live life on his terms. Ellie was a woman to be admired. He liked so many things about her, and he didn't know what he was going to do about his growing romantic attachment to a ghost. *Where did that thought come from?*

"Did you know your company is still operating?"

Ellie smiled. "I do. I saw some of my designs in the store I visited."

"Does it surprise you that your uncle kept it going?" Mae asked.

It took a few seconds before Ellie responded. "In a way, I guess it is surprising. I don't know how he found the time. He wanted to retire. But he knew I had an excellent assistant, Rob Harmon. Rob was capable of running the company."

"Do you know why your uncle didn't sell your home?" Steele asked.

Ellie shook her head. "No. I thought he might come here occasionally, but he hasn't. At least, not when I'm there."

Steele thought it was time to discuss what happened to Ellie that night on the beach, so he said, "Ellie, Mae wanted to talk to you about what she saw last night."

Ellie noted Steele's serious tone and she looked at Mae. "What did you see?"

"When I touched your arm last night, I saw you on the beach the night you were murdered. You were looking out over the ocean and suddenly you turned around. A man was standing behind you, pointing a gun at you and he pulled the trigger."

Ellie looked at Steele for a moment and then she whispered, "Did I know him?"

Mae said, "I had the feeling you did, but you seemed—shocked."

Steele gave Ellie a moment to process what Mae told her. He glanced at her wrist and saw her bracelet. "Mae and I saw your bracelet in a store today."

Ellie looked surprised. "Really? When you asked me if it was a gift, I couldn't remember."

"The one we saw had a little gold tag with your initials," Steele told her.

Ellie looked down at her bracelet and turned it on her arm. Her eyes widened as if she remembered something important. "Yes, this one had the little tag . . . it was here, and now it's gone." She looked at Steele and said, "I remember now! I designed this bracelet."

"Do you know what happened to the tag?" Mae asked.

"No, I don't." Her brow furrowed in confusion. "There's something I think I should remember . . . but . . ." She rubbed her forehead and Steele could hear the frustration in her voice when she said, "Why can't I remember?" Several seconds passed, and she whispered, "Hearts . . . hearts . . . hearts."

Suddenly, her body started to flicker in and out, much as it did earlier.

"Uh-oh," Steele said.

"What's happening?" Ellie's voice sounded far away, more like an echo.

When Ellie flickered again, Mae reached for her, but her hand went through her arm.

Another flash and she was gone.

Mae stared open-mouthed and wide-eyed at Steele. "What just happened?"

"Scotty beamed her up again."

CHAPTER TWENTY-EIGHT

Tug of War

Ellie roamed the displayed cases in the jewelry department at *Infinities.* She hadn't intended to leave Steele and Mae, but her mind was on hearts, and for some reason, she ended up in the store. Seeing her heart bracelet displayed in the glass case, she pulled it out.

The department manager, Brad Conrad, was showing a well-dressed woman at the adjoining counter an expensive ring. Both turned to see a bracelet dangling in the air, and the woman said, "What's going on?"

Brad stood in stunned silence. When the bracelet rotated in the air, he backed away a few feet.

The woman said, "Is this some kind of joke? I don't think it's funny."

"I . . . can't . . . explain . . . that," Brad finally uttered.

The woman walked to the floating bracelet and grabbed one end. A tug-of-war ensued between the woman and an invisible force.

"Lady, I'm looking at this bracelet. You can see it when I'm finished," Ellie said.

The woman couldn't hear Ellie, and she was not deterred. She continued to yank on the bracelet.

Brad walked closer to the counter and watched the bracelet moving back and forth in mid-air.

"What's holding this thing?" The woman asked.

Looking around, Brad said, "I don't know." He moved his hand back and forth over the bracelet, thinking maybe some sort of wire or thread was suspending the piece. Nothing was there.

"Oh, you can have it. I don't want you to break it," Ellie said, releasing the bracelet.

The woman stumbled backward and landed on her butt in the middle of a display table. When she got to her feet, she threw the bracelet at Brad. "I don't know what you're trying to do, but I don't think this joke is funny! You just lost a customer!" She harrumphed loudly, turned, and stormed out of the store.

"She's wearing one of my designs," Ellie said to Brad, who was unaware of her presence.

Brad glanced around the store to see if anyone had noticed the entire incident. Seeing no one was watching, he placed the bracelet back inside the glass case.

Ellie noticed more of her designs in the display case. She removed a gold heart necklace and held it to her neck. Pulling the mirror on the counter closer, she looked at her reflection. It was a beautiful piece. Watching the necklace float through the air, and the mirror sliding across the counter, Brad's eyes nearly popped out of his head. He threw his hands in the air and ran away screaming.

Ellie watched him run away. *I wonder what's wrong with him.* She shrugged and glanced at the price tag. *My goodness, I had no idea it would be this expensive.* She pulled out all of the pieces she'd designed before her—she didn't like the word *death. I think demise is more palatable.* Every piece of jewelry was designed with hearts, her favorite symbol of love. She was amazed the store was carrying so many pieces. *It must be for Valentine's Day.*

Steele and Mae remained on the patio, waiting to see if Ellie would return. Thinking Mae might be tired of getting inside people's heads, Steele kept the conversation light.

"I guess since you planned a date with Morgan, you're not in a relationship."

"No, I'm not. I haven't found many men brave enough to date a woman who they think can read their mind."

Chuckling, Steele said, "Tom said the very same thing."

"What about Morgan? Do you think he's up to that challenge?"

"Oh, yeah. Morgan's not afraid of much."

Mae stared at him. "You do know that Ellie likes you—a lot."

"I like her a lot."

"I know, and I imagine that makes this situation difficult for you."

"Yeah, I've never been attracted to a ghost before."

CHAPTER TWENTY-NINE

Semantics

At dusk, Steele and Bear sat on the patio, watching the storm roll in over the ocean. The dark gray low-hanging clouds were barely distinguishable from the churning sea. Steele enjoyed watching the storm, though thoughts of Ellie filled his mind. It was difficult for him to wrap his brain around the fact that he'd fallen for a ghost. And fallen hard. Referring to her as a ghost didn't sound as final as saying she was dead.

Semantics.

The sad fact was that Ellie wasn't alive. He couldn't plan a future with her. He'd heard about love at first sight, but it had never happened to him.

Until Ellie.

He fell in love that first day he'd spoken to her. He'd liked the women he'd dated in the past, but he'd never been in love.

Damn my luck.

When the wind picked up, the rain blew onto the patio forcing Steele and Bear to move inside. Mae was in the kitchen cooking something, and Steele said, "Something smells delicious."

"I found everything I needed to make spaghetti. I hope you don't mind."

"Mind? Are you joking? It's nice to eat someone else's cooking. And I love spaghetti."

Turning to face Steele, Mae held up a bottle of wine and said, "Care for a glass?"

Steele nodded. "I'll pop the cork."

"Since I wasn't having any luck connecting with Amy, I thought I would cook. It always relaxes me."

"Give your mind a break tonight. We'll try again tomorrow." After Steele opened the wine, he walked to the window facing Ellie's house. "There's still no light on at Ellie's."

"Do you think she'll walk the beach tonight in this horrid weather?"

"I don't know. This is the worst storm I've seen in months." Steele knew he would stay awake late tonight to see if Ellie was on the beach. He dreaded seeing her in the same condition as the last time, but he didn't want her to be alone.

"I know if she's out there, you'll be with her."

Steele nodded. "It's not right that she's had to face that alone every night. I don't think she remembers, but I do."

Mae set two glasses of wine on the counter, and after Steele filled Bear's food bowl and refreshed his water, he poured wine into the glasses before he sat down. "Were you able to reach any of your psychic friends today?"

"Yes, I talked to three friends whom I consider to be the best in the business. They've never seen or heard about anyone with Ellie's abilities, and they're quite intrigued. They've made themselves available if I want their help. I told them we may need to call on them at some point." Mae sipped her wine, then added, "Every spirit we've encountered before has never appeared in what we would describe as a *solid* form. When I touched Ellie's arm, it was like touching your arm."

"Yeah. She's warm and soft and feels so alive." Steele knew the question he wanted to ask was going to sound crazy. But after he took a drink of wine, he asked anyway, "Have you ever seen a ghost . . . come back to life?"

Mae stared at him for a moment and then said, "You mean to come back from the dead?"

"Yeah, that's what I mean."

Mae shook her head. "I've seen some strange things, Steele. But I don't think that's possible. I don't know how it would be done."

Steele heard his landline ringing in his office, so he jumped up and ran to answer. He grabbed the receiver on the fourth ring. "Hello."

"Is this Steele Harper?"

"Yes. How can I help you?"

"My name is John Marlowe."

Quickly recognizing Ellie's uncle's name, Steele said, "What can I do for you, Mr. Marlowe?"

"To be honest, I'm not quite sure. I was out earlier, and when I returned home, there was a note on my desk for me to call Steele Harper in Siesta Key. There was no number, but you were the only Steele Harper in that area."

"Who left the note for you?"

Mr. Marlowe chuckled. "That's the strange thing. I have no idea."

Steele had a feeling he knew who had left the note.

"Where do you live in Siesta Key?"

"Next door to Ellie's home."

CHAPTER THIRTY

Straitjacket

The next morning, Steele and Mae returned to the mall. They spent an hour walking around, but Mae was unable to connect with Amy.

When they returned home, Mae packed her overnight bag and was getting ready to leave. When Steele started to pick up her bag to carry it to her car, he saw Amy's teddy bear on top.

"You don't mind if I take Amy's teddy bear with me, do you?"

"Not at all."

"If I can connect with her, I'll call you."

"Morgan and Tom will be here this weekend, so feel free to join us."

Driving to Palm Beach gave Steele time to think about the events over the last few days. Last night, there wasn't a light at Ellie's home, so he'd watched the beach to see if she would return during the storm. Bear stayed by his side, and Steele knew he was waiting for her, too. They watched the driving rain for an hour, and finally, just before midnight, Ellie appeared.

He told Bear to wait for him, and as he walked to the beach he tried to brace himself for what he would see. The first time he'd seen her with blood flowing over her garment, he'd been so stunned that his brain froze, and he was unable to react quickly.

When he reached her on the shore, it was a repeat of the night she was murdered. Again, when she turned to him, she was covered in blood. When he tried to pick her up to carry her home, she disappeared. Even though he knew what was going to happen, seeing her go through that again was difficult to handle.

Arriving at the address Mr. Marlowe had given him, Steele stopped at the guardhouse, lowered his window when the guard approached his car and handed him his business card. "Steele Harper to see Mr. Marlowe."

"Yes, sir. He's expecting you." The guard opened the gate and motioned him through. After parking in the circular driveway, he walked to the double-door entrance and pressed the doorbell.

A housekeeper opened the door and greeted him warmly. "Welcome, Mr. Harper. Mr. Marlowe is in the library. Please follow me."

Entering the library, John Marlowe was seated behind a large mahogany desk in a beautifully appointed room. Marlowe rose, walked around his desk, and extended his hand. "John Marlowe. Thank you for coming, Mr. Harper."

"Call me Steele, please." Steele took the measure of the tall, distinguished man with a commanding presence, a firm handshake, and a direct manner.

"And call me John. May we offer you something to drink? I know you've had a long drive."

"Coffee would be good."

Mr. Marlowe nodded to the housekeeper, and she quietly left the room.

"Steele, as I mentioned last night on the phone, there was a message left on my desk to call you. My housekeeper said she didn't leave the message, and quite frankly, I don't know who left the message or why I was supposed to call you."

"John, I was going to call you to discuss Ellie. As I said, I live next door to her."

"You mean where Ellie did live? I'm afraid I haven't had the heart to sell her home. I pay to have the house kept in good condition, and a lady cleans the place once a week." He glanced at a framed photograph on his desk, picked it up, and showed it to Steele. "I was very close to my niece. Her father was my brother, and he was killed in a plane crash with Ellie's mother when Ellie was young. Ellie came to live with me. She was a beautiful child and a wonderful young woman."

Steele stared at the photograph of a smiling Ellie with her uncle. There was a noticeable difference in her appearance. Ellie's complexion wasn't pale in the photograph, and her eyes sparkled with life. Though she was beautiful now, he didn't see the sadness in her eyes in the picture. "She's beautiful."

"Yes, she was." Once he returned the photograph to its position, John turned his attention to Steele. "Why do you think someone left a message for me to call you?"

"Because I'm investigating Ellie's murder. As you know, the case was never solved."

Marlowe leaned back in his oversized leather chair. "Yes, I'm well aware. I've even hired two private firms to investigate her murder, but they haven't been successful. Who hired you to investigate?"

"No one. I'm doing this for me."

Leaning forward, Marlowe braced his elbows on this desk and looked Steele in the eyes. "Why? Did you know Ellie?"

Taking a deep breath, Steele thought, *here we go—how do I tell him I'm talking to a ghost? He'll probably think I'm completely crazy and have me wearing a straitjacket within the hour.*

Maybe I am nuts.

"John, this is an unusual story."

CHAPTER THIRTY-ONE

Make it a Double Shot

Steele tried to organize his thoughts before he spoke. How was he going to break the news to John Marlowe that his niece was—well, not exactly alive—but he could see her and talk to her?

"John, this is going to sound like I should be in a hospital for the mentally insane, but . . ."

As if Steele had conjured up Ellie, she appeared by her uncle's desk and said, "Hi, Uncle John." She smiled at Steele and shook her finger at him. "I thought you were going to let me ride along when you came here."

Steele's eyes bounced from Ellie to John. "I . . . um . . ."

John was looking at him, his brows raised as if he was asking him to continue what he was saying.

"Um, Ellie, your uncle . . ."

"Yes, that's Uncle John," Ellie said, pointing to her uncle.

"I know, but I don't think he can see you. You know, like Morgan and Tom can't see you."

Steele glanced at John. He was leaning back in his chair, trying to distance himself from the madman in front of his desk.

"He can't?" Ellie asked.

Steele shook his head back and forth.

"What is wrong with you?" John asked.

"Well, he obviously got the message I left for him," Ellie said.

"Yes, he did, and he called me," Steele replied.

John watched the man in front of him having a one-sided conversation. He jumped up from his chair, but he remained behind his desk. "I think you need to leave."

"Uncle John, Steele needs to talk to you. Don't be rude," Ellie said.

"He's not being rude, Ellie. He can't see or hear you."

John looked like he was watching a tennis match, his eyes bouncing back and forth from Steele to the space where Steele was looking as he continued his crazy conversation.

"Uncle John!" Ellie shouted.

Steele rolled his eyes. "It doesn't matter how loudly you speak. He can't hear you. He can't see you."

"Did you just roll your eyes?" Ellie asked.

Steele rubbed his temples. "Well, yeah. I mean, your uncle is listening to a one-sided conversation. I'm sure he thinks I'm from Pluto—you know—out there."

John reached for his phone and picked up the receiver, all the while keeping a close watch on Steele. "I'm calling the police."

Ellie walked around the desk and snatched the phone from his hand. "Now listen to me. Steele needs to talk to you!"

Eyes wide, John slumped back to his chair and backed away as the phone dangled in front of him. "What the devil?"

Steele had a thought. "Ellie, write him a note."

"What do you want me to say?"

Throwing his arms in the air, he said, "I don't care, just something he'll recognize that it's from you."

Too stunned to move, John watched as a pen floated in the air, and then a piece of paper was torn from his notepad. "What's going on here?"

Ellie wrote the note and held it in front of his face. "Hi, Uncle John, or should I say Babo?"

"Ellie?" He looked around the room, and his eyes landed on the only person he could see. Steele. "Can you explain this?"

Steele was grateful John wasn't running from his office screaming. "I'll try."

Ellie wrote another note. "Sit back and relax, Babo. Steele will explain everything."

The housekeeper walked into the office with a tray holding a coffee pot, cups, and some cookies. She glanced at her boss and noticed that he was as white as a ghost. "Mr. Marlowe, are you all right?"

Trying his best to collect himself, he said, "Yes, thank you, Mrs. Baker."

"Hi, Mrs. Baker. Steele loves brownies. Do you have any made?" Ellie said.

No response.

Ellie looked at Steele and said, "Please tell Mrs. Baker I said hello."

Steele shook his head.

"Why not?"

Steele didn't want any more complications, so he simply pursed his lips and softly said, "Shhh."

"Mrs. Baker, please close the door, and I don't want to be interrupted," John said.

"Yes, sir."

"Before you begin, Steele, I think I need a bourbon, not coffee. How about you?" John asked as he walked to the bar.

Steele wanted the whole bottle. "A bourbon would be good right now."

"He could have asked if I wanted one," Ellie pouted as she sat on the arm of Steele's chair.

"I thought you couldn't drink," Steele replied.

John turned to him and said, "Who told you I couldn't drink?"

"Not you—Ellie."

"Ellie doesn't drink bourbon," Mr. Marlowe said.

Ellie smiled. "He remembered."

"No, she doesn't. She doesn't drink anything now."

"I see." John poured them both a double shot.

After he handed Steele his drink, he said, "If Ellie's in the room right now, where is she?"

Steele looked at Ellie, who was still sitting on the arm of his chair, swinging her crossed leg back and forth, distracting him. If her uncle wasn't in the room, he might have pulled her onto his lap. "She's sitting on the arm of my chair."

Ellie gave Steele a heart-stopping smile. "I'm still upset that you didn't let me ride with you."

"I'm sorry."

"Oh, for what?" John asked.

"Ellie wanted to ride with me when I came to see you, but I didn't see her this morning."

"Ask her what we did on her sixteenth birthday," John said.

"She can hear you." He glanced at Ellie, waiting for her response.

"I always wanted to go to Paris, and Babo took me there for my birthday."

"Paris," Steele said.

"Oh, my . . ." John didn't finish his sentence. He tossed back his bourbon, grabbed the bottle, and poured another.

Steele said, "I'm sorry, this is good bourbon, and I should be sipping, but . . ." Steele tossed back the double without tasting a drop. He cleared his throat and said, "I know this comes as a shock. I know how I felt when I met your niece. I didn't even realize she was a—spirit until I introduced her to my friends. They couldn't see or hear her."

John handed Steele the bottle. "So, you can talk to ghosts?"

CHAPTER THIRTY-TWO

Soulmate

With Ellie sitting on the arm of his chair, Steele found it difficult to concentrate. He told John about meeting his niece and everything that had happened since, but his eyes kept drifting to Ellie. She was *very* distracting.

John listened intently without interrupting, and when Steele finished, he said, "This is an unbelievable story. To tell you the truth, I don't know what to think."

"How can you not believe Steele?" Ellie asked.

Steele put his hand on her knee. "Ellie, look at it from his point of view. A madman shows up in his office and tells him he can see and speak to his long-departed niece. It is hard to believe."

Ellie stared at his hand on her knee. She placed her hand over his. "That feels . . . so good."

Steele gazed into her eyes. He *really* wanted to pull her onto his lap. But if he did that, then he'd want to kiss her senseless.

John looked at Steele and asked, "Is she still sitting beside you?"

"Yes."

"It must be very distracting when she talks, and you're trying to conduct two conversations at the same time," John said.

Steele chuckled. He wanted to say, *you have no idea, but he said,* "Somewhat. At times, I feel like my head might explode." *Like right now.*

John smiled and said, "She distracted a lot of men before her . . . well . . . it was because she was so lovely."

Looking into Ellie's eyes, Steele thought if another man looked at her cross-eyed, he shoot them. "That's understandable."

They stared at each other a few seconds before Steele resumed his conversation with John. "Anyway, when I found out Ellie was murdered, and it was an unsolved case, I knew I had to find the person responsible."

"What makes you think you can solve her case when the police and two private firms haven't been successful?"

Sharing his background with John, Steele said, "I'm good at what I do, John. I will find out who did this." He glanced at Ellie again. "I have a vested interest."

Ellie placed her palm on Steele's cheek and smiled. "You know you are very handsome."

Steele had a feeling she was enjoying frustrating him. He tried to concentrate on his conversation with John. "John, would you mind answering a few questions for me?"

"Perhaps you would like to join me for dinner, and we can continue our conversation."

Glancing at his watch, Steele hadn't realized how late it was. "I appreciate the offer, but I left my dog home alone."

"Why didn't you bring Bear with you?" Ellie asked.

"I didn't know if your uncle liked dogs," Steele replied.

"You stay and talk with Uncle John, and I'll take care of Bear. I wish I could bring him back with me," Ellie said.

"Thank you." Steele turned to John and explained, "Ellie offered to take care of my dog, so I can join you for dinner."

John said, "You mean she can go to your home and let the dog out?"

"Yes. She thinks about where she wants to go, and in the next moment, she's there. She's very fond of my dog."

"Ellie always loved dogs."

Once Ellie left, Steele thought he should have told her to return so she could ride home with him. He enjoyed her company.

As they ate dinner, Steele remembered the questions he wanted to ask since Ellie wasn't there to distract him. "When was the last time you saw Ellie before . . ."

"We had dinner in Palm Beach the night before her death."

"Did she act normal? Was anything troubling her?"

"No, it was a perfect night. Everything in her life was going well. Her business was successful, and she was about to launch her new jewelry line."

"Ellie told me she had an excellent assistant."

John nodded. "Rob Harmon. He runs her company for me now. I moved the headquarters to Palm Beach to make it more convenient for me, and Rob was keen to move here. He's an exceptional young man with an excellent head for business and he's very creative."

Steele told John he needed to speak with Rob. Then, he asked, "What about Ellie's personal life? Was she seeing anyone?"

"Not at that time. She'd been dating Clay Ford, but they'd broken off their engagement six months before her death. She may have had a date here or there, but she wasn't serious with anyone."

Steele had heard that name before. "Is Clay Ford a property developer?"

"Yes, and his headquarters is in Palm Beach."

"How long were they engaged?"

"I think about a year."

Steele concentrated on his steak for a few minutes before he asked, "Who broke off the engagement?"

"Ellie did."

"Do you know why?"

"She said he wasn't her soulmate."

After dinner, Steele and John drank brandy in the library. Since Steele didn't know if or when Ellie would return, he thought he would tell John what Ellie experienced every night since her murder.

"You mean she relives her murder every night on the beach?"

"Yes, and the moment just before her murder, my two friends saw her. But they can't see her at any other time."

"I would love to see her, but I don't think I could handle seeing her like that."

Steele understood. "I wouldn't advise it."

CHAPTER THIRTY-THREE

Head Over Boots

Steele was leaving John's home when Ellie returned.

"I was hoping you would come back," Steele said when she appeared in the library.

Her eyes widened, and she said, "You were?"

"Yes, it'll be nice to have company on the drive back."

"I take it that she's reappeared," John said.

Steele nodded and pointed to where Ellie was standing. "She's right there."

Ellie walked to her uncle's side and kissed him on the cheek. "Bye, Babo."

John reached up, touched his cheek, and glanced at Steele, his brows drawn together in question. "Did she just . . ."

"Yeah, she kissed your cheek and said goodbye."

Teary-eyed, John's voice quivered when he said, "Tell her goodbye and to come back. She can always write me notes."

"She heard you. She said she would visit again," Steele told him.

After Steele started the car, Ellie leaned over and changed the radio station. "Do you know how long it's been since I've been in a car?"

Steele turned and smiled at her. "A year?"

Ellie laughed. "Guess I walked into that one."

"Seatbelt."

Ellie arched her brow at him. "Seriously?"

Steele grinned. "Just teasing."

He listened to the tune on the radio—*Head Over Boots*—and glanced at Ellie. "Country?"

"Don't you like country music?"

"Yes, I do, but I didn't know you did. You don't remind me of a country music gal."

"I may have many surprises in store for you, Mr. Harper. Wait until you see my boots."

"I can't wait."

Ellie laughed and sang along with Jon Pardi.

Listening to the words of the song, Steele thought, *damn, I'm already head over boots for her.*

When the song ended, Steele asked, "Do you remember where you drove the last time you were in a car?"

"I've thought about that before. I think the last time I drove was the day of my . . . murder, but I can't remember where I went. I know the day before, I was at a fashion show and then I visited my uncle."

Steele didn't intend to discuss her murder tonight. He wanted the drive to be fun for her. Her smile faded as soon as she started thinking about that fateful night. He changed the subject and said, "Was Bear glad to see you?"

Ellie was looking out the window, watching the palm trees zip by. "Yes, he misses you when you're not there. He likes going for rides with you."

"How do you know he misses me?"

Turning in the seat to face him, Ellie tugged her skirt over her knees. "He told me. Mae might be able to read Bear's mind, but I can talk to him."

"How does Bear talk? Does he have a deep voice?"

"Very funny, wise guy. I guess it's similar to the way Mae reads his mind—telepathy. The difference is that he understands what I'm thinking without words. We can have a conversation."

"He doesn't understand what Mae is thinking?" Steele asked.

"I don't know."

Steele was about to ask another question when his phone rang. Glancing at the screen on the dash, he saw it was Morgan calling. Pushing a button on his steering wheel, he said, "Hey, Morgan."

"Steele, have you heard the news today?"

"I've been on the road today. Ellie and I are on the way back home now. What's up?"

"Tell Ellie hi," Morgan said.

Ellie waved at the steering wheel, and Steele said, "She says hi, Morgan. Now, what's going on?

"A twelve-year-old girl is missing from the same shopping mall where Amy Carson was snatched last year."

"I was at that mall with Mae early this morning. When did it happen?"

"Sometime early afternoon," Morgan replied. "She was shopping with her mother, and she wanted to go to a different store. Her mother said the store was next door to the one where she was shopping, so she let her go alone."

Steele knew that girl's mother would regret that decision for the rest of her life. "Did anyone see anything?"

"Not one lead so far."

CHAPTER THIRTY-FOUR

A Predators Paradise

Lying in bed the next morning, Steele thought about what Ellie experienced every night. After they'd returned home from Palm Beach last night, Ellie disappeared. But Steele knew she would appear later on the beach. There was one question he couldn't answer, and he wanted to know. *Would she disappear forever once he solved her murder?* He would hate it if he never saw her again, but he had to try to solve her case. There was no way he could do nothing and watch her suffer every night on the beach.

After opening the door for Bear, Steele showered and then turned on the local news. He heard the report about the missing twelve-year-old. Merilee Martin. They flashed her picture on the screen with a number to call if anyone had information. Steele knew it would be an all-out effort to find the child within the first twenty-four hours.

The news reporter mentioned the girl was abducted from the same mall where Amy was abducted a year ago. They showed Amy's picture and briefly discussed the lack of information on her case. It was heartbreaking that it took another abduction for Amy's case to be mentioned again by the local press, but Steele was thankful they showed her picture. One thing he'd learned during his years in law enforcement was that sometimes it could take months or years before that one person came forward with information that helped to solve a case.

After feeding Bear and taking him outside for his morning sniffathon, Steele's first phone call was to his contact in the local police department. He found out someone saw a man driving a white van who left the mall in a hurry, but they didn't get a license number. That was not what he would call a credible lead.

Steele's next call was to Mae.

"I heard about it," Mae said as she answered the phone. "Steele, I don't have a sense that the two cases are related."

"You answered my question before I asked. I'm impressed."

Mae chuckled. "Bad habit."

They discussed what they'd heard on the news about the latest abduction, and then Steele filled her in on his meeting with Ellie's uncle. "By the way, Ellie can write notes."

"Ellie's talents are very interesting. I've decided I'll take you up on your offer and see you this weekend."

Just in case Mae was wrong, and Amy's case was related to the latest kidnapping, Steele and Bear jumped in his car and drove to the mall. If the same person or persons abducted the two girls, and he uncovered any information on Merilee's disappearance, it might lead him to Amy.

He spent the next hour speaking with a few of the same people in the *Infinities* store, but this time he was asking about the most recent abduction. Again, no one saw anything. He then walked to the shop next door since Merilee's mother said that was where her daughter went to the shop.

Steele had previously been to all of the shops, and when he reached Lilly's Boutique, he saw the poster he'd had printed with Amy's picture and the offer of a reward for information. Glancing inside the shop, Steele was surprised that it was already overflowing with young girls. The boutique carried inexpensive jewelry and other items that catered to teenage girls.

A predator's paradise.

Steele turned around and glanced at the parking lot. So many places for one of those predators to sit and watch.

Glancing down at Bear, he said, "We're going inside, so no jumping on anything."

Bear nudged Steele's thigh.

"I need to ask Ellie if you can understand me."

Bear nipped at his fingers.

Once they were inside, Steele didn't have a chance to speak to the woman behind the counter because he was swarmed by young girls oohing and aahing over Bear, and asking so many questions that Steele couldn't keep up with them.

"What's his name?"

"What kind of dog is he?"

"How old is he?"

"Does he swim?"

"Does he like the ocean?"

"Do you take him everywhere?"

"How did you train him?"

Steele felt like he was in the middle of a gaggle of geese. While they focused on lavishing attention on Bear, he turned to the woman at the counter and showed her his identification.

"Did you happen to see the little girl who was kidnapped, Marilee Martin?"

"Yes, she was in here and bought a pair of earrings."

"Can you show me what she purchased?" Steele asked.

The woman picked up a pair of earrings from the display on the counter. "She brought what every young girl has purchased for the last two weeks. It's our Valentine's Day special."

Steele looked at the silver heart earrings with a bright red crystal heart in the center. *Hearts.*

"How long was she in here?" Steele asked.

"I'm not sure, maybe twenty minutes or so. Like I told the police, we are always very busy, and it's hard to keep track of everyone."

"Was she alone?"

"I didn't see anyone with her. But I heard on the news that her mother was shopping next door."

Pointing to the poster in the window, Steele said, "Do you happen to remember the girl who was abducted last year?"

"Of course, it was such a sad event. Nothing like that had ever happened before in the mall."

"Did you see her that day?"

The woman shook her head. "No, but she was in the shop before."

One of the young girls stroking Bear's fur yanked on Steele's shirt. "I saw Amy that day."

CHAPTER THIRTY-FIVE

Lost Puppy

Glancing down at the young girl yanking on his sleeve, Steele said, "Are you sure you saw her?"

"Yeah. I was in here, and she was looking in the window."

"How did you know it was Amy?"

"She was in my class."

"How do you remember it was the same day she went missing?" Steele asked.

"Because I told my mom I saw her when we heard on the news that she was missing."

Several of the other girls were listening to their conversation, so Steele asked if anyone else had seen Amy that day. Two sisters came forward and said they'd also seen Amy outside the shop.

One of the other girls spoke up, "She had an ice cream cone."

"Did she come inside the shop?"

Both girls shook their heads from side to side. "When we walked outside, there was a man who asked us if we'd seen a puppy. He said it jumped from his car, and he needed help to find him."

Steele was somewhat encouraged by this information since no one had previously mentioned a man looking for a puppy before. "Did you help him?"

"No, our mom was shopping next door, and we told her we would be back in fifteen minutes. We were already late."

"Was Amy still there?" Steele asked.

"She walked to the bike rack."

"Can you tell me what this man looked like?"

The girls looked at each other, and then one spoke up, "He was tall, and I think he had dark hair. I can't remember anything else."

It occurred to Steele that these girls were much younger than they looked. Their outfits were too provocative for their ages. He wasn't the fashion police, but he did question why parents didn't veto some of their children's clothing choices. In the past, he'd heard parents say their children had a *right* to dress how they wanted. While that was true, Steele figured he'd seen too many predators attack girls because the way they dressed drew attention. So common sense took precedence over their rights. While it might not be fair, parents had to draw the line with their children. It was more important to keep them safe.

"Was there anything about this man that frightened you?" Steele asked.

"No, he seemed very nice," the oldest girl said.

Steele raised his voice and said, "Listen up, girls." Once every girl in the store turned to look at him, he said, "Never, and I mean *never,* go with anyone, man or woman, who says they have a lost dog, puppy, cat, penguin, or anything else."

When the girls giggled, he knew they were listening. "Got it?"

Every girl nodded.

"Are all of you shopping with a friend?"

Again, every girl nodded.

"Good. Always shop with a friend." He gave each girl his business card and added, "Give this to your parents, and if you hear anything about the day Amy Carson went missing, tell them to call me."

Steele and Bear walked outside, and he stood against the building and looked at the surroundings. He couldn't believe the number of girls shopping without their parents or an adult. Since a girl was abducted the day before, he would've expected every parent in the area to keep their children close. He didn't know if people were too trusting or if they thought nothing like that would ever happen to them. Too many people thought it would never happen to them—until it did.

If the guy with the missing dog story was involved in Amy's disappearance, there was nothing in the file about him. Had the police overlooked an important detail? He was probably grasping at straws since the police were usually thorough when a missing child was involved. Those were the cases every man and woman in the department took personally—it could have been their child.

He was frustrated. He needed a break in this case.

Someone had to see something.

That afternoon, Steele turned his attention to Ellie's murder. His first phone call was to Rob Harmon.

"Mr. Harmon, I'm Steele Harper, and I'm investigating the murder of Ellie Marlowe."

"Mr. Marlowe told me this morning that you would be calling. How may I be of assistance?"

"How long did you work for Ms. Marlowe?"

"Ellie hired me almost five years ago."

"During that time, did she ever have problems with anyone?"

Harmon chuckled slightly. "I'm sure you know this can be a real cut-throat business, but everyone loved Ellie. I can't think of anyone who would do her harm. They might copy one of her designs, but I can't fathom anyone committing murder."

"What about the men she dated? Any problems with personal relationships?"

"She was engaged to Clay Ford. If you live in Florida, I'm sure you've heard of him," Harmon replied.

"What can you tell me about their relationship?"

"I know he wasn't pleased when she broke it off."

"How do you know?"

"He called her *every* day for weeks, trying to get her to reconsider. But Ellie had made up her mind. Clay wasn't right for her."

"What do you mean *wasn't right*?"

"Clay was into being seen, you know, attending all the parties of the high rollers. There wasn't a big event that he missed. I think he likes his photo all over social media. Ellie isn't . . . I mean, Ellie wasn't that kind of person. She preferred smaller, intimate dinners at home. For someone rather famous, Ellie was a private person."

"Do you think Harmon just wanted to be seen with her, or do you think he loved her?"

There was a brief silence, then Harmon said, "Interesting question. I'm not sure since I don't know him well. Ellie was an attractive woman, and many men asked her out. I imagine Ford's intelligence and charm attracted Ellie at first. And he did all of the right things—at least he did the things most women seem to want."

"Right things?"

"You know, flowers, expensive gifts, and dinners at the most exclusive places. His big mistake was assuming Ellie was like most women he knew. I don't think he took the time to discover what she liked."

When Steele ended the conversation, he googled Clay Ford. In addition to his bio, there were thousands of photographs of him. In the most recent photographs, he had a different woman on his arm at every event. Scanning through the older pictures, he saw Ellie with him at various events. Even as much as he hated to admit it, Ford was an attractive guy, and he was wealthy. Steele thought he was probably catnip to women. It would be easy to be jealous of a guy like Ford. But he reminded himself that Ellie was the one who ended their engagement.

I bet that didn't happen often to a guy like Ford—if ever.

CHAPTER THIRTY-SIX

It's In His Kiss

Taking a break from his phone calls, Steele said to Bear, "Grab your Frisbee and let's go play."

Bear ran to the bedroom and came back with his red Frisbee clutched between his teeth. Steele chuckled as the excited canine raced out the door. "Are you in a hurry?"

Bear didn't stop until he reached the shore.

When Steele caught up with him, he took the Frisbee and tossed it down the beach. Bear took off and snagged it in the air. Several people walking on the beach stopped to watch Bear, commenting on his athletic abilities. Bear didn't disappoint his audience; not once did he let the Frisbee hit the sand. And as Steele had already discovered, the big Lab was tireless. Steele walked into the water and tossed the Frisbee in the ocean, thinking it would take Bear longer to retrieve. Without hesitation, Bear swam out with him, grabbed the Frisbee, and made his way back to the shore to wait for Steele to emerge from the surf.

After he swam for a few minutes, Steele headed back to shore. To his surprise, Ellie was sitting next to Bear.

"Hi. What have you been doing today?" Steele asked as he sat down with Bear between them. If anyone walked by and saw him talking, they would assume he was talking to Bear.

"Thinking. I'm tired of not being able to remember so many things."

He could only imagine how frustrated she must be. "Ellie, I spoke to Rob Harmon today."

Ellie looked surprised. "You did? Why?"

"I'm interviewing everyone you knew to see if they have any idea why someone would want to kill you. I don't think your murder was random."

"Why not? I started to say I don't think I recognized the person, but then, I don't know since I can't remember."

"The circumstances point to a planned murder. I think someone knew your routine. They knew you would be on the beach at that time of night. I just can't see someone walking the beach late at night hoping to see a stranger to murder."

Ellie looked away for a moment before she said, "That makes sense. But I can't think of anyone who would want to kill me. Did Rob have any ideas?"

"No, he didn't. Was there any professional rivalry with Rob?"

"No, I think he enjoyed working with me. We never had creative differences, and that is fairly unique in our industry. I know he wanted to start his own business one day, but he told me that was a few years in the future."

From what Ellie's uncle told him, Rob was pretty much running Ellie's business now. While Ellie might trust Rob, that didn't mean Steele would trust him until he was thoroughly investigated. People were often not what they seemed. "Can you think of anyone who was a professional rival that wasn't a friend?"

"I . . ." Ellie stared at his face, but Steele knew she wasn't seeing him. After a few moments, she said, "I don't know . . . I feel like there's something I should remember."

Steele reached over and squeezed her hand. "That's okay. You'll remember when you're ready." A few minutes ticked by, and Steele debated whether or not to ask her about Ford. He decided he wanted to know. "Rob told me about Clay Ford. He said Ford was upset that you broke your engagement."

"Yes, he was at first. Clay's a nice person, but he enjoys the limelight. Attending all of the functions every night of the week was draining. He didn't understand that I preferred a different kind of life."

"Do you think he was angry with you?" Steele asked.

"He wasn't thrilled. But if you are asking me if he murdered me over a broken engagement, the answer is *no*. He had many women who wanted to date him."

"But he hadn't asked another woman to marry."

Ellie shook her head. "He wouldn't murder anyone. He loves his life, and he wouldn't jeopardize that."

Bear laid his head on Ellie's lap and fell asleep as she gently stroked his fur. Steele thought if he ever died, he would like to be reincarnated as Bear.

Like Bear, Steele wanted a nap. The sun, sand, and surf had worn him out. "What do you think about going inside and taking a nap with us?"

Ellie arched her brow at him. "Together?"

Steele gave her a mischievous grin, then said, "On the sofa." He didn't give her time to think about her response. He stood, and Bear immediately jumped to his feet. Steele held his hand to Ellie and said, "I promise I'll be on my best behavior."

Once inside, Steele and Bear both drank some water, and then they all stretched out on the oversized sofa. Steele lay beside Ellie, and she rested her head on this chest while Bear wedged his body between their legs.

Ellie looked up at Steele and said, "Thank you for helping me."

"I know I said I'd be on my best behavior, but . . ." He stopped talking and kissed her gently. When their lips parted, he said, "Ellie, do you enjoy kissing?"

"Oh, yes. It feels . . . wonderful."

It made no logical sense that a spirit could feel anything, but he liked her description of his kiss—*wonderful.*

He wrapped his arm around her waist and pulled her close. He fell asleep wondering if she could feel everything.

CHAPTER THIRTY-SEVEN

XOXOXO

A light puff of air ruffled Mae's hair as she poured herself a cup of coffee. Without turning around, she said, "Hello, Ellie."

"How did you know it was me?" Ellie asked.

"I'm psychic."

Ellie laughed. "I was worried I might frighten you."

"I don't frighten easily. I'm glad you came to visit," Mae walked around the counter and into the living room. "Please have a seat."

Glancing around the room, Ellie admired the soft gray and aqua décor. "I like how you've decorated. The colors are soothing."

"Thank you. I find softer colors are easier to live with."

"I agree." Ellie sat on the sofa a few feet from Mae. "It's nice to talk to someone about design."

"I must admit that I had to utilize the talents of a professional decorator. I can choose colors, but I can't seem to manage a logical seating arrangement if left to my own devices. I could have used your help."

Ellie chuckled. "I love to decorate, but someone gave you good advice."

"Did I tell you how much I love your jewelry designs? I drove back to *Infinites* yesterday and purchased a pair of your heart earrings."

Ellie unconsciously twirled the heart bracelet on her arm. "I had so much fun designing the heart pieces for Valentine's Day."

Mae saw the melancholy look on her face. "I think you're a romantic."

Ellie's eyes met hers. "You didn't say you *were*. That makes me feel . . . alive. You and Steele are the only two people I've met who can see and talk to me . . . at least, living people. I can't tell you how much I've wanted to talk to someone over the last year. I was beginning to think I would never have anyone to talk to."

"I'm glad Steele contacted me. I know you get lonely for companionship, and you're welcome to visit with me whenever you want."

"The other . . . spirits are always so angry that it's impossible to have a conversation with them. They tried to talk to me, but I didn't believe I was dead. Once they saw I could go where I wanted to go, they didn't want me around. I think they considered me a freak of nature."

"You mean they're generally confined to one area?" Mae asked.

Ellie nodded. "I've seen a few on the beach when I walk. I see more in cemeteries. They want to leave, but for some reason, they can't, or they're afraid to try. They've told me most spirits couldn't leave the place where they were murdered, or where they were buried. I've tried to explain how I go where I want, but it doesn't seem to work for them. They aren't patient and don't want to continue to try if it doesn't work the first time. I understand how they feel. They're angry because they don't understand what happened to them."

"That's what I've found with the spirits I've contacted before."

"Do you think I will ever know what happened to me?"

"I know Steele will do everything in his power to find out. And I will help in any way I can."

Clasping her hands together, Ellie's voice was almost a whisper when she said, "I wish I had met Steele—before. I haven't known him long, but I think he's a wonderful man."

"I haven't known him long, either. But his friends think a lot of him, and that says all I need to know. I've worked with Morgan and Tom, and they are both great guys. They are willing to do what they can to help Steele find your murderer."

"I'm so fortunate to have found all of you. And I owe it all to Bear."

Mae reached over and covered Ellie's hand with hers. As soon as she touched her, she read her mind. "You're in love with Steele."

Steele awoke at 7:00 a.m., and Ellie was nowhere in sight. After he opened the patio doors for Bear, he walked to the kitchen to make coffee and saw a note on the counter.

Bear told me you wanted to ask me if he understood you when you spoke to him. The answer is yes, and he asked me why you don't understand him. Ellie. xoxoxo

Smiling at the hugs and kisses sign-off, Steele thought he'd like to be giving her hugs and kisses early in the morning. He reached for the canister of coffee and dumped some into the filter. His hand stilled in the air as another thought hit him. *I don't want to lose her.*

Bear ran back inside just as Steele filled his food bowl.

"Did you hear me filling your bowl?" Steele asked him.

Emitting a sound somewhat like a groan, Steele looked at him and chuckled. "I'm glad you understand me, Bear. You're a great dog."

Bear nudged his leg, earning him a head rub.

"And I wish I could understand you right now because I'd like to know where Ellie went." Steele's hand stilled over Bear's head. "Bear, I just had an idea. I need to ask Ellie about eavesdropping."

CHAPTER THIRTY-EIGHT

No News is Good News

After spending his morning on the phone, when Steele ended the last call, he jotted some notes down on Amy's case. He'd learned there were few deliveries to the stores in the mall the day Amy was kidnapped. It didn't take long for him to eliminate the delivery drivers as suspects.

He called the local police to find out if they were aware of the man trying to lure young girls with the lost puppy story on the day Amy was kidnapped. Detective Rogers told him it was the first time he'd heard about this man. And considering that a year had passed, it would be almost impossible to find him with so little information. Each time Steele thought he might have a valuable lead, it turned out to be a dead end.

The police secured footage from the security cameras from that day, but the detective told him they didn't provide any credible leads. The cameras at the back of the buildings were focused on the delivery docks. The field beyond wasn't visible from the angles of the cameras. Steele wanted to see the tapes, and the detective agreed he could have a look at them. No doubt, he had Morgan to thank for that since he was a college chum of Detective Rogers.

He also found out in his conversation with Rogers that there were no suspects in the latest kidnapping from the same shopping mall.

Picking up his cell phone, he made two more calls. After scheduling an appointment with Clay Ford and Rob Harmon for the next day, he went for a swim with Bear. He did his best thinking when he exercised, and hopefully, exhausting his body would prevent him from waking up in the middle of the night.

Returning to his house without an answer to the direction he should take on Amy's case, he was more frustrated than ever. He needed to work on his other cases, but Amy's case, and now Ellie's case, was consuming his time and brainpower.

As much as he hated to call Amy's parents, he had to find out if Amy would have fallen for the lost puppy ruse from a stranger. He knew each time he called Amy's parents, they probably expected that he would have good news. He didn't. This wasn't the case that *no news is good news.* Still, the call had to be made.

Steele explained the reason for his call, and Amy's mother said, "She loved dogs. We were going to get her a puppy for her birthday. I'm sorry to admit this, Steele, but I never thought to warn her about such a situation."

"Do you think she would have helped the man?"

There was a long silence, and then Mrs. Carson said, "Yes, I think she would have helped. She wouldn't have gotten in the car with him, but she would have searched the area for a puppy."

Steele heard her voice break, and he said, "I'm sorry." He didn't know what else to say. There was nothing he could say that would keep her heart from breaking.

"Please . . . call whenever you know anything."

"You have my word, Mrs. Carson. I won't give up."

When he set his phone on his desk, he picked up the poster with Amy's picture on it and carried it to the kitchen. Bear walked into the kitchen and nudged his leg. He held the poster for Bear to see.

"I need to find Amy, Bear."

Bear sat down and stared up at him.

"Do you have any ideas? I need all of the help I can get."

Bear just stared at the poster until Steele placed it on the counter. "I'll ask Ellie what you have to say when she returns." Speaking of Ellie, he wondered where she was. He hadn't seen her since last night's kiss. He hoped that hadn't been a mistake, but she seemed to like it. She didn't object when he pulled her closer, and it was the first time he'd felt her body next to his from lips to toes. His body reacted just thinking about it. He wanted a repeat. *Hell, who am I kidding? I want a whole lot more.* He pulled a glass from the cabinet and poured himself a shot of bourbon.

Then, he pulled a bone from the pantry and gave it to Bear. "Are you getting hungry?" He glanced at his watch. "I didn't realize it was so late. I guess it's almost time for dinner."

Bear gobbled his bone, walked to the pantry door, took the doorknob in his mouth, and opened it.

Steele chuckled. "I guess you are hungry."

CHAPTER THIRTY-NINE

Good Timing

Steele didn't see Ellie until later that night on the beach when they suffered through the nightly ritual. As he walked home with Bear, he wondered if he would ever be able to put an end to her agony.

The next morning when he awoke, Ellie was sitting on the bed next to him.

Quickly glancing down at the lower half of his body, he was relieved to see that the sheet was covering him. "What are you doing here?"

Ellie's eyes widened. "Oh, I thought you would be happy to see me." She started to get up, but Steele grabbed her arm.

"Stay there." Propping the pillow up on the headboard, he sat up, dragging the sheet with him. "I *am* happy to see you. It's just that I sleep . . . in the buff."

Giving him a mischievous grin, Ellie said, "I know. Who do you think covered you up?"

Steele didn't know if she was teasing or not. "You didn't—did you?"

Ellie just smiled at him. "You're bronze all over. Do you sunbathe in the nude?"

"Of course not." He lowered the sheet a few inches past his waist and pointed to his tan lines. "See, there are tan lines."

She laughed, and Steele realized how much he liked that sound. "You were teasing me."

"Well, no, not exactly, I did cover you, but you were lying on your stomach. She swung her legs over the side of the bed. "Don't move. I have coffee ready." When she reached the bedroom door, she turned back to him and said, "You have a nice, white rear."

Steele tossed a pillow at her, but he was laughing.

Ellie returned with a large cup of steaming black coffee for him. She climbed back into bed, and they sat side-by-side discussing their plans for the day.

"I was hoping you'd be here this morning. I wanted to know if you would like to ride to Palm Beach with me. I'm going to see Rob Harmon and Clay Ford today."

"Why on earth are you going to do that?"

"I told you, I'm talking to everyone you knew. I have to understand what was going on in your life. I'm going to take Bear, so why don't you ride with us?" Steele looked at her, waiting for her answer, and he thought she had tears in her eyes.

It was difficult for her to keep her emotions to herself. Steele was the only one who was willing to help find her murderer. "Thank you for asking me. I'd like that."

"But today, you'll have to be quiet. It won't be like it was visiting your uncle. I won't tell them that you're in the room. And you have to promise that you won't distract me. Which reminds me of something else I wanted to ask you."

Ellie's brows drew together in question. "What?"

"Would you mind visiting Harmon's office occasionally? I might ask you to do the same thing at Ford's office. It all depends on what I find out today."

"Why do you want me to do that?"

"I realized what an advantage it would be to know what was said after I questioned people. You could hear what they say when I leave, or just drop in on them from time to time to see if you hear anything suspicious. You could even follow them, and they would never know."

"Do you think they had something to do with my murder?"

"I'm not saying they do or they don't. It would be nice to know what they do when they think no one is watching."

Ellie thought about it for a few seconds, and said, "Does that mean I'll be your partner."

Steele smiled at her. "Yes, you'll be my partner."

"I'll do it. I'm not sure I'll find out anything since I don't think either one knows anything about my murder."

Steele leaned over and placed his cup on the nightstand. "When you didn't come here yesterday, I thought that I upset you."

"What would make you think that?"

He looked into her eyes, and then his gaze slid to her full lips. "I thought you didn't like my kiss."

Ellie gazed at his lips, and without realizing it, she drew closer to him. "I . . . I liked your kiss. I just thought you might get tired of seeing me."

Steele leaned closer. "Never." He wrapped his arm around her and pulled her closer. Without another thought, he kissed her. It wasn't his intention to let his kiss get out of hand, but the next thing he knew, he was lying down, and Ellie was on top of him with only the sheet between them.

Ellie's eyes widened when he held her tightly to his body. She could feel every inch of him through the sheet.

He gave her a sheepish grin. "Sorry, it's morning."

"Hmm . . . I should let you get ready."

Steele didn't want to move—didn't want her to move. But he glanced at the time on his ceiling and realized he had to leave in twenty minutes if he was going to make his appointments on time. "Ellie, I like talking to you in bed in the morning."

Ellie smiled. "I like it too."

At that moment, Bear jumped on the bed and stared at them.

"He's hungry," Ellie said.

Steele arched his brow at her. "So am I." He was hungry for her. He reached over and rubbed Bear's ears.

"Good timing, buddy."

CHAPTER FORTY

A Lie Could Cost You Everything

Steele quickly showered while Ellie took Bear outside and fed him breakfast. After Steele dressed, he walked to the kitchen and spotted a plate of cinnamon rolls on the counter. "Where did these come from?"

Ellie picked up two rolls and wrapped them in a paper towel. "You don't have time for breakfast, so I thought these would be good to eat while you drive."

Steele smiled. "Yeah, I guess I can't let you drive."

Ellie laughed. "Probably not. She poured a cup of coffee into a mug. "Bear told me he's excited to be going with us today. He likes to ride in your car."

Steele gave Bear an ear rub. "Good, it's a long drive." He looked at Ellie, who was holding his coffee mug and cinnamon rolls. "Thanks for feeding me. You're sort of handy to have around." He leaned over and kissed her cheek. "I'll give you an ear rub later."

"I don't know what I can tell you that I didn't tell you on the phone," Rob Harmon stated.

"Did Ellie date someone before Clay Ford?"

Rob ticked off a few names, and added, "They were just occasional dates, nothing serious."

"That's true," Ellie said. "I had forgotten all about them."

Steele glanced at the chair where she was sitting, but he didn't respond.

At one point during their conversation, Harmon saw Steele staring at the empty chair. "Is something wrong?"

Something was wrong. Ellie was so beautiful and so damned distracting, even when she was quiet, he could stop looking at her. "No. Just thinking. Did the same employees stay with the company after Ellie's death?"

"Yes, but I think we've added two new people since then."

"Would you have any objections if I spoke with them?" Steele asked.

"Not at all."

Steele noticed Ellie had left her seat and was looking at some papers on Rob's desk. He thought she was going to pick up a piece of paper, so he quickly stood and said, "Would it be possible for me to speak with your employees now?"

"Of course." Harmon stood and said, "I'll introduce you."

Ellie waited until Rob left the office with Steele before she resumed nosing through Harmon's desk.

"Did you find out anything interesting from the people in the office?" Ellie asked as they walked back to the car.

"No, but they all enjoyed working for you," Steele said. "What were you looking for on Harmon's desk?"

"Some of his designs. Actually, they were *my* designs."

"Do you mean he's putting his name on your designs?"

Ellie shook her head. "No, well, I don't know, but . . . there was something odd about a note I saw on his desk. He wrote to another designer, saying he had some designs that he might be interested in. That makes no sense."

"Hmm. Do you share designs with your competitors?"

"Absolutely not."

"Did you know the designer?" Steele asked.

"Yes, but I didn't know him well. Truthfully, I didn't care for him."

Steele glanced at his watch. "We have just enough time to get to Clay Ford's office."

Clay Ford was exactly the kind of man Steele expected him to be. He was an attractive, well-dressed man, close to his height at six-two, in excellent physical shape, charismatic, and his luxurious office telegraphed success. It was understandable why women found him appealing and, most likely, excellent marriage material. He glanced at Ellie to gauge her reaction to seeing Ford again, but her expression didn't change.

"As I told you on the phone, I'm investigating Ellie's murder," Steele began.

"You mean Eleanor. I preferred her given name," Clay said with a smile that wasn't genuine. "And you were hired by whom?"

"No one hired me."

Ford's brows drew together. "Then why are you investigating her murder?"

"I live next door to Ellie . . ."

Ford interrupted him. "Next door to where *Eleanor* used to live."

"Yes. Anyway, I learned that *Ellie's* murder was not solved, and I took an interest in her case."

"Have you spoken to her uncle about reopening her case? I can't imagine he would be pleased to hear about this."

Steele nodded. "I have spoken to Mr. Marlowe, and he approves of my investigation. And her case was not closed, just cold. Is there any reason you would object to answering some questions about *Ellie's* case?" Steele could feel Ellie's eyes on him, but she remained quiet.

Clay shook his head, but Steele noticed his jaw clenched. He barely masked the irritation in his voice when he said, "How can I help you? I have a hectic schedule, but I can give you a few minutes."

"It's my understanding that Ellie broke your engagement just before her murder."

When Clay's eyes narrowed, Steele almost smiled. He'd cracked that cool professional exterior and hit a nerve.

"Yes, we ended our engagement just days before. Why is that important?"

"Was there someone else in her life?" Steele asked, intending to give him a subtle jab.

"Steele, I told you there was no one else," Ellie said.

Steele refused to look her way.

"Why would Eleanor waste her time with anyone else? We had different priorities. My life is extremely challenging, and she couldn't keep pace with the demands on my time."

Ellie let out a loud puff of air. "That's not true, and you know it, Clay! I didn't *want* to live your lifestyle."

It was obvious to Steele that Ford had a huge ego. "Did Ellie ever mention having problems with anyone, professionally or personally?"

"She was *just* a designer. I can't imagine that her occupation garnered enemies."

"Just a designer?" Ellie turned to Steele. "See, that's another reason I didn't want to marry him. He didn't think my career was important."

"Did you support her career?" Steele asked.

"I can't see what this has to do with your investigation, but no, I wanted her to be my wife, and that didn't include her career. Being my wife is a full-time occupation."

"I see. So you aren't aware of any problems in her life?"

"None."

"When was the last time you saw her?"

"We had dinner the night we decided to end our engagement."

"Where were you the night of her murder?"

Standing, Ford walked around his desk and pointed his finger at Steele. "I don't like your implication."

"I not implying anything; I'm asking everyone I interview that question."

"I was at a social function. And I'm certain there are thousands of photographs to confirm that." He inclined his head toward the door. "If you have further questions, you can contact my attorney."

Steele stood and tossed his business card on Ford's desk before he walked to the door, allowing Ellie to precede him. "Have your attorney call me if you remember anything useful."

Once they were outside, Ellie said, "What was that all about? You didn't find out anything from him."

"I just wanted to see what kind of guy he was," Steele replied honestly.

"What did you think?" Ellie asked.

"Did anyone ever tell you not to expect honesty from people who lie to themselves? Someone once told me the truth doesn't cost you anything, but a lie could cost you everything. Clay Ford is a liar."

CHAPTER FORTY-ONE

Creepy

By the time Morgan and Tom arrived Friday night, Steele had steaks on the grill and potatoes in the air fryer.

"I can't believe you're cooking," Tom said.

Morgan slapped Steele on the back as he grabbed a beer from the cooler. "You must have missed us."

Steele expertly flipped the steaks. "No, I just knew I needed to feed you if I wanted your help."

"Where's Ellie?" Tom asked.

"I haven't seen her since early this morning." Steele thought Ellie was unusually quiet this morning. The last few days, when he awoke, she was sitting beside him with a cup of coffee in her hand, and they chatted comfortably until it was time to start his day. This morning, he wanted to ask her if something was wrong, but he didn't want to alienate her by asking too many questions—like a detective.

He'd never thought about waking to a woman every day, but he found himself looking forward to the mornings. And he'd even started wearing boxers to bed. They held each other and kissed in the mornings, but he didn't let things go too far. It wasn't that he didn't want to make love to her. He did. Badly. But he didn't know how that worked with a spirit. And he wanted to take things slow until he figured out what the future held for them.

As far as he was concerned, the only negative aspect of the time they spent together was what they faced each night. As the appointed hour approached, it was difficult to think about anything else, and it placed a pall over their evenings.

Morgan pulled Steele from his thoughts when he asked, "How's the case going? Learn anything new about Ellie?"

Steele told them about his interviews with Ellie's friends and her uncle while they ate dinner. "And I met Clay Ford."

"So you got to meet the man Ellie was engaged to?" Tom asked.

"Yeah."

"And?" Morgan said.

Steele shrugged. "I wasn't impressed."

Tom and Morgan exchanged a glance, and Tom said, "So he was good-looking, successful, and rich?"

Grinning at them, Steele said, "That pretty much sums him up."

Tom laughed. "Damn, I can see why you weren't impressed. Not much there to like."

"Well, Ellie did break it off, right?" Morgan asked.

"Yes, before she was murdered."

"You don't suspect him, do you?" Tom asked.

"I didn't care for him, but no, he's not on the list."

"You just wanted to know what kind of man Ellie was attracted to, didn't you?" Morgan asked.

Steele just smiled.

"I would've done the same thing," Tom admitted.

They moved on to discuss Amy's case, and Morgan said, "Steele, it's a dead end. We have no new leads to follow. I know you don't want to give up on this case, but I don't have any suggestions."

Steele looked at Tom, who nodded his agreement with Morgan.

Setting his plate aside, Steele said, "I'm not throwing in the towel yet. I have a feeling I'm not connecting some dots. Maybe I'm crazy, but I think something will come together for me. Maybe Mae will have a breakthrough. By the way, Mae will be here in time for lunch tomorrow."

"Good morning, beautiful," Steele said when he opened his eyes and saw Ellie beside him holding his cup of coffee.

"You're just calling me that because I have your coffee," Ellie teased.

Steele winked at her. "I wasn't looking at the coffee."

"Sweet talker. I guess you want some brownies to go with your coffee."

Moving to a sitting position, Steele took the coffee cup from her. "I'll have to arm wrestle Morgan and Tom for them." He thought he'd rather have her for breakfast, but he kept that thought to himself.

"I visited Rob Harmon's office yesterday," Ellie said.

Turning to look at her, Steele said, "Did you have a reason to go back so soon?"

"The note I saw on Rob's desk. Remember, I told you he was sending a note to another designer?"

"Yes, but you didn't tell me the name of the designer."

"His name is René Bouchard, and he lives in Palm Beach," Ellie said.

"Did you find out anything interesting?"

"The note was gone, but I decided to go to an exclusive women's boutique in Palm Beach that carried my designs. They are still carrying my brand, but I noticed a few of the designs with René's labels were my designs."

"Let me get this straight. This Bouchard guy was a competitor, and yet, some of the clothing he's selling are your designs?"

Ellie nodded.

"Could it just be an accident? Is it possible that he came up with the same designs?"

"I guess it's possible, but they are *exactly* the same—down to the color combinations I wanted to use."

"Tell me about this guy Bouchard."

"As I told you the other day, I didn't care for him, but he was a friend of Rob's. I saw him occasionally at shows, and he'd visited our office fairly often."

"Why didn't you like him?" Steele asked.

Ellie furrowed her brow. "It's hard to explain, and I feel like I'm forgetting something, but I think I found him sort of . . . creepy."

"Creepy?"

Frustrated, Ellie expelled a loud breath. "I can't remember why I thought that."

"Mae is coming today; maybe she'll have some suggestions to help you remember."

Steele pulled her closer to his side. "I hope you don't find me creepy because I like waking up to you in the mornings."

CHAPTER FORTY-TWO

Crime of Opportunity

Mae joined Steele, Morgan, and Tom on the patio and said, "I'm going to Ellie's house, and we're going for a walk. I think if I can help her to calm her mind, she'll be able to remember what she's been blocking." She glanced at Steele and added, "I know you've seen how tense she becomes when she can't remember something."

Steele nodded. "She gets very frustrated, and I don't know how to help her. It's easy for me to tell her to *relax*, but she's the one facing death every night. While she may not remember the pain, she knows it's going to happen every day."

Mae gave him a slight smile. "That night was traumatic for her, and I understand why it's difficult for her to bring those memories to the surface. When she came to visit me, I think we made some headway, and she started talking more freely about her life."

"Don't forget we're having dinner tonight," Morgan said. "Alone."

Tom punched him in the arm. "You mean you're not inviting us on your *date*?"

"That's right. Three's a crowd, and four is a pain in the . . . neck," Morgan replied.

Mae grinned at Morgan. "I won't forget our date."

Steele called out to her, "Mae, take Bear. Ellie is more relaxed when Bear is around."

"You were right, Mae. I do love Steele," Ellie said as they walked along the shore. "I don't need to explain to you why we have no future together. That's the reason I don't want him to know the depth of my feelings."

"I understand, but I know Steele cares for you," Mae responded.

"He feels sorry for me, and I know he wants to help. It will be easier for him when I disappear or go wherever I'm meant to go if we are not involved."

"Ellie, if you had a choice to stay here, would you want to?" Mae asked.

Ellie stopped walking and looked at her. "How would that be possible? You mean to remain here as a spirit?"

"Would you want to remain as a spirit forever, knowing that only a few people could see and interact with you?"

Ellie reached down and rubbed Bear's ears. "I don't know. Before I met Steele and Bear, I prayed for something to change. I was so lonely and confused. But now, since Steele and you can see me, I don't feel so alone. It's nice to have people I can talk to. I might be afraid to move on now. I guess it's the unknown that's so terrifying. And I think my prayers were answered. Maybe what I am right now is my future."

They walked in silence for several minutes before Mae said, "Tell me about all of the people you remember interacting with during the last few weeks before your last night."

They strolled for a long time, and Mae listened as Ellie told her as much as she could remember.

Just as they started to turn around and walk back toward Ellie's home, an older man appeared in front of them.

"Have you uncovered what happened to you, young lady?" the man asked Ellie.

Ellie nodded toward Mae. "My friend is trying to help me find out."

Mae could see the older gentleman. He was dressed in formal 1800s Regency period clothing, and Mae smiled at him. "Hello."

The man tipped his tall beaver hat and bowed slightly. "A pleasure. Once you help this lovely young lady, perhaps you could help me find my murderer."

Mae started to ask a question, but the man disappeared.

Steele asked Morgan and Tom to review his notes on Amy's and Ellie's cases. While they read, Steele closed his eyes and thought about what his next move should be on both cases.

After Morgan finished reading, he said, "Steele, do you know what both of your cases have in common?"

Steele gave him a puzzled look. "What?"

"Hearts."

"Amy was abducted just before Valentine's Day, and Ellie was killed the same night."

"Yes, but it's more than that," Morgan said. "Amy loved hearts, her blouse had hearts on it, her phone cover had hearts on it, and her bike had heart stickers."

Steele furrowed his brow. "Her mother told me Amy loved hearts, but I don't see a connection."

"Ellie wears a heart bracelet, and you said Ellie's heart jewelry was displayed in that store," Morgan explained.

"Yeah, but it was almost Valentine's Day. Every store in the mall had something with hearts in the windows. The owner of Lilly's Boutique told me the week before Valentine's Day every item she sells has hearts on it."

Morgan shrugged. "It probably means nothing, but I did find it interesting."

"You said Ellie goes to that mall," Tom said. "Do you know if she was there the day she was murdered?"

Steele shook his head. "She can't remember where she was. It will be a big help if Mae can help her to remember what she did that day."

"Have you uncovered anything that would lead you to believe that the recent kidnapping of Marilee Martin has anything in common with Amy's case?" Tom asked.

"Not really. Lilly's Boutique caters to young girls, and Amy was seen looking in the store's window that day. Marilee was inside Lilly's Boutique the day she was kidnapped."

"Do you think Amy's kidnapping was a crime of opportunity or preplanned?" Morgan asked.

"My gut tells me it was a crime of opportunity," Steele replied. "She wasn't taken by a family member or acquaintance, and no one contacted the family for ransom."

"So we're left with trafficking, intent to assault, or murder," Morgan said.

"Someone may have wanted a child permanently. Maybe a woman who lost their child and went off the deep end," Tom added.

They looked at each other, and Steele said, "I don't like any of those options."

CHAPTER FORTY-THREE

Happy Wife, Happy Life

After going over the details of both cases with Morgan and Tom, Steele said, "Let's try to think outside the box. Maybe I need to come at this from a different angle. Morgan, you said that hearts were the common theme in both cases. I have never asked the shop owners if they saw Ellie the day of Amy's kidnapping."

"You did say Ellie shopped at that same mall," Morgan said.

"She still goes to *Infinites* to look around," Steele told them.

"Even if Ellie was there on the same day, how would that connect to her murder? She wasn't killed at the mall in the middle of the day. She was killed on the beach at night," Tom said.

Steele shrugged. "True, and I may be grasping at straws, but what else do I have right now?

Morgan interrupted, "I agree that we should check it out. Let's go to the mall right now. I'll leave a note for Mae in case they get back before we return."

They jumped up, grabbed their shoes, piled into Steele's car, and headed to the shopping center.

"Why does Ellie go to that store now that she can't shop?" Tom asked.

"She enjoys seeing her designs in the store. She hasn't said this to me, but I think it's her way of staying connected to her prior life," Steele replied.

"I'm surprised that her uncle kept Ellie's business open," Morgan said.

"He certainly didn't need the income. After spending some time with him, I think he didn't have the heart to close her business. He told me how hard Ellie worked to get it off the ground and make it a success. He wanted to keep her contribution to the fashion world alive. He didn't want her to be forgotten."

"That's a nice tribute to his niece," Morgan said.

"Yeah, he's a fine man," Steele replied.

Steele stopped at one of the jewelry display counters where the manager, Brad, was working.

"Brad, I don't know if you remember me, but I spoke to you before about the young girl who was kidnapped last year."

"Yes, sir, I do remember you. How can I help you?"

Steele pointed to the display case where Morgan and Tom were looking at Ellie's designs. "I'm also working on Eleanor Marlowe's murder."

Recalling his last experience behind that jewelry counter, Brad glanced warily at Steele and replied, "Ms. Marlowe used to come in here often. She was such a lovely woman."

"Would you happen to remember if she was in the store Valentine's week of last year?"

Brad didn't hesitate to respond, "Actually, I do remember seeing her the very day of her death. I remember because I noticed the heart bracelet she was wearing. She told me she was designing an entire line of heart jewelry. The bracelet she was wearing was a beautiful piece, and I told her we'd love to carry her designs. We're selling that very bracelet right now. I remember how shocked I was to hear about her death the next day."

"Was she with anyone that day?"

Brad shook his head from side to side. "She was always alone."

"Thanks, Brad. I appreciate your help." He turned to Morgan and Tom and said, "Come on, we're going to get some ice cream."

"Hello, Steele," Mr. Simpson said as soon as the men walked inside the Yum Yum Ice Cream Shoppe.

"How are you doing, Mr. Simpson?" Steele asked.

"Keeping busy. Are you having any luck on Amy's case?"

"Not much. But today, I have another question for you." Steele introduced Morgan and Tom and said, "I promised them some ice cream."

After Mr. Simpson filled their order, Steele said, "I wanted to ask if you knew Eleanor Marlowe."

"I did. Well, I can't say I would have known who she was if not for my wife. My wife told me she was a famous designer. As it happens, I just bought a Marlowe bracelet for my wife for Valentine's Day from *Infinities*. The wife dropped hint after hint, and it cost as much as my first car." He gave Steele a sheepish grin and added, "You know how it is . . . if the wife is happy then . . ."

Steele chuckled. "Happy wife, happy life."

"You've got that right. Are you working on Ms. Marlowe's case?"

"Yes. I know you were busy the day of Amy's kidnapping, but do you happen to remember if you saw Ms. Marlowe that day? I have reason to believe she was in the mall the day she was killed."

"I do remember seeing her because when I later saw the news about her death, I told my wife that she'd been in the shop. She liked plain chocolate ice cream on a waffle cone. Her death came as quite a shock. She was a lovely lady. I couldn't imagine why anyone would want to kill her."

CHAPTER FORTY-FOUR

Screaming All the Way

It was raining by the time Steele, Morgan, and Tom returned home. When they ran inside, Mae and Ellie were sitting in the living room drinking hot tea. Bear ran to greet them.

"How was your walk?" Steele asked as he rubbed Bear's ears.

"Very nice, and we returned before the rain," Ellie replied.

Steele headed to the kitchen to get drinks for the men, and he grabbed a treat for Bear. Once he passed everyone their drink, he sat beside Ellie, reached for her hand, and brushed a kiss over her knuckles. Bear plopped down by their feet and chewed on his bone.

Morgan chuckled. "Steele, I just want you to know, it's weird watching you kiss the air."

"Yeah, if anyone is watching you they'd think you are a candidate for the funny farm," Tom said.

Steele couldn't help but smile. "Usually when we're outside, Bear is with us, so I'm sure everyone thinks I talk a lot to him."

He looked at Ellie and said, "We were at the shopping mall, and it seems you were there the same day that Amy Carson was kidnapped."

Ellie's eyes widened. "I was? I saw her poster on your desk, but I don't remember seeing her before."

"Mr. Simpson, The owner of the Yum Yum Ice Cream Shoppe, said he bought one of your bracelets for his wife. Do you remember him?"

Ellie smiled. "I do. He is such a nice man, and he's crazy about his wife."

"He liked you," Steele replied.

The conversation eventually turned to dinner when Steele said he was hungry.

"I think Morgan and Mae should take us to dinner with them," Tom teased.

Morgan laughed. "No way. I'm not taking you two along to mess up my date night."

Steele thought he heard a knock on the patio door, and he glanced that way. He stared at the door for a full minute before he said, "Did someone fail to mention that we were having a costume party?"

"What?" Morgan asked as he turned around to look at the patio doors. Seeing nothing there, Morgan turned back to Steele. "What are you talking about?"

"You don't see them?"

"See who?" Tom asked.

Everyone turned around to look at the door, and Ellie and Mae said in unison, "Oh, no!"

"I take it from that response that you two know these gentlemen," Steele said.

"Uh . . . we saw the Englishman from another era, on the beach earlier, but we didn't see the cowboy," Mae replied.

"I don't see anyone at the door," Morgan said.

"I don't either," Tom added.

Steele told Tom and Morgan about the men as he walked to the door. "As Mae said, one is dressed as an Englishman from another time, and the other man is a cowboy wearing a pistol on his hip."

Mae and Ellie jumped up and followed Steele to the door. When he opened the door, the two men started talking at once. Steele held up his hand and said, "Whoa, one at a time."

"What do you want?" Ellie asked.

The Englishman spoke to Ellie, but he pointed to Mae, and said, "You mentioned on the beach that this kind lady was going to help you find out who killed you." He then inclined his head to the cowboy at his side. "This is my friend, Ace Barton. We have been on this beach for many, many years, and when I told him about your lady friend, we came here to plead our case for your assistance."

"How did you find me?" Ellie asked.

Cowboy Ace spoke up, "We followed you."

Steele said, "I'm Steele Harper, and I'm investigating Ellie's death." He pointed to Mae and said, "This is Mae Rogers, and she's helping me."

The Englishman nodded. "The pleasure is ours, Mr. Harper, Miss Rogers. I'm Edward Hamilton, Duke of Bedford. Mr. Harper, am I to understand that you are a local constable if you are investigating a death?"

"No, sir, I'm a private investigator."

"Do we call you Duke?" Ellie asked.

"Please call me Edward." He glanced at Mae. "Are you an investigator as well?"

"No, I'm a psychic."

Edward arched his brow. "Interesting. How does one enlist your assistance to discover our murderers?"

"Why don't you come inside, and we can discuss this?" Steele said.

Both men hesitated, and Edward said, "I fear if we enter your premises, we may disappear."

"Why do you think you'll disappear?" Mae asked.

"That is what we were told by other spirits. They seem to think that only Ellie can go hither and yon from the beach." He glanced at Ellie and added, "Your abilities cause great consternation among the other spirits. They are quite envious of you."

"Come inside, and if you disappear, you can always come back," Ellie suggested.

"I'll leave the door open, and we'll see what happens," Steele said.

"Capital idea!" Edward responded.

The Duke of Bedford and Ace hesitantly stepped over the threshold. They didn't take another step, waiting to see if they would disappear. When they didn't, they exchanged a grin.

Steele directed them to the sofa, saying, "These are my two friends, Morgan and Tom. They can't see or hear you two, so when I repeat our conversation, it is for their benefit."

Edward bowed politely, removed his beaver hat, and waited for the women to take their seats before he sat down.

"Ace is a real cowboy?" Morgan asked.

Ace removed his Stetson, grinned, and said, "The genuine model."

"Yes, he is, and he has an authentic Colt .45 on his hip," Steele replied.

"Yessir, the best pistol ever," Ace said.

"Steele, can you put something beside them, like coffee cups in various colors, so we'll know to whom we are speaking?" Tom asked.

"Good idea." Steele retrieved cups from the cabinet and said, "Ellie is pink, Ace is blue, and Edward is purple."

"How I wish this was filled with a proper cup of English tea," Edward said longingly.

"You couldn't drink it," Ace reminded him.

"Edward, you said you have been on the beach for years," Ellie said.

"Yes, we have."

"When were you killed?"

"1835. I sailed from England to New York. Sadly, I do not remember much of what transpired after that."

Steele looked at Ace. "What about you?"

"1888. I worked on a cattle ranch here in Florida, and I came to the coast to meet a friend the night of my murder."

The cowboy had a hole in his chest, much like Ellie did when she relived her murder at the beach every night. Steele wondered why her wound wasn't always visible like Ace's, but he didn't ask. He said to Ace, "I take it that you were shot."

Ace pointed to the hole in his chest. "Good guess, partner."

Steele didn't see a wound on Edward, so he asked, "What happened to you?"

"According to the doctor who examined me after my death, I was poisoned."

Steele repeated the conversation to Morgan and Tom.

"Exactly how many people have been killed on this beach?" Morgan asked.

"Ace and I have probably seen at least one hundred spirits over the years," Edward said.

"And you've never tried to leave the beach?" Ellie asked.

"No, we have not." Edward looked at Ellie and asked, "Where would we go? This is the first time we have been visible to living humans as far as we know."

Ellie understood their dilemma. "Steele was the first one to see me."

Ace leaned forward and looked at Mae. "Ma'am, exactly what is a psychic?"

After Mae explained her abilities to the cowboy, Steele asked, "Do you relive your murder every night?"

Ace frowned. "Are you asking if I see myself being murdered over and over?"

"Yes. Ellie goes through her murder every night."

"Oh, my heavens, no! That's horrendous." Edward looked at Ellie and shook his head. "That must be terrible for you, my dear. I had no idea. We will stay beside you in the future."

Ellie was touched by their concern. "Steele has been with me lately."

"Sir, considering this terrible fact, you must focus on Ellie's murder before we impose our troubles on you," Edward insisted. "Ace and I have discussed why we've never moved on to another place, but I'm afraid we have no answers."

"Have you ever seen a spirit move on? Can you tell us what happens?" Morgan asked.

"We have not seen anyone going up, but we have seen a few going below. The earth opens up, and red hot flames shoot from the earth, and these ghastly creatures escort the departed down through the opening. It is a frightful sight, to be sure. It is certainly not something that anyone wishes to witness."

"The departed are screaming all the way down," Ace added.

CHAPTER FORTY-FIVE

Doc Holliday

Edward and Ace entertained them for a few hours with stories of their lives before their murders. Their experiences were so interesting that Morgan and Mae decided to postpone their date—again. Steele ordered pizza so they could keep talking.

"Why can you see us and your friends cannot?" Edward asked Steele.

"I don't know. I've never seen spirits before, or I wasn't aware if I did," Steele said.

"Most peculiar," Edward replied. "Would you kindly share what you have uncovered about Ellie's murder?"

After Steele told them about his investigation, Edward said, "I understand why it is difficult to solve a crime after so much time has passed. How may Ace and I assist you in your efforts?"

Steele couldn't immediately think of a reply, so he repeated Edward's question to Morgan and Tom. They both shrugged, and Steele said, "Edward, could you ask the spirits on the beach if any of them saw Ellie's murder?"

"We can certainly do that."

"With Ellie's ability to travel to various places, she has helped me with my investigation."

Edward looked at Ellie and smiled. "Perhaps you can instruct us how to go from place to place."

Ellie smiled. "I'm not sure I do anything special. I just think about the place I want to be, and that's where I end up. We'll try it together tomorrow."

When the hour approached for Ellie to return to the beach, Steele motioned for her to join him in the kitchen. "I know it's about time, and you always disappear for hours afterward, but I wanted to tell you to come back as soon as you can."

"When I go to the beach and then . . . well, after that, I don't know where I go from there."

Steele leaned over and kissed her cheek. "Come to my room, and if I'm asleep, wake me."

Everyone insisted on going to the beach with Ellie that night. As they waited beside her on the shore, Ellie's shorts and tee shirt transformed into a long, flowing white dress.

"Does that happen every night?" Mae asked.

Steele nodded. "One minute, she's wearing something different, and the next moment the same white dress appears."

Everyone grew quiet when Steele checked his watch. They saw the dread on his face, and all eyes fixated on Ellie as she stood stoically, staring at the moonlight on the water. As she did every night, she turned, and her expression was one of surprise.

Steele thought she must have heard something that night that made her turn around. Or her killer said something to her.

"Ace! Shoot the villain! Shoot him!" Edward exclaimed.

Steele and Mae turned toward Edward and saw him pointing to something they couldn't see. Their eyes slid to Ace, and they watched in stunned silence as he drew his Colt .45 and pulled the trigger.

Ellie slumped to the ground with blood flowing from her wound. Steele immediately picked her up and held her in his arms for a brief moment.

Then she disappeared.

Steele said, "Edward, what did you see?"

"You mean you did not see the scoundrel?"

"I saw no one," Steele replied.

Edward turned to Ace. "You saw him clearly, did you not?"

"Yes, but my Colt didn't fire."

"It has not been fired in years. Perhaps it's waterlogged," Edward said.

Steele held up his hand. "Wait . . .wait . . .wait! Are you two telling me you saw the man who shot Ellie?"

Edward and Ace nodded at the same time. Edward said, "Mae, did you see him?"

"No."

"What's happening?" Morgan asked.

"It's damned frustrating not to know what's going on, Steele," Tom added.

After Steele explained to Morgan and Tom what happened, Edward asked, "Where did Ellie go?"

"I don't know. She can't remember where she goes right after her murder." Steele then asked him, "Could you describe the man you saw?"

"Yes, he was a rather well-dressed man," Edward said.

"Did you get a good look at his face?" Steele asked.

"I can certainly describe his features."

"A friend of mine who is a sketch artist works with the local police. I'll call her to see if she can come over tomorrow. Edward can give me the description, and I can relay the information to her," Mae said.

Steele looked at Ace and asked, "Could you describe him as well?"

"He looked a little bit like Doc Holliday, but he didn't have a mustache."

Steele pulled out his cell phone and pulled up a photograph of Doc Holliday. He held it for Ace to see, "Is this Doc Holliday?"

"Yes, it is!" Ace pointed to the cell phone and said, "How did Doc Holliday's likeness get in that little box?"

"Ace, that's one of those contraptions everyone is always looking at on the beach," Edward said.

CHAPTER FORTY-SIX

Too Bad They Were Dead

Steele opened his eyes and looked at the ceiling—*5:47 a.m.* His first thought was of Ellie and, of course, her murder. After a few minutes of staring at the ceiling, deep in thought, he turned on his side and saw her sitting motionless beside him. He'd never seen her eyes closed before, and it alarmed him.

"Ellie," he said softly.

She immediately turned to him and smiled. "I didn't want to wake you."

He noticed she was wearing a yellow dress with thin little shoulder straps. "How long have you been here?"

"I just arrived. I was debating how long I should let you sleep."

He propped up his pillow, leaned back, and pulled her into his arms. "Do you remember where you went this time?"

She laid her head on his chest. "No. I was at home a few minutes ago, and then I came here."

"Are you tired?" He chuckled. "I don't even know if you get tired."

"No, I don't get tired."

"Just my luck," he teased. "I was going to ask you to lie down beside me."

She looked up at him and grinned. “I don’t have to be tired to do that.”

As if he’d been invited, Bear chose that moment to jump on the bed and maneuver his big body between them, plopped down, and exhaled loudly.

They both laughed, but Steele thought Bear had just destroyed his romantic moment. “Bear, didn’t anyone ever tell you that three’s a crowd?”

Ellie rubbed Bear’s head. “He’s our chaperone.”

Staring into her eyes, Steele said, “Do we need a chaperone?”

Ellie gazed at him a few seconds before she said, “Are you asking if . . . if . . .”

Steele nodded. “That’s exactly what I’m asking.”

“I . . . don’t know. How do I feel . . . how does my body feel to you? I mean, do I feel alive?”

Steele reached for her hand and brought it to his lips. “You feel very much alive. When I hold you, I feel like my arms are full. I feel your breath on my chest. Your lips are soft, warm, and pliant when I kiss you.”

“How is that possible?” Ellie asked breathlessly.

“I don’t know, and I’m not questioning it. It feels too good, and I’ve waited a long time for you.” He placed her hand on his bare chest over his heart. “Do you feel what you do to me?”

Ellie felt his heart hammering, and with featherlike strokes, she caressed his chest.

Steele thought he would explode from the sheer pleasure of her touch. He leaned over and kissed her softly. He lifted his lips and asked again, “Do you want to see if we need a chaperone?”

Her seductive smile was the only invitation he needed. In one swift move, he climbed over Bear, and supporting his weight on his forearms, he kissed her passionately. When his lips left hers, he nibbled his way slowly to her neck as he expertly lowered the spaghetti straps on her dress. He stopped long enough to whisper in her ear, "Are you sure?"

"Very sure."

Mae introduced Steele, Morgan, and Tom to Sondra Bryant, the sketch artist.

Steele said, "Thank you for coming on such short notice."

"Mae said it was rather urgent, and I must admit I was intrigued when she explained the situation."

"Sondra, as I mentioned on the phone, we have three spirits with us. Two spirits will describe the features of the man they saw to me, and I will tell you what they are saying."

Steele found himself waiting for Sondra to run from the house screaming, but the older woman surprised him. She sat down, pulled out her pencils, and opened her sketch pad.

"Sondra, I'm surprised you are handling this situation like it was just another day at the beach," Steele said.

Sondra smiled at him. "Mae and I have been friends for many years, and I know she wouldn't pull a prank. But I must admit, this is a first for me."

"If it makes you feel any better, this is a first for me and Steele," Mae replied.

Sondra said, "I'm ready when you . . . or when *they* are."

Everyone chuckled, and Steele said, "Thanks for handling this so well."

Steele, Ellie, Morgan, Tom, and Bear sat on the patio while Sondra worked. Steele left the patio doors open, and he could hear what Edward and Ace were describing to Mae. He knew it couldn't be easy going through a third party, but Sondra displayed a lot of patience. Fortunately, Edward and Ace agreed on the description of Ellie's murderer. Having worked with many witnesses, Steele was impressed by their meticulous details. They were good witnesses.

Too bad they were dead.

CHAPTER FORTY-SEVEN

Buzzard Bait

"Steele, why do you think you can see spirits and we can't?" Morgan asked.

"I have no idea. It makes no sense to me," Steele replied.

"It's frustrating not being able to interact with them," Tom said.

Steele jumped up and said, "I have an idea." He walked inside and asked if Sondra would have time to do two more sketches today."

"Yes, I do. What do you need?"

Glancing at Mae, Steele asked, "Mae, when you finish with our suspect, would you mind describing Edward and Ace to Sondra?"

Mae's eyes lit up. "What a great idea. Yes, I'll describe them to her."

"Capital idea, Steele," Edward shouted.

"That'll be interesting. It's been a long time since I saw myself," Ace said.

"So it's true that spirits can't see themselves in a mirror?" Steele asked.

"Regretfully, it is a fact," Edward replied. "It would be helpful if I could see if my cravat is properly tied."

Glancing at the clothing Edward was wearing, Steele thought he was definitely a dandy. "It looks good to me."

"Sondra is almost done with this sketch," Mae said.

"Great." Steele returned to the patio to see three people smiling at him. Well, two people and one beautiful spirit.

"It'll be nice to see what they look like. Now, if we could hear them," Morgan said.

"I'm not a miracle worker," Steele teased. He turned to Ellie and asked, "Can you see your reflection in a mirror?"

She leaned closer to Steele and whispered, "Yes, I can. I didn't want to mention that to Ace and Edward."

Steele smiled at her. "Right. One thing at a time."

Within minutes, Mae asked them to come back inside to see the finished sketch.

Ace pointed to the drawing and said, "That's the low-down, cold-blooded murdering skunk. He should be in the hoosegow."

Sondra held the sketch for everyone to see, and Ellie gasped.

"Ellie, do you recognize this odious villain?" Edward asked.

Ellie's eyes remained fixed on the face of evil staring back at her. She looked at Edward and Ace. "Are you sure this is the man you saw?"

"Yes, ma'am," Ace said, and Edward concurred.

"Do you recognize him? Who is he?" Steele asked.

"René Bouchard."

Steele recognized the name. "Isn't that the designer whose designs look like yours?"

"Yes. Remember, when we were in Rob's office, he was writing a note to René. When I returned later, the note was gone."

Steele nodded and looked at the drawing again. "But why would he murder you?"

"I have no idea. It doesn't make sense. I didn't know him well."

Steele explained to everyone Ellie's relationship with René Bouchard before he said, "Ellie, you said Bouchard was a friend of Rob's. Maybe they're both involved."

"I can't believe Rob would be a party to my murder," Ellie said.

Hearing her voice quiver, Steele pulled her into his arms. He knew it was difficult for her to think someone she considered a friend would be involved in her death. "We'll figure this out."

"You mentioned he might be stealing Ellie's designs. Do you think Ellie found out about it before her murder?" Morgan asked.

"I wasn't aware of anything like that. But I'm positive he's passing off some of my designs under his label right now. I still have my drawings at my house, and I think anyone could see the obvious similarities," Ellie replied, and Steele repeated her response.

"Ellie, you said René Bouchard's business is located in Palm Beach, right?" Steele asked.

"Yes."

"I'll pay him a surprise visit tomorrow."

"Tom and I will see what we can find out about him," Morgan said.

"Ellie and I can go to *Infinities* tomorrow, and she can show me those designs," Mae said.

"Ace and I would like to assist," Edward said.

"I'd like to find a way to get my Colt working again so I can shoot the varmint the next time. He'd be buzzard bait in two seconds flat," Ace said.

Steele thought Ace would be a good man to have around in a battle—if his Colt worked. He repeated Ace's comment to Morgan and Tom. They both arched their brows at him. He knew they were thinking the same thing he was thinking.

How do we make that Colt work before Bouchard shoots Ellie?

CHAPTER FORTY-EIGHT

Then What?

Sondra completed the additional sketches, and Tom and Morgan were excited to see what the spirits looked like. Sondra surprised them with a sketch of Ellie.

"Edward and Ace look like I expected, and Ellie is stunning," Tom said.

"Steele, you're one lucky guy," Morgan added.

Steele stared at the sketch. "Don't I know it."

Mae and Sondra decided to take a walk on the beach, and Edward and Ace accompanied them.

Ellie said she needed to do some things at home, giving Steele, Morgan, and Tom time alone.

While they were sitting on the patio, Morgan picked up the sketch of Ellie. "She is beautiful, Steele. I can see why you fell in love." He exchanged a glance with Tom and then asked Steele what they were both thinking about. "How is that going to work out?"

Steele gazed at the endless sea and shook his head. He'd asked himself the same question time and time again. He didn't have an answer, but in his heart, he knew he couldn't let her go. "I have no idea. But you're right. I'm crazy about her."

"What if we solve her murder and she disappears forever—then what?" Tom asked.

Steele didn't want to become emotional, so he didn't respond.

"Remember what Ace said earlier about his Colt," Morgan said, then shook his head. "I know this is probably going to sound crazy, but do you two think there is any way we can alter a past event?"

"Do you think we could do what Ace suggested and shoot the *murdering varmint* before he shoots Ellie?" Tom asked.

Morgan smiled and shrugged. "Yeah. I know it sounds far-fetched, but what if it's possible?"

Tom leaned forward in his chair and said, "Let's say something like that could be done. Then what? We'd have a dead body, and I can see us explaining it to the first officer on the scene, *Uh, yeah, officer, you see, we wanted to save this ghost, and the man who shot her originally, well, he comes back every night to shoot her again. So we thought we'd have another ghost shoot him before he could kill the ghost. Now we have an alive ghost and another dead person who will probably be a ghost.*"

Morgan grimaced. "When you put it like that . . ."

"Then what? How in the world would we explain an alive Ellie Marlowe after she's been dead for a year?" Steele asked.

Morgan and Tom stared at him.

"I hate those two words," Morgan said.

Tom glanced at Morgan and furrowed his brow. "What two words?"

"Then what."

"Oh, those two words. The nemesis of every logical thinking human," Steele replied.

"It wouldn't be difficult to manufacture a new identity for Ellie," Tom said.

"True. We know enough criminals who could handle that small detail," Morgan agreed.

"We don't even know if the Colt is a real gun. I mean, is it solid, or is it . . . I don't know . . . transparent?" Tom shrugged and looked at Steele. "Do you know what I mean?"

"I do. I don't know if I can actually feel the gun or if I just see it. Ellie is solid, like any living person. But I haven't touched Edward or Ace."

"Do you mean Ellie isn't—ghost-like? When you put your arms around her, you can actually feel her?" Morgan asked.

"Yeah. She's not like the ghosts you'd see in a movie." Steele had another thought. "The bracelet that she wears is real, just like the clothing in her closet. One night she took it off and when I looked at it, I noticed it was solid gold. I think Ace's Colt would be the same if I held it."

"I'd like to know if we can see the bracelet if you are holding it," Morgan added.

"We can see her clothing in the closet." Tom looked to his right, then to his left to see if anyone was near. "This is crazy, and I hope to hell no one ever hears our conversations about this. We'd all be in straitjackets."

"I would shoot Bouchard if I could see him," Steele said.

"I thought about that too. I wonder why you can't see him," Morgan said.

Tom dropped his head in his hands. "Maybe we are ready for the nuthouse."

Morgan ignored Tom's momentary lapse into the nuthouse. "I guess the first thing we need to do is see if the Colt can be fired."

Morgan hesitated, and Steele asked, "What is the second thing we need to do?"

"We need to see if a ghost can actually kill a live person."

"I see what you mean. But Ace had no problem drawing it from his holster and pulling the trigger. You wouldn't believe how fast he was," Steele replied.

"Let's take a look at that Colt tonight," Morgan said.

CHAPTER FORTY-NINE

The Love of Money is the Root of all Evil

Later that night, everyone was at Steele's house waiting for Ace and Edward. Morgan and Mae discussed going to dinner, but they wanted decided to postpone their evening out again.

Steele had Ellie remove her bracelet, and as soon as he held it in his hand, Morgan and Tom could see it. Hopefully, they would be able to see Ace's Colt .45.

They didn't have long to wait until Edward and Ace walked through the patio door.

"We've been waiting for you," Steele said.

"I hope we are not intruding, but we enjoy your companionship," Edward said.

Steele motioned for them to sit down. "Not at all. But I do have one favor to ask."

"Name it," Edward said.

"Don't tell other spirits that I can see you. At least, not right now."

Edward held up his hand and said, "Say no more. We will honor your request."

Ace nodded his agreement.

"Ace, we've been talking about your pistol. We want to see if Morgan and Tom can see your Colt if I hold it."

Ace's eyes lit up. "I didn't think about that. Do you think you can repair it?"

"We'll see what we can do."

Ace pulled his Colt, flamboyantly twirled it a couple of times, and then handed it to Steele.

Steele took the gun, and his gaze slid to Morgan and Tom to see their reaction. "It's too bad that you can't see how expertly Ace handles this gun."

"At least we can see the gun," Morgan said.

Tom's mouth hung open. "I'll never question if we're crazy again."

Everyone laughed and then gathered around as Steele disassembled the Colt.

"You know your way around a revolver," Ace said.

"A lot of parts are rusted, and you need a new firing pin," Morgan said.

"We can order those online," Morgan said.

"Is that your general store?" Ace asked.

Steele repeated Ace's question for Morgan and Tom.

Tom said, "Ace, things are a bit different today. Everything is done on a computer, and we'll have to order parts since this is an old pistol."

"What's a computer?" Ace asked.

"We'll have to save that answer for later." Steele thought about all the inventions since Ace was alive. If Edward and Ace were going to stay around, they had a lot to learn.

"Steele, you know what we were talking about earlier? Do you think we could put a different weapon in Ace's holster?" Morgan asked.

"I think we need to think that through and consider the consequences if it did work." Steele didn't want Ellie to go through her death each night, but they needed to have a plan in the event Ace could shoot René Bouchard, and they changed history.

"What are you talking about?" Ellie asked.

Steele looked at her and smiled. "I'll explain later."

Once they wrote down all of the parts they needed to order, Steele reassembled the Colt and handed it back to Ace.

Morgan reminded Steele to see if Ace and Edward felt *solid* like Ellie. Steele grasped Ace's arm and said, "He feels solid."

"What do you mean?" Edward asked.

Once Steele explained, Edward said, "I assumed that ghosts were . . ." he flapped his hand back and forth, trying to think of the right word, "transparent."

"That's what we thought. But Ellie feels solid, and we were wondering if you and Ace felt like her," Steele replied.

"Yet, we have had people walk through us on the beach. It's most disconcerting," Edward said.

Steele looked at Ellie. "Has that happened to you?"

"Yes. We don't like it."

"Ellie, do you think we can change clothes like you? I would prefer my attire to be more modern," Edward said.

Ace frowned. "What's wrong with the way I'm dressed?"

Edward looked him up and down and arched his brows. "It is rather out of fashion."

Steele chuckled. "Ace, you don't have to worry. There are still cowboys around who still wear the same gear."

The next morning, Steele rose early and drove to Palm Beach. He didn't make an appointment with René Bouchard since he wanted his visit to be a surprise. He was relieved that Ellie and Mae were spending the day together. They were going to take care of Bear, and he didn't have to worry about Ellie distracting him. Ellie was also going to work with Edward and Ace to see if she could help them *travel* to various locations, and learn to change their attire.

Morgan and Tom returned to Miami, and they were going to begin their investigation into Bouchard's background. Steele didn't question that Bouchard was Ellie's killer. She didn't hesitate to identify him from Sondra's drawing. But what was Bouchard's motive? By Ellie's account, she didn't know him well. Steele's gut told him Bouchard and Rob Harmon were in *this* together. Whatever *this* was. Why would Harmon betray Ellie? She had supported his career, and by all accounts, they were friends. Ellie and Harmon didn't have a romantic relationship, so he ruled out jealousy, obsession, and rage. He found nothing in Ellie's background to consider revenge could be a motive. Everyone loved her.

That left financial gain.

He remembered the shocked expression on Ellie's face each time she turned to face her killer.

Was money the motive?

CHAPTER FIFTY

Because Murder is Illegal

Steele walked inside the ultra-modern studio, and the young, pink-haired girl behind the reception desk was looking at her cell phone. When she looked up at him, her expression telegraphed that he'd interrupted something much more important. "Yeah?"

"I'm here to see Mr. Bouchard."

Her face was expressionless. "Do you have an appointment?"

"No."

"You need to make an appointment." She glanced back down at her phone, summarily dismissing him.

Steele pulled out a business card and plucked a flower-topped pen from a jar on the counter. On the back of his card, he wrote—*I have questions about Eleanor Marlowe's murder*. He held the card in front of the receptionist's face. "Please give this to Mr. Bouchard. I think he will see me."

The girl's eyes left her screen long enough to look at his card. She stood, gave a loud exasperated sigh, rolled her eyes, and walked away with phone in hand.

Four minutes passed, and Pinky returned and said, "Follow me."

Steele had to give her credit, her eyes remained glued to her phone and she didn't run into anything. They reached the door to Bouchard's office, and Pinky motioned for Steele to enter the room.

Bouchard was standing at a table with his back to the door looking at swatches of material. When he turned to face him, Steele noticed he looked exactly like Sondra's drawing. *Doc Holliday, minus the mustache.* There was no question that this was the man Edward and Ace saw kill Ellie. Steele judged Bouchard to be about thirty-five years old, five-nine, lean, with dark hair and eyes.

Bouchard extended his hand. "Mr. Harper, nice to meet you."

Steele noticed he was still holding his business card in his other hand. "Thanks for seeing me."

Bouchard motioned for him to take a seat in one of the four chairs circling a table. He sat in a chair opposite Steele. "You said this is about Eleanor Marlowe's murder. I don't know how I can help you. I didn't know her well."

"As you may be aware, her murder has never been solved." Steele waited to hear if he had a response.

Bouchard glanced away, then he said, "No, I didn't know. I'm sorry I didn't follow the case."

"I see. Have you known many people who have been murdered?"

Bouchard's brows drew together as if he was confused. "No, why do you ask?"

Steele shrugged. "Most people don't know someone who has been murdered. If they know the victim, they generally follow their case closely. If for no other reason than to make certain the perpetrator is arrested."

"I'm very busy, and as I said, I didn't know her well. Of course, I was sorry to hear of her death."

"Her murder," Steele countered.

Bouchard shifted uncomfortably in his chair. "Well, yes. It was very unfortunate for someone so young to be murdered."

Steele stared at him for a couple of seconds. "I'm interviewing everyone Ms. Marlowe knew or worked with. What can you tell me about your relationship with her?"

"Again, I didn't know her well. I met her through a friend of mine, Rob Harmon."

"What is your relationship with Mr. Harmon?" Steele asked.

"We've known each other for years. I guess you could say we're good friends."

"How many times were you in Ms. Marlowe's studio?"

Bouchard looked away again before he responded. "I'm not sure. Perhaps ten times. Rob may have a better memory about that."

"Other than Ms. Marlowe's studio, did you ever see her anywhere else?"

"I can't recall. Perhaps we saw each other at a few parties since we traveled in the same circles."

"Was Rob Harmon satisfied with his position at her company?"

"As far as I know, he was quite happy. He runs the company now."

"Do you think he had a reason to murder Ms. Marlowe?"

Bouchard frowned. "I can't imagine Rob would have a reason to murder anyone."

"Did you hear any gossip about her murder?"

"Not her murder per se. I heard she'd broken her engagement with Clay Ford just before her death."

"Who told you about that?" Steele asked.

"It must have been Rob. Yes, yes, it was Rob because he told me Ford kept calling the office several times a day."

"I understand you're a designer as well."

"Yes, I am."

"Were you a competitor of Ms. Marlowe's?"

"I guess you could call us competitors, but my designs are quite unique."

Steele thought that was an interesting response. "How would you describe Ms. Marlowe's work?"

Bouchard hesitated, then said, "I don't want to sound callous, but her designs were . . . well . . . pedestrian. Of course, that is only *my* opinion."

Steele wanted to punch him in the nose. "It's my understanding her designs are fairly expensive."

Lifting his chin in the air, Bouchard said, "Some consumers are not as discriminating as they should be."

Steele *really* wanted to knock that sneer off of his face. He reminded himself that murder was illegal.

Before Steele could ask another question, Bouchard said, "Isn't it difficult to solve a murder after a lengthy amount of time has passed?"

"It can be. It's easier when a witness comes forward."

Bouchard's eyes widened. "Do you have a witness?"

"I can't discuss the details of the investigation. Do you own a gun?"

"Me?" He chuckled. "I'm afraid I wouldn't know which end to use."

Steele arched his brow. "So, that's a no?"

"I don't own a gun."

Steele stood and looked him in the eyes. "If you think of anything, you have my card. I'm sure we will see each other again."

CHAPTER FIFTY-ONE

Time for an Exorcism

"Let's hold hands, and we'll close our eyes and concentrate," Ellie said to Edward and Ace. She'd been working with them for two hours, but they were so anxious to go somewhere new that they wouldn't stop talking and pay attention to what she said. "Mae and I are going to a store called *Infinities.* I want you to *silently* say the name of the place where you want to go. Don't talk. Focus on the name of the place. Ellie didn't know if it would work, so she suggested holding hands with them to see if her powers could transport the three of them. She looked at Mae before she closed her eyes and said, "Mae, if we disappear, drive to *Infinites.*"

"I will." Mae smiled at the two men and added, "Good luck."

"I think a stiff drink is needed more than luck," Edward replied.

"Yep, instead of going to a general store, can't we go to a saloon? I'd even try a shot of rotgut right now," Ace said.

"*Infinities*, Ace," Ellie reminded him.

They closed their eyes, and a minute later, they disappeared.

Mae grabbed her keys and headed out the door. By the time she reached *Infinites* and walked inside the store, the place was in chaos.

In less than two seconds, Mae discovered the reason for the mayhem. Edward and Ace were walking through the store, picking up items, totally oblivious to the customers in the store running at break-neck speed to the front doors. Ellie was snatching things from their hands and placing the items back on the tables, trying her best to get them to behave, but they were tuning her out. The employees of the store had the same shocked expression on their faces as the customers.

"This is all ladies' apparel. Where are the gentlemen's cravats?" Edward bellowed.

"I ain't never seen a general store like this. Where are the Colts?" Ace asked as he picked up a lacy see-through bra and held it in the air by a delicate strap. "Ain't much material on this here thing. Is this what they call a chemise now? Dang, I'd like to see this on a woman."

Mae hurried to them and spoke sternly as if they were two misbehaving children. "You need to stop picking things up. Think about what you're doing. You're scaring the customers to death—remember they can't see you. All they see are items floating through the air. It's total bedlam in here." She snatched the lacy bra from Ace's hand and tossed it back on the table.

Edward and Ace looked around the store and saw everyone making a mad dash to the front door.

"Oh, my." Edward promptly dropped the pair of ladies' red silk panties that he was holding, and they drifted to the table. The woman behind the counter let out an ear-piercing scream before she backed away and ran into a dressing room.

Edward and Ace looked properly chastised.

Edward's gaze slid from Mae to Ellie. "I do apologize. We are being churlish."

"Yep," Ace agreed, but he had no idea what churlish meant. Reluctantly, he pulled his gaze from the lacy garments that fascinated him. "Can I at least look at the Colts?"

Ellie's rolled her eyes. "They don't sell weapons here. Just follow us to the designer area. There's something I want to show Mae, and remember she will not talk to us, or people will think she's crazy. And *don't* pick up one thing."

Edward and Ace both nodded their agreement and trailed Ellie and Mae through the store without touching anything.

After Ellie showed Mae her designs, she pulled out some of Bouchard's dresses. Mae took photos with her phone, so she could show them to Steele.

"I must say, Ellie, I have never seen such lovely gowns," Edward said. "If you were a seamstress in my day, you would have made a fortune."

Ellie thought he might be trying to sweet-talk his way out of the doghouse, but she graciously thanked him.

"Ellie, let's go to your house, and you can show me your drawings," Mae said.

Ellie turned to Edward and Ace. "Let's hold hands again, and this time think of going to my house."

Mae waited for them to disappear before she walked to the jewelry department. She had a hunch that if Bouchard copied Ellie's designs or stole them, he might do the same with her jewelry. While she was looking at Ellie's jewelry, she heard two employees gossiping nearby about the items floating in the air.

The man said to the woman, "There's something very strange going on in this store. This is the second time I've seen something like this. I told my boss we should ask a Catholic priest to perform an exorcism."

CHAPTER FIFTY-TWO

Mother Teresa–A Criminal?

Steele left Bouchard's studio, and he called Ellie's uncle to see if he could stop by his office.

Twenty minutes later, John Marlowe greeted him like an old friend. "Steele, it's good to see you again. I'm glad you called. Come in and have a seat."

"Thanks for seeing me on such short notice." After they exchanged pleasantries, Steele told John about Bouchard and the night on the beach. "Two spirits who know Ellie and are helping in my investigation. They saw Bouchard a moment before he shot Ellie. We had them describe Bouchard to a sketch artist. Ellie recognized Bouchard."

"I know Bouchard. I met him through Rob, and he often visits Rob at the studio. Are you saying you know for certain that he shot Ellie?"

"Yes, but now I have to prove it. I'm afraid the testimony of two spirits who can only be heard by me and a psychic will get us nowhere."

John leaned back in his chair and sighed. "Yes, that is a problem. How can I help?"

"Ellie thinks Bouchard is selling some of her designs under his label. I don't know if this has something to do with her murder or not. But Rob may be selling Ellie's designs to Bouchard, and if he is, someone in that business may be aware. If you hear anything about Bouchard's business experiencing financial problems, let me know."

By the time Steele arrived home, Ellie had finally successfully taught Ace and Edward how to change clothes.

After Steele kissed Ellie, he glanced at Edward and Ace and smiled. "You two look sharp. I like the new clothing."

"Is *sharp* a compliment?" Edward asked.

Steele chuckled. "Yes."

"Did you see my new holster, Steele?" Ace asked.

"Yes, and hopefully, when the parts get here, your Colt will be like new."

"I hope so. I want to kill that murdering polecat."

Steele didn't comment. He was still considering the consequences if Ace killed Bouchard.

"Ellie and I have something to show you, Steele," Mae said.

Ellie reached for Steele's hand, led him to the dining table, and opened her portfolio. "Here are some of my designs that I completed before my death."

Steele flipped through the pages, and Ellie pointed to the swatches of fabric attached to each drawing. "These are what I selected for the materials and color combinations for the designs."

After Steele reached the last page, Mae handed him her cell phone. "I took these today while we were at *Infinities*."

Steele scrolled through the photographs and then looked at Ellie's drawings again. "So Bouchard did copy them."

Ellie said, "Rob is the only person who knew about my new designs. We had copies in my studio."

Steele nodded. "Do you know if Bouchard's business was doing well before your death?"

"I don't know, but his designs were not carried in the high-end stores."

Steele told her about his interview with Bouchard. "I also stopped by your uncle's office. He told me to tell you to visit him, and to give you a kiss." He kissed her forehead. "That was from your uncle." He then kissed her lips, but when his phone rang, he reluctantly pulled away to glance at the screen. He saw the call was from Morgan. Before he answered, he said, "That last kiss was from me, and there'll be more where that came from later."

"Hey, Morgan."

"Hi, Steele. I wanted to fill you in on what we found out about Bouchard. He's from Miami, and he started his design company six years ago in Palm Beach. He's never been married and has no children. He dates a lot of women, but no relationship has lasted for over a year. I can't find one piece of dirt on this guy. I mean, he makes Mother Teresa look like a criminal. Tom is contacting some of his business associates, so we'll touch base with you in the morning."

Steele told him about the theft of Ellie's designs. "I don't know if that is a motive for murder, but we've both seen stranger things."

"That's the truth. What did you think of him?"

"He's a liar. I didn't like him."

"Shorthairs stand straight?" Morgan asked.

"Oh, yeah. But I wouldn't trust anyone whose office didn't have a speck of dust."

Morgan laughed. "Yeah. There's something that's just not right about that. Textbook criminal behavior."

"Text me the name of Bouchard's last girlfriend. Maybe she can give us some insight into the man behind his pretentious mask."

CHAPTER FIFTY-THREE

A Way to a Woman's Heart—Bragging?

Ellie woke Steele the next morning by holding a hot cup of coffee near his nose.

He opened his eyes and smiled at her. "Smells good."

"I started to make you a vanilla latte."

Steele frowned at her. "That's not a man's drink. Don't mess with perfection—black and the stronger, the better."

Ellie laughed, and Steele thought about how much he enjoyed waking up with her beside him. She was better than coffee any day. He reached over and clasped her hand in his, causing her heart bracelet to jingle. He glanced down at the broken heart. For some inexplicable reason, that broken heart worried him. *Had someone intentionally taken the other half?* "I know a jeweler who does excellent work. I'm sure he can repair your bracelet."

Ellie stared at her bracelet. The broken heart troubled her too, but for some reason, she didn't think she should change it. "I can't explain it, but something about the broken heart feels important.

If you don't mind, I would rather wait until . . . I don't know . . . it doesn't make sense, but it just seems significant. I want to wait until I remember what it is."

Steele brought her hand to his lips and kissed her palm. "We'll wait. If it's important to you, it's important to me."

"Thank you. I have a question for you."

"What is it?"

"Why are you repairing Ace's pistol?"

Steele told her about the conversation he'd had with Morgan and Tom. "We were kicking around the possibility of Ace killing Bouchard before he shoots you. I don't know if it's even possible, and if it is, then that could present a whole new set of problems."

"I don't see how that could work. You can't change history."

"I'm not certain I know what's possible or impossible. I mean, two months ago, I wouldn't have thought it was possible to be sitting in bed beside a spirit that I can see and talk with."

Ellie looked into his eyes. "Have I told you how much I appreciate what you've done for me?"

Steele grinned and held his cup of coffee in the air. "There are some benefits besides waking up to a beautiful woman. But I do think she's forgotten what attracted me in the first place."

Arching her brow at him, Ellie asked, "And what was that?"

"How quickly one forgets. Your brownies."

Ellie leaned over and kissed his cheek. "I'll see what I can do."

Steele wanted to give her a real kiss, but his phone rang, interrupting his next move.

"Hi, Tom. Morgan said you would call."

"Yeah. He told me you had a theory about Bouchard stealing Ellie's designs. You might be onto something. I found out Bouchard wasn't meeting his financial obligations before Ellie's death. About six weeks after her murder, he signed several large contracts. His business associates say he's difficult to work with, and while they were careful about how much they revealed, not one had anything positive to say."

"Interesting. So money was a problem for him?"

"Not really. He comes from money, but his creditors weren't happy that it took him so long to pay his bills. I get the feeling that he's the kind of guy who thinks he shouldn't have to pay. He has an expensive lifestyle, and he lives in an exclusive community in Palm Beach County. His place has been featured in local magazines. It takes an act of Congress to get past the front gate."

"Not exactly the usual kind of murderer," Steele said.

"No, it doesn't make sense that he would have to murder to steal designs. Steele, there's another thing you need to see. Morgan texted you the name of Bouchard's last girlfriend. We looked at her social media accounts, and you're not going to believe this, but there's a group of Bouchard's ex-girlfriends who post comments about him on social media. They have a page dedicated to him on all platforms."

"You're kidding."

"Nope. And the list is long. You need to take a look. I'll send you the link. These women say Bouchard is just plain weird."

"Weird, how?" Steele asked.

"He's the kind of guy who gets ticked if everything is not perfectly organized. They said he's a control freak and a narcissist. One woman said he spends money freely and knows all the best places to go, but he was a lousy lover. All of the women said he bragged about how good he was in bed and boasted about his . . . ah . . . anatomy, but he was all talk."

Steele laughed. "The way to a woman's heart—bragging."

"I didn't say he was bright—just rich. They all said he's a jerk. These women are brutal. It tells me nothing is private anymore. And you know that old saying that *hell hath no fury like a woman scorned?* Well, when you read these comments about Bouchard on social media, you'll understand."

"Were any of these relationships long-term?"

"No. He doesn't date anyone for long."

"Did they date him because he was rich?" Steele asked.

"Yeah, they admitted that was their motive. And they knew they would be photographed frequently, which helped them to get clicks on their social media accounts. They said they weren't in love with him. If they did love him, that love turned to hate."

CHAPTER FIFTY-FOUR

Whiter Than a Ghost

Steele and Ellie sat in his office reading the social media comments written by Bouchard's ex-girlfriends. Tom wasn't exaggerating when he said the women were brutal. He didn't know if they were being objective or if emotions overrode their logic.

"Do you think these women want to embarrass Bouchard, or are they trying to warn other women about him?" Ellie asked.

"I don't know. I can't understand why anyone would go public with personal information. It makes no sense to me. People put *way* too much information on social media today." Steele's cell phone rang again, and he said, "It's Morgan."

"Hi, Steele. Have you listened to the news today?"

"No, why?" Steele immediately picked up his remote and clicked on his television.

"They found the girl who was kidnapped from the mall. She's alive, but she's in the hospital. They found ten girls in this one house. They were abducted by sex traffickers. Amy Carson was not among them."

Steele sat back in his chair and released a long breath. "I guess that's a blessing in disguise."

"Yeah, I know what you mean," Tom said.

They spoke for a few more minutes, and when Steele hung up, he told Ellie the news.

Ellie leaned over and kissed his cheek. "I know you'll find Amy."

Steele tossed his phone on his desk. "It's so frustrating not to have one lead." He glanced at the television, and a banner scrolling along the bottom of the screen indicated they were discussing the abducted girls. Turning up the sound, he heard the reporter give the location where the girls were found. "I'm going there to see what I can find out. Will you watch Bear?"

"Of course."

Once Steele was on the scene, one of the detectives recognized him and told him what information the police had. "When we arrived on the scene, the kidnappers were nowhere to be found. The girls were drugged and were in no condition to answer questions."

For the next two hours, Steele spoke to the neighbors, trying to get a lead on the people who led the sex trafficking ring. Frustrated that he didn't uncover any useful information, he decided to return home and make some calls. When he arrived home, Ellie and Bear were not around, so he sat outside on the patio and called Bouchard's last girlfriend, Colleen Day. Steele didn't divulge he was investigating Bouchard for murder. He told Colleen he was considering doing business with her ex-boyfriend. Colleen didn't hesitate to talk to him, and she didn't hold back with her unflattering opinion of Bouchard.

"I guess you can tell I don't like him," Colleen said. "But you should know, the man is *very* strange. I mean, he's forty-two, and he likes young women . . . I mean, *really* young—the younger, the better. I think he likes to *groom* them. I'm twenty-three, and I was too old for him. He likes control, but he can't control me. He would get angry if I left the room without him—he'd even follow me to the restroom. His home is huge, so maybe he thought people might steal something. It was weird."

Steele thanked her for her honesty, and when he hung up, he decided to call some of the other women to see what they had to say. Their comments about Bouchard were similar to Colleen's. Just as he ended his last call, Ellie and Bear walked from the beach and joined him on the patio.

He reached for Ellie's hand and pulled her onto his lap, and Bear jumped up on top of her.

Steele laughed. "You two are heavy."

"Watch it, or you won't get your surprise," Ellie teased.

"Ah . . . I meant to say Bear is heavy. You're as light as a feather."

Ellie laughed. "Good save. Didn't you see your brownies in the kitchen?"

"You mean I've been home almost an hour, and I could have been eating brownies?" He quickly removed Ellie and Bear from his lap.

"Discarded for a brownie," Ellie teased.

Steele was already through the door, but he turned back and said, "*A* brownie? Try five or six."

Once in the kitchen, Steele tossed Bear a bone and snagged a couple of brownies for himself. "Have you seen Ace and Edward today?"

Grinning, Ellie said, "I saw more of Edward than necessary."

Steele's mouth was full, but he arched his brow at her.

"They were on the beach earlier, and Edward was wearing swimming trunks. I've never seen legs so white."

"As white as a ghost?" Steele joked.

Ellie punched his arm. "Very funny. They told me they were going to visit Mae. They wanted some *live* company, and they know you're busy."

Steele shoved the second brownie in his mouth. When he finished chewing, he said, "Do you think they can return without your help?"

"Yes, they successfully transported themselves several times today. I did make them promise not to make a spectacle of themselves if they visited a store."

"Good. When they come back, I have a job for them."

CHAPTER FIFTY-FIVE

Einstein's Ghost

Steele knew Amy's parents would have heard the news about the abducted girls who were found, and he wanted to let them know that Amy wasn't among them. As he pushed their number on his cell, he braced himself for what would be another emotional phone call. He liked the Carson's but talking to them when he didn't have positive news was draining for both parties. Without fail, they expressed their appreciation for his efforts and thanked him for continuing his investigation.

After dinner, Steele and Ellie were watching television, but she could tell he wasn't paying attention. He'd been unusually quiet throughout dinner, and she knew something was troubling him.

"Do you want to talk about what's on your mind?" she asked.

Steele looked at her and smiled. "Not really. Just mulling over some of my cases." He didn't want to tell her that he was thinking about what would happen if he or Ace shot Bouchard. He had another thought—*what would happen if he moved in front of Ellie just as Bouchard pulled the trigger?* He tried to play out each scenario in his mind. This was all uncharted territory for him. And who could he ask about altering a past event? Maybe if he saw Einstein's ghost, he could ask him. Note to self: *Ask Edward and Ace to find Einstein during their walks at night.*

Ellie knew he was thinking about her murder. "Steele, why don't you stop going to the beach with me at night?"

Steele turned and looked at her. "Why would you ask me that?"

"I know seeing me in that condition every night is troubling you. It might be best if you stayed here."

He pulled her onto his lap. "I don't want you to go through that alone." After he brushed a kiss over her lips, he whispered, "Don't ask me that again. Please."

Ellie didn't argue. She was comforted by his presence and wondered how she'd managed to face her death each night alone for a year. She wanted to lighten the mood and forget about what they would face later that night, so she said, "Can you play chess?"

"Yes, but I haven't played in a long time. Can you play?"

"My uncle and I used to play often."

Steele smiled at her and said, "Did anyone ever tell you that you're more than a pretty face? But I can think of a few things that take my mind off of business. And I would pursue one of those more pleasurable pursuits, but Ace and Edward might appear."

Ellie grinned at him. "I guess we play chess then."

Steele left the room to get his chess set. They played for an hour before they took a break, and Ellie asked, "What job do you have for Edward and Ace?"

Steele leaned back against the sofa. "I thought I would have them watch Bouchard for a couple of days."

"I could do that."

"Ellie, he's the man who killed you. I don't want you to be around him."

Ellie smiled. "Did you forget he can't see me?"

"No, but I . . ." he hesitated because he didn't want to scare her by admitting that when he'd talked to Bouchard, all he wanted to do was beat the hell out of him. "I just don't want you near him."

"Okay, but I think I should take Edward and Ace to Bouchard's studio the first time they go. They haven't been that far from home."

"Do you consider the beach your *home*?"

"In a way. It's hard to explain, but this is where we always return."

"In Ace's and Edward's case, they've been here longer than anywhere. So it's understandable."

"True. I'm fortunate that I have an actual home to go to."

"Do you think Ace and Edward would like a home to go to at night?" Steele thought he would tell them they could stay with him if they wanted a place to go at night.

"I told them they were welcome to stay at my home, but I think they were afraid they wouldn't be able to leave. Now that they know they can come and go as they please, they may change their mind."

Steele suddenly changed the subject and asked the question he'd thought about earlier when they were looking at the women Bouchard dated, "Did Bouchard ever hit on you?"

Surprised by the sudden change in conversation, Ellie's eyes widened. "What?"

"Did Bouchard flirt with you or ask you out?"

Ellie recalled one day in particular when Bouchard was visiting Rob. "I hadn't thought about this in a long time—well since I died. Remember, I told you I thought there was something creepy about him, so I always tried to avoid him when he came to see Rob. But one day, when I was in my studio working on some designs, I felt . . . something . . . sort of an eerie feeling that someone was watching me. I turned around, and René was at my door. I thought my door was closed, but it wasn't. He was just standing there staring at me. It made me very uneasy."

"What did he say?"

"He asked if I wanted to grab some lunch. Of course, I declined. I was very surprised he'd asked since I rarely said more than a few words to him."

"Did you notice that all of the women Bouchard dated were blonde?"

"I didn't notice. I guess that's why you're the detective."

"You called him creepy. What was it about him that creeped you out?"

Ellie shrugged and looked away. "It was just the way he stared at me. He made me uncomfortable. And everything was *too perfect* about him. He's the type of man who spends more time in front of a mirror than a woman."

Steele chuckled. "Yeah, I can see why you thought that. He would give Edward a run for his money in the *dandy* department."

Ellie laughed. "True. But Edward isn't weird."

CHAPTER FIFTY-SIX

The Talisman

Before daylight, Steele's cell phone rang, and when he didn't wake, Ellie touched his shoulder and said, "Steele, wake up."

Steele turned over and blinked his eyes open. "What is it, honey?"

"Your cell phone is ringing."

Steele glanced at the ceiling—4:07 a.m. He shook his head, trying to clear the cobwebs before he reached for his phone on the bedside table. "Yeah?" he said gruffly as he turned on the lamp.

"Steele, I'm sorry I woke you, but I just had a vision. I went to sleep holding onto Amy's teddy bear last night."

Steele had no idea who was talking, and he ran a hand over his face trying to get his thoughts in order. "What? Who . . ."

Ellie leaned over and whispered, "It's Mae."

Steele gave her a grateful smile. Softening his tone, he said, "Mae? Are you okay?"

"Yes, I'm sorry to call so early, but I had to tell you what happened."

"It's okay, Mae, I'm awake now. What do you need to tell me? What happened?"

"I had a vision of Amy."

Steele sat up, propped his pillow against the headboard, and leaned back. He put the call on speaker so Ellie could hear their conversation. "Did you say you had a vision of Amy? Is she . . . was she . . ."

"She's alive. She's not harmed in any way, and she looks like someone is taking good care of her. She was clean and wearing blue pajamas with pink hearts. She's in a beautiful room that's decorated with hearts on everything. The wallpaper has little pink hearts, and there's a large pink heart-shaped, puffy pillow on her bed. I just don't know where the room is, but I know she can't escape. She was lying on her bed, and she was holding something in her hand. I couldn't see what it was, but I had a feeling it was some sort of talisman. I tried a telepathic connection with her, but I wasn't successful."

Steele was momentarily speechless. He tried to temper his excitement knowing that Mae could be wrong. "How does a telepathic connection work?"

"I go into a deep meditative state, and I try to pick up on Amy's energy, thoughts, and emotions."

"But if she doesn't know she can connect with you, then what?"

"She doesn't have to do anything, but I'm hoping she will be guided by her intuition. If not, I still think I will be able to pick up her thoughts."

"Did you say you were holding onto Amy's teddy bear?"

"Yes, I fell asleep with it in my arms. Something woke me up. I think it was my unconscious mind telling me Amy was awake, and I was making some sort of connection."

This conversation was almost too much for Steele to take in at 4:00 a.m., but he was trying to keep up. "It's a relief to know she's alive. Mae, I don't want to put pressure on you, but I'm at a dead end with leads. To be honest with you, you're my only hope right now."

"I wouldn't have called if I wasn't encouraged by this connection, Steele. I've been thinking about the reason she hasn't been abused or harmed in any way. Maybe someone wanted a girl, and they kidnapped Amy. Not for any nefarious reason. They just wanted a child to love. Maybe it was a woman who lost a child, and her mind couldn't cope."

"Tom suggested that very thing not long ago. I hope you're right about that." Steele didn't know what he believed, but Mae's theory was the most optimistic, so he was inclined to go with her version. Unfortunately, in his line of work, he'd seen too many cases that didn't turn out that way. But he refused to go there as long as there was hope. Until he knew what happened to Amy, she was alive in his mind, and he wouldn't allow himself to think otherwise.

"Steele, I'll try later today to reconnect. Right now, I'm exhausted, and I need to get some rest."

"Thank you, Mae. Call me later." Steele put his phone back on the nightstand and turned to Ellie. "Lie down beside me, honey. Let's go back to sleep."

Ellie snuggled to his side and rested her head on his bare chest. "I like it when you call me *honey*."

Bear jumped on the bed and plopped down on Steele's other side.

Steele hugged both of them. "I think this is what it means to be *as snug as a bug in a rug*."

CHAPTER FIFTY-SEVEN

Right Between the Eyes

Ellie transported herself along with Edward and Ace to René Bouchard's studio. They walked down the hall peeking into offices until they saw Bouchard sitting at a desk.

"There he is. I will leave you here, but stay out of trouble." She gave them a little wave before she disappeared.

"She didn't even close her eyes before she disappeared," Ace said.

"She's been doing this a lot longer than we have. I'm sure we will soon be as adept," Edward replied.

They walked into Bouchard's studio, and Ace stared at Bouchard. "If my gun worked, I'd shoot the scoundrel right between the eyes."

"I understand how you feel. But you can't shoot him until he's on the beach preparing to shoot Ellie. If you shoot him now, we'll never know if the past can be altered."

"I keep forgetting that part." Ace gave him a wicked grin, and said, "There's no reason we can't have a little fun with him and make him think he's crazy."

Edward smiled. "After we see what we can find out, I promise we'll make Bouchard question his sanity."

When Ace frowned, Edward added, "But I see no reason we can't give that rude, pink-haired girl in the front office a lesson in manners. Do all people have their faces stuck in their phones as she does?"

"We see enough people on the beach doing the same thing. Those little phones are the most important things in their lives. They ignore the people they're with, they run into people, and they don't even look at the ocean, much less go in for a swim. I don't know why they bother to go to the beach."

"Too true. Do you remember when we saw Ellie on the beach before she was shot? She was never on her phone," Edward said.

"I remember. She loved the beach and playing with Bear."

When Bouchard picked up his cell phone and made a call, Edward and Ace stopped talking so they could listen to his conversation. The call didn't seem important, so they stood over his shoulder and read everything they could see on his desk. Edward walked to a table behind Bouchard's desk and looked through his drawings. Bouchard must have heard a sound because he turned and looked at the table where Edward was standing. Luckily, Edward saw him and didn't move anything until Bouchard turned around.

Bouchard ended his call and left his office. Edward and Ace thought that was their opportunity to riffle through every piece of paper on his desk. Bouchard's cell phone was lying on top of a stack of papers where he'd just left it. Ace smiled to himself as he intentionally hid it under a notepad.

Edward chuckled at Ace's antics. He wanted to join in the fun, so he picked up a pen and doodled designs on some of Bouchard's drawings.

Ace was watching over his shoulder and said, "I think you made them look better."

Edward opened more portfolios and looked through the drawings. "Ace, take a look at this."

"What is it?"

Tapping the bottom corner of the drawing, Edward said, "Right here. It's Ellie's signature."

Ace pushed his Stetson back on his head. "Well, I'll be. How'd that skunk get his hands on Ellie's work? We should take these and show them to Steele."

"We can't walk out with these because they would still be visible to people," Edward replied.

"Remember how we got here—we just *thought* our way here. Maybe we can take them with us that way."

"Let's give it a try." Edward held the drawings in one hand and placed his other hand on Ace's shoulder. "Concentrate."

Seconds later, Edward looked down at his empty hand and said, "It didn't work."

"Nope, but we're back where we belong," Ace said, pointing to the sea rolling to shore. "At least we did something right."

"I guess we better go back to Bouchard's," Edward said.

Minutes later, they were standing inside Bouchard's studio again. Bouchard had not returned to his office, so Edward picked up the portfolio from the floor. "We need to find a good hiding place for this and tell Steele where he can find it."

"I guess we can't put it behind the wall," Ace said.

"No, we can't move items through walls." Edward looked around, trying to find a good hiding place. Suddenly, he looked up and said, "I've got it. I was watching a restaurant being renovated on the beach, and those ceiling pieces move." He pointed to the ceiling tiles and added, "You're taller than me, and if you stand on the table, you can lift one of those rectangles and put the drawings up there."

"Great idea." Ace jumped up on the table and easily lifted one of the tiles. Edward handed him the portfolio, and Ace slid it above the adjoining tile brackets.

Edward was at the doorway watching for Bouchard. "Hurry, Bouchard is walking this way."

Ace positioned the tile back in place and jumped to the floor just as Bouchard walked through the door.

CHAPTER FIFTY-EIGHT

Let's Have a Rope Party

The first thing Bouchard noticed when he returned to his studio was sand on the floor. He glanced around the room and spotted sand on top of his design table. *What the heck?* All of his drawings were haphazardly tossed about, and his desk was in total disarray. His office was at the end of the hallway, and it would have been impossible for someone to walk that way without being seen. So how did sand get on the marble floor? Someone had been in there and intentionally made a mess of everything. He stalked out of the studio and down the hallway, yelling for the receptionist.

Steele and Bear were watching the late afternoon Florida cloudburst from the comfort of his sofa when Edward and Ace suddenly appeared. They were in the middle of a conversation, and both men were excited and talking over each other. They reminded Steele of two children who had just experienced the thrill of their first theme park.

When they finally took a breath, Steele managed to hear enough of their conversation to piece together the gist of what they were saying. "Did you say you hid the drawings in the ceiling?"

"Yes, we did. At first, we tried to bring them with us, but it didn't work, so we had to go back and hide them," Ace said.

"They were Ellie's drawings, and we thought they might be a valuable piece of evidence," Edward added.

Steele didn't know how this would help him, but he didn't want to dampen their enthusiasm. He motioned for them to sit down. "Those drawings could come in handy if I can prove Bouchard killed Ellie."

Ace threw his arms in the air. "We know he killed her. Why can't you go to the sheriff and tell him?"

"We have to be able to prove it in a court of law," Steele answered.

"Steele cannot tell the authorities that two ghosts saw Bouchard shoot Ellie," Edward reminded Ace.

"I know." Frustrated, Ace plopped down on the sofa and pushed his Stetson back on his head. "Maybe vigilante justice wasn't such a bad idea in my day. In Bouchard's case, we could have one heck of a *rope party*."

Steele chuckled. "I'll admit the thought holds some merit."

"Steele, I'm sorry, but I don't think we heard anything that would be of help to you. Though we did hear Bouchard make a lunch engagement with Rob Harmon tomorrow," Edward said. "And we did notice Bouchard's penchant for orderliness. Even the pencils on his table were perfectly aligned. There was not one item out of place in his studio. He's rather fastidious—a real *dandy*."

Steele could hardly keep a straight face hearing Edward describe Bouchard as a *dandy*.

At that point, Ace did crack a smile. "Yeah, we messed everything up when Bouchard left the room. That ruffled his feathers."

Steele grinned at them. "I'm sure that drove him nuts."

"What do you hope to find about Bouchard that would help with your case?" Edward asked.

"I thought he might slip up and say something incriminating to someone. Usually, criminals can't help themselves from boasting about their crimes, but Bouchard may be too intelligent to be so careless. He's not the average criminal."

"It might not be a bad idea to make him question his sanity," Edward said.

Steele stroked his five o'clock shadow. "You might be onto something. Maybe Ellie could take you to Bouchard's home when he's working. She could leave some things like her drawings, or a piece of jewelry for him to find."

"I like the sound of that," Ace said.

"Bouchard lives in a gated community, and all visitors must be approved by him. He'll never figure out how things magically appear in his home. If we're lucky, he'll think Ellie's ghost is haunting him."

Ace rubbed his palms together. "This is going to be fun."

"Ace and I cannot take inanimate objects with us. Can Ellie do that?" Edward asked.

Steele shrugged. "I don't know, but she can think of something like a cup of coffee, and it appears."

"I wish I could do that," Ace said.

"Edward, you said Bouchard is meeting Harmon for lunch tomorrow. Did you happen to hear where they were meeting?"

"A place called Table Six. Why?"

"I'll drive to Palm Beach tomorrow and *accidentally* run into them at the restaurant and invite myself to join them. I'll tell them about strange events happening at Ellie's home and drop a few hints that

I think the place is haunted. While I'm with them, the three of you can visit his home."

"Steele, that's brilliant, particularly if you want to drive Bouchard insane. Is that your goal?" Edward asked.

"I agree with Ace—I'd like to shoot the SOB," Steele admitted. "Since I can't kill him, I don't care if I drive him right into a straitjacket. But I don't want him to confess until I figure out a way to change what happened to Ellie. Right now, I'll settle for making him so paranoid that he'll feel like he needs security beside him to take a leak."

Edward and Ace laughed so hard that Bear howled. Steele couldn't help laughing with them. He couldn't remember the last time he'd laughed so hard.

When their laughter died down, Edward asked, "By the way, where is Ellie?"

"She's visiting her uncle today."

"Would you prefer to have some time alone to work on your cases?"

Steele shook his head. "No, I have a question for you two."

"Ask away," Edward said.

"I want to know if all of the spirits you see on the beach were killed there."

"Not all of them. There's a policeman who was killed in another part of the city a few months ago, but he loved the beach, so this is where he spends his time," Edward replied.

"I remember that case. He was a detective and was just a week away from retirement when he was shot."

"That's him. A very nice fellow. It is such a sad story. He had promised his wife they would travel when he retired, and then he was murdered. He visits his wife often, but it's difficult for him to see how much she misses him."

"I think I heard that his case wasn't solved," Steele said.

"No. I guess he's stuck here like we are."

"Do you ever see the spirits of young children?" Steele asked. He'd been thinking about that earlier when he was watching the rain, but he wasn't sure he wanted to know the answer.

Edward and Ace exchanged a look, and they both shook their heads from side to side.

"No, never."

CHAPTER FIFTY-NINE

Much Ado About Nothing

When Ellie returned, Steele told her about his lunch plans for the next day. She suggested that he should call her uncle to meet him. There was no way Rob Harmon and Bouchard would dare object to Steele joining their luncheon if her uncle was present.

Steele called John, and Ellie was right, he readily agreed to meet him at Table Six and play along with Steele's story that Ellie's house was haunted. John even made the reservations and requested a table for four which ensured Harmon and Bouchard had no reason to refuse to join them.

Table Six was the place to be seen in Palm Beach, and it didn't surprise Steele that Bouchard made reservations at the trendy restaurant. It was Bouchard's kind of place. Steele preferred the House of Bourbon down the street, where they had a great selection of good Kentucky bourbon and superb burgers.

The next afternoon, Steele walked into the restaurant and spotted John seated at a table. They shook hands, and Steele said, "I appreciate your help today."

"Thank you for including me. You know I'll help in any way I can."

"What I want to do today is play with Bouchard's mind. As I told you last night, I'm going to convince him that Ellie's house is haunted."

"To tell you the truth, my first thought was to confront Bouchard today. But I understand why you want to wait until you have proof to charge him. Are you trying to frighten him into confessing?"

"John, I want him to incriminate himself, but I'm also trying to find a way to stop him from shooting Ellie." Seeing John's puzzled expression, Steele said, "Let me explain."

He told John about Edward's and Ace's roles in the investigation. "They helped to identify Bouchard as the murderer. "I don't know if we can change history, but I would like to find a way to reverse that night. I want Ellie to live."

John leaned back in his chair, stared at Steele for several seconds, and said, "You're in love with my niece."

"Yes, I am."

"I don't know if you can reverse what has happened, but I'll do whatever I can to help." John glanced at the door to the restaurant and saw Harmon and Bouchard walk inside. "They're here." He stood and said, "I'll bring them back to our table."

Steele watched as John feigned surprise at seeing the pair dining at the same restaurant. From across the room, he heard John insist they join him for lunch. His treat. As expected, they did not refuse his invitation.

"Rob, I believe you know Steele Harper," John said when he returned to the table with both men. He glanced at Bouchard and added, "Steele, this is René Bouchard."

"We've met," Bouchard said, quite obviously surprised that he was having lunch with John.

"How odd to find you two dining here," Rob said.

"Steele was just updating me on his progress into Ellie's murder." He looked at Bouchard and added, "Steele is investigating the death of my niece. Sadly, her murder has never been solved, so he's kind enough to keep me informed of any new developments."

"How interesting. Have there been new developments?" Bouchard asked.

"In a way. I was just telling John that I'm beginning to think that Ellie's house is haunted."

Rob's eyes widened, and Bouchard laughed.

"Why on earth do you think Ellie's home is. . ." Rob stopped talking when the waiter appeared and placed a bottle of Pellegrino sparkling water at each place setting. After he handed the men a menu and recited the chef's special, he said he would return after they had time to peruse the menu.

Rob wasted no time asking his question, "Why do you suspect Ellie's home is haunted?"

"Are you aware Steele lives next door to Ellie's home?" John asked.

"You mean Eleanor's former home," Bouchard said.

"Yes, well, I haven't listed the home, so as far as I'm concerned, it's still Ellie's home," John replied.

"I told John that lights come on at night, and after the first couple of times it happened, I went over to investigate. I thought someone had broken in, but no one was there. Some days the patio doors are open, and I hear music coming from the house."

"Perhaps the lights are on a timer," Rob suggested.

"No, I haven't installed timers in the house," John replied.

"I thought about timers, and I looked around but didn't find any. There was no reason for the lights to come on. But that's not all . . ."

The waiter reappeared, and the men placed their order, though no one had looked at the menu.

Steele resumed his story when the waiter disappeared. "I saw a blonde woman walking from the beach and into the house. I had two friends over, and they didn't see her, but I saw her as plain as I see you," he pointed to Bouchard for emphasis. "I walked over to the house, and the patio doors were wide open. I walked through every room, and no one was there."

"Your mind must be playing tricks on you," Bouchard said.

Rob was so pale it looked like he'd seen a ghost. "What kind of music did you hear? Ellie listened to music in her studio all day long."

"Classical," Steele responded.

"That's what she loved best," Rob whispered as if Ellie's ghost might pop up beside him if she heard him.

"Rob, surely you don't believe in these ghost stories," Bouchard said.

Before Rob could reply, John said, "Well, whether I believe in ghosts or not, something strange has been happening in my office. I found notes that could only have been written by Ellie."

Steele almost laughed at the shocked expression on Bouchard's face.

Bouchard said, "What makes you think they were written by Eleanor?"

"I recognize her handwriting. She always draws a heart beside her name. The same heart that is on all of her jewelry."

"That's true. I've seen her do it thousands of times," Rob said. "What does she write to you, John?"

"Different things—she misses me, and she hopes to see me soon."

Their food arrived at the table, and the discussion continued as they ate.

"The strangest thing I've seen is a woman on the beach each night around midnight. She's wearing a long white gown and looking at the moon over the ocean. Suddenly, she turns around, and blood is soaking her gown down the front, and then she disappears."

"How can you see her blood on her gown from your home?" Bouchard asked.

"I saw her several nights in a row, so I decided to go to the beach and wait for her. That's when I witnessed what happens every night at the same time. The woman is Ellie," Steele said before he took a bite of his forty-five-dollar burger. He noticed Bouchard hadn't touched his Kobe beef steak with white asparagus.

"Someone is pulling a prank. That's all it is," Bouchard said.

"Don't you believe in ghosts?" Steele asked.

"Of course not. No rational person would."

"I think there are many things that we do not understand. I would never say we know everything that happens in the world around us," John stated.

"I still think it's nonsense," Bouchard said.

"I tell you what, Mr. Bouchard, you have an open invitation to come to my home any night that would be convenient and see for yourself." Steele hadn't thought about issuing that invitation, but once he'd put it out there, he was glad he did.

"Would you include me in that invitation, Steele?" Rob asked.

Bouchard stared at Rob and said, "You can't be serious?"

"I most certainly am. I'd like to see this for myself. If you're not afraid, come with me," Rob replied.

"I think it would be a waste of an evening. Allow me to quote Shakespeare, and say it will turn out to be '*much ado about nothing.*'"

"Could I impose upon your hospitality and invite myself, Steele?" John asked.

"You are all welcome. I'll even grill all of you a steak since Mr. Bouchard doesn't seem to be enjoying his."

Bouchard looked at his uneaten plate of food. "I wasn't very hungry."

Steele wondered why he'd ordered the most expensive item on the menu if he wasn't hungry. There was always rabbit food to order. "Well, if you aren't going to eat that steak, my dog, Bear, would love it."

CHAPTER-SIXTY

You Got Any Dynamite?

"Bouchard keeps his home the same way he keeps his office. Not one item out of place," Edward said.

Ellie's eyes swept the expensively appointed room. "I feel like I'm in an upscale antique store."

"It doesn't look comfortable," Ace said, pointing to the Louis XVI chairs. "It's not like your place, Ellie. I mean, your home looks like a woman lives there, but a man can relax in your place. This place doesn't look like a man's place. I mean, there's no boot jack by the door and no place to hang your hat or gun belt."

"I know what you mean, Ace. It's too foppish," Edward replied.

Ace shrugged. "Well, I don't rightly know the meaning of that, but if you say so."

"How about—too dandyish."

Ace smiled. "Yeah, that sounds about right."

Ellie laughed at their comments, but she agreed. "Let's see if we can find anything in his library."

Just like the entire home, Bouchard's library was spotless. Ellie saw a portfolio next to his desk, and when she opened it, she found drawings of her heart jewelry.

"The scoundrel! He has your drawings everywhere," Edward said. "I'd like to run him through! I was quite handy with my sabre in my day."

"That gives me an idea." Ellie thought about removing a heart from her bracelet and leaving it on his desk, but she didn't want to part with one. Instead, she picked up a pencil, grabbed the drawing of her heart bracelet, and traced the broken heart from her bracelet below the original drawing. Then she signed her name.

"Why did you choose that heart?" Edward asked.

Ellie looked at the drawing. "I don't know. Maybe because he's torn my life in half."

"Do you have another piece of your jewelry that we could leave for him to see?" Edward asked.

"No. My bracelet is the only one I have. The stores carry them, but I can't buy them."

"Do you want me to stage a hold-up?" Ace asked.

Edward chuckled. "You mean like the highwaymen in my day?"

"Yeah, stagecoach and train robbers used to steal women's valuables," Ace replied.

Ellie shook her finger at them. "There will be no robbing. I imagine I can conjure up a piece of jewelry. I'm not sure it will be mine, but I can try."

"You mean like you do a cup of coffee? Steele *really* likes that," Ace said.

"Yes. I've never tried to see if it works with anything other than food or drink for Steele." Ellie closed her eyes and concentrated.

A second later, a replica of her bracelet appeared in her hand.

Edward and Ace were rendered speechless—for a moment.

"You really must teach us how to do that," Edward finally whispered.

Ellie examined the bracelet and said, "All I do is think about what I want."

"Is that how you got Steele?" Ace asked.

Ellie turned and looked at him. "What do you mean?"

"Did you concentrate to get a man like Steele?" Ace explained.

"Not really. I just prayed every night for someone to help me. I didn't think of anyone specific."

"You got lucky," Ace said.

"Yes, very lucky."

Edward examined the second bracelet. "This one doesn't have a broken heart. Why don't you leave the damaged bracelet here for Bouchard to find, and you keep the new one?" Edward asked.

Ellie glanced at the two bracelets. "I just have a feeling that I need to keep the broken one."

"Let's look around some more," Edward said. He walked around the room and noticed an odd bust of Nero on a pedestal table. It didn't appear to be as expensive as the other items in the room. He moved closer to examine the bust, and he saw that there was a space between the head and the neck. It looked like the head could turn. When he twisted the head, one wall opened, sliding behind a bookshelf. "What the devil?"

Ellie and Ace joined Edward in front of a steel wall that had a combination lock in the center of the steel doorway.

"What is this?" Ace asked.

"It's probably a panic room."

At their puzzled expressions, Ellie explained the reason for a safe room.

"Let's walk through and see what he has in there," Edward suggested. He took one step forward, and instead of going through the wall, he slammed his nose against the steel. "What the . . .?"

Ellie tried to go through the wall and had the same result. Ace wisely did not try. "I like my nose as it is."

"I've never seen a wall I haven't been able to walk through," Ellie said.

Edward held his ear to the steel door. "I hear nothing."

"Why don't we look for the combination to the lock? It might be in his desk," Ace suggested.

The three hurried back to the desk and started rifling through everything.

"I could always dynamite it open. Ellie, can you round me up some dynamite?" Ace asked.

Ellie and Edward stopped thumbing through papers and stared at him.

"Ace, exactly what did you do in your former life?" Edward asked.

"I wasn't a safecracker if that's what you're asking. I told you, I worked on a ranch." He grinned. "That's not to say I haven't learned a few tricks from outlaws over the years. I did spend a few years out West. It came in handy to have friends on both sides of the law."

CHAPTER SIXTY-ONE

Blow That Wall to Kingdom Come

Lunch ended, and Steele walked with John to his car. "I have a feeling Harmon will take me up on my offer and come to see my ghost. Do you think Bouchard will come with him?"

"I think he'll be too curious not to come, and I imagine Harmon will make sure he does." John slapped Steele on the back and added, "When Bouchard goes home tonight and finds whatever surprise Ellie, Edward, and Ace left behind, that will probably make him even more paranoid."

Steele laughed. "I'm counting on it."

The men said goodbye, and Steele walked to his car carrying the small box holding Bear's dinner. When he left the elevator in the parking garage, he saw Ellie, Ace, and Edward standing beside his SUV. They turned and waved to him.

"This is a nice surprise," Steele said.

"We went home to take care of Bear, but we thought we would come back and ride home with you," Ellie said.

"What's in the box?" Ace asked as they piled inside his vehicle.

"A steak for Bear, compliments of Bouchard."

"He bought a steak for Bear?" Edward asked.

"No, it was his lunch. I guess you could say I ruined his appetite."

They laughed, and Edward said, "Then wait until he goes home. He's in for a shock."

The three told Steele about Bouchard's home, and Edward said, "Ellie left a bracelet on top of his desk. He's as fastidious in his home as he is in his office. He won't miss the gift Ellie left for him."

"You wouldn't even know someone lived there. I only saw one daguerreotype in his home. I guess he doesn't have a family," Ace said.

"You're right, Ace. I didn't see one photograph," Ellie said.

"It was on the whatchamacallit by his bed," Ace said.

"The nightstand?" Edward clarified.

Ace snapped his fingers, yet there was no sound. "Yeah, that's it. And there was something weird about the daguerreotype."

"It most likely looked strange since it was colorized," Edward said.

Ellie and Steele's eyes met and they smiled at each other.

"Did you find anything besides your drawings?" Steele asked.

"Tell Steele about that strange wall we couldn't walk through," Edward suggested.

After Ellie described the wall, Steele asked, "Ellie, was this the first time you were unable to walk through a wall?"

"Yes. It must be some reinforced steel or something."

"What would make a man so afraid that he needs a room with a combination lock?" Edward asked.

Steele shook his head. "I know panic rooms are popular today, but I wasn't aware they required combination locks. Maybe he has something of rare value hidden behind that door."

"Maybe an art collection. Expensive paintings?" Ellie suggested.

"Perhaps stolen art," Edward said.

Steele nodded. "That might make sense."

"Yeah, we know he likes to steal things," Ace added.

"I doubt he steals art, but he might purchase stolen art. And I'm not so certain he stole Ellie's designs. I think he bought them from Harmon," Steele said.

"Do you think Rob knows Bouchard murdered me?" Ellie asked.

Steele thought about her question. Even though he didn't like Harmon, he didn't think he was aware Bouchard shot Ellie. "I don't know beyond a reasonable doubt, but my gut says he didn't know."

"They're both blaggards, in my estimation," Edward said.

"If that means lowdown, dirty skunks, I agree," Ace replied.

Steele nodded. "I couldn't have said it better. Ellie, when we get home, I want you to draw me a layout of Bouchard's home."

"Why? You can't get into his building without passing through the security gate?"

Steele glanced at her and grinned. "You never know. I might know a spirit who can unlock doors when I find a way around the security."

Ellie smiled at him. "I can go inside and unlock the door, but how will you get around security?"

"I'm sure I also have two friends who could distract the men posted at the gate with some imaginative antics."

"Be assured, sir, *that* we can do," Edward said.

"And I'll find us some dynamite so you can blow that wall to kingdom come," Ace said.

CHAPTER SIXTY-TWO

If Only

The next morning, Steele awoke, and without looking, he knew he was alone in bed. It surprised him how quickly he'd grown accustomed to having Ellie beside him in the mornings. He missed her. Turning toward her pillow, he noticed her leather-bound journal lying open on the bed. He picked it up and saw today's date on the page. He'd seen her write in her journal before, and while it never occurred to him to read what she wrote, for some reason, he thought about the day she died. He wondered if she had recorded anything on that day.

He flipped through the journal until he found the day she was murdered.

Something happened to me today—but I can't remember what it was. I awoke on my patio disoriented, and I had a terrible headache. I felt like I was sleeping soundly, and abruptly awoke and nothing made sense. I can't even remember the date or day of the week. I can't remember anything about the entire day. I have a large bump and a small cut on my forehead. Did I fall? I noticed my bracelet was broken, and it wasn't before. And where is my car? It's not in the garage, but I don't remember leaving it anywhere. Perhaps I walked somewhere today. I read my journal from yesterday, but I didn't write my plans for today. Maybe after I walk on the beach tonight, I will remember something.

Steele closed the journal and leaned back on his pillow. Ellie's car was missing. He didn't know why it made a difference at this point—the killer was identified. But it was a curious piece of information. It would be nice to know why Bouchard killed her. He couldn't wrap his brain around Bouchard murdering Ellie because he was stealing her designs. The theft seemed like a weak motive for murder? Was Bouchard jealous of her as a competitor? For some reason, he wasn't satisfied with that motive either. Yet, as every cop knew, the reasons for murder made no sense.

Steele glanced at her journal again. He wondered what Ellie was writing this morning. He picked it up again and looked at the last entry.

If anyone read my story, they would think they were reading fiction. But this is my life. I was murdered, and I'm a spirit. I can't move on, and I can't come back. A wonderful man entered my life and he's trying to help me. If only I'd met him before . . . I died. I can't give him a normal life, and I don't want him to live his life with a spirit. I want him to have someone he can introduce to his friends; someone he can take to dinner or the movies. How do you give up someone you love? I want to pray for answers, but does anyone hear a spirit?

If only—two very sad words.

Steele laid aside the journal again, threw off his covers, and walked to the patio. Ellie was on the beach with Bear. As if she knew he was staring at her, she turned to him and waved. Bear raced toward him, with Ellie trying to keep up with him.

Bear greeted him as usual—like he hadn't seen him in weeks. Bear always lightened his heart. When Ellie reached him, he pulled her into his arms and whispered in her ear, "I'm sorry, but I read a few pages of your journal. You are *not* going to leave me. You aren't ever going to leave me. I wouldn't have a life without you. We'll find a way. If not, this will last forever. No more thinking *if only*."

Ellie wasn't upset that he'd read her journal. But his words made her cry. "I can't ask you to live like this."

"It's not your choice." Steele kissed her. He pulled back and looked at the tears trailing over her cheeks. He brushed them away and smiled at her. "Where's my coffee?"

She smiled slightly. "I guess you want cinnamon rolls too."

"I do. You've spoiled me."

Steele sat at the counter drinking coffee as Ellie prepared the cinnamon rolls. As soon as she pulled the rolls from the oven, she placed a plateful in front of Steele.

"I wish Ace and I could eat cinnamon rolls," Edward said from behind them.

Ellie jumped at the sound of his voice. "You scared me, Edward."

Edward chuckled. "I must say it is quite enjoyable to sneak up on people. But as I was saying, I wish we could taste cinnamon rolls; they always smell divine."

"I'd settle for biscuits and red-eye gravy," Ace said.

Edward's brows drew together in question. "And what is red-eye gravy?"

CHAPTER SIXTY-THREE

I'm a Ghost–Not Dead

After Steele ate his cinnamon rolls and drank his second cup of coffee, he called Ellie's uncle. "John, this is Steele. I need to ask you something?"

"Of course."

"What happened to Ellie's car?"

"It's in my garage. I haven't been able to part with it. It's a 1985 Alfa Romeo Spider, and Ellie loved that little car. Why do you ask?"

"Was the car at her home the day she was killed?" Steele asked.

"No. Several days after her murder, the police found it at the shopping center not far from her home. What's this about Steele?"

"Probably nothing. She'd written in her journal that she couldn't remember what had happened that entire day. She didn't know where she'd left her car. I was just trying to put some of the missing pieces together."

"I see. I also have some news for you. Before your call, I just ended a call with Rob Harmon. He asked if I could schedule a time to go to your home. He said Bouchard called him first thing this morning and said he'd changed his mind. Rob said Bouchard is now very interested in going to Ellie's home. I told him I would call you to set the day."

"Let's do it before Bouchard changes his mind. What about tomorrow night? Is that good with you?"

"Tomorrow works for me. I'll call Rob right now and set it up."

Steele walked outside to the patio and sat beside Ellie, who was talking with Edward and Ace.

"Harmon and Bouchard are coming here tomorrow night with your uncle."

Edward smiled wide. "I think that means we are going to have some fun, Ace."

"No dragging chains," Steele teased.

Pursing his lips, Edward said, "Nothing as droll as that, my dear fellow."

"Yeah, we can think of something better than that," Ace agreed.

"I wanted to ask all of you a question," Edward said.

Everyone looked at him, and Steele said, "What do you want to know, Edward?"

"I'd like to know if you believed in ghosts before you met Ellie."

Steele said, "That's a good question."

Ace was the first to reply. "My grandmother told me a story about moving into a home with five children when she was a young mother. People told her and my grandfather that the home was haunted, but my grandmother wasn't afraid of anything. They moved in. She said when they would come home from town, they'd see an old woman in the field taking care of the garden. But when they got closer, the woman would disappear. They'd hear noises in the house, but they ignored them. But one time, when the old lady appeared sitting in the rocking chair, my grandfather saw her and insisted they move that night."

Steele laughed. "I take it that your grandfather wasn't as brave as your grandmother."

Ace chuckled. "Not by a long shot. But I believed in ghosts because my grandmother wouldn't lie about anything. She was the most honorable person I ever knew."

All eyes turned to Ellie, and Edward said, "What about you, Ellie? Did you believe in ghosts?"

"I don't think I thought much about it one way or the other."

"Edward, did you believe in ghosts?" Steele asked.

"Truthfully, I could not fathom such a thing," Edward replied.

"What about you, Steele?" Ellie asked.

"I've always thought there are many things in this world and beyond that we don't understand. Morgan and I talk about UFOs and Bigfoot all of the time. We both believe in keeping an open mind. Tom thinks we're nuts, but we think Tom is afraid to admit that there are too many things in this world that we can't explain. I guess I never ruled out the possibility of ghosts."

"I agree that we should keep an open mind," Edward said. "Particularly now."

Everyone laughed, and Steele said, "Let's make plans for tomorrow night. Naturally, I want the lights turned off and on. Ellie, I want you to play classical music. I think you guys could pick up some things and carry them around. It would look like they are just floating through the air."

"Ellie, we could open your portfolio and flip through the pages," Edward suggested.

"You could have another bracelet appear and drop it in his lap," Ace said.

"Steele, what if I take something from his home and have it appear in front of him? Maybe one of his statues?" Ellie suggested.

Steele grinned at her. "Oh, that's devious. Remind me never to get on your bad side."

"In case you haven't noticed, Steele, Ellie doesn't have a bad side," Ace said.

Steele arched his brow at Ace. "I've noticed, but I'm surprised you have."

"I'm a ghost—not dead," Ace replied.

CHAPTER SIXTY-FOUR

Séance Anyone?

"You grill a delicious steak, Steele," John Marlowe said.

"Yes, you do, and it was kind of you to prepare dinner," Rob Harmon said.

"It's my pleasure. I'm just glad to have all of you here tonight to witness what happens next door. I don't want anyone to think I'm going off the deep end." Steele glanced at Ellie, Edward, and Ace and winked.

Ellie pointed to Bouchard's plate and said, "He doesn't seem to be enjoying his dinner."

Edward closed his eyes and inhaled deeply, appearing to have a pleasant memory. "The steaks smell wonderful. I would savor every bite."

Steele didn't care if Bouchard ate his steak or not since Bear would be happy to have it for his dinner.

"Bear told me to tell you that he would eat his steak," Ellie said to Steele. "He said he doesn't like Bouchard, but he loves your steaks."

Steele almost laughed aloud. It was as if she knew what he was thinking. He didn't like the thought of Ellie being in the room with her killer, but she was handling it well. In truth, she handled it better than he did.

Harmon looked out at the ocean at the sun dipping below the horizon. "It will be dark soon."

"Do you think that's our signal to get moving?" Ellie asked Ace and Edward.

"Let them eat steak—we will have our fun," Edward said.

Steele looked at his watch. "You will see the lights come on next door in a few minutes."

"Should we go over to the house and make sure no one is there? I still think someone could be slipping inside and causing the mischief," Bouchard said.

"As I said at lunch, I've walked over there several times at night, and I've never seen anyone there."

"I brought my key, so we can have a look around if you like," John said.

Steele refilled their wine glasses. "Let's finish our dinner, and we'll walk over."

Ellie waved to Steele and blew him a kiss. "We'll be waiting for you."

While his guests finished their wine, Steele carried the dishes to the kitchen. He sliced Bouchard's steak into small pieces and added it to Bear's dry dog food. It took him two minutes to eat the entire bowl of food.

As they walked to Ellie's, a light came on in the house.

Harmon pointed to the house. "Do you see that light? It wasn't on a moment ago!"

"I told you, it happens every night," Steele said. "I've had friends over, and they've seen the same thing several times."

John pulled out his key, but as they neared the house, they heard music coming from the patio. They altered their course and walked to the patio, where they found the doors wide open.

"That's Tchaikovsky, Ellie's favorite," Harmon said.

Steele had heard the music before, but he didn't know it was Ellie's favorite. He still had a lot to learn about her, and he wanted to spend his life learning all of her likes and dislikes."

"I see you brought your weapon," Bouchard said to Steele.

"Yes, but I doubt that anyone is here. You're welcome to stay out here while I check."

"I think we should all go inside. Force in numbers," John said.

Steele pulled his pistol and said, "Stay behind me."

They walked through the entire house until Bouchard and Harmon were satisfied that no one was there.

"Why don't we sit in the living room for a while? It's nice being inside Ellie's home again. It brings back such pleasant memories," John said.

"Her clothes are still in the closet," Harmon said. "And I swear I smell her perfume."

"I always smell her perfume." Steele wasn't lying. He loved the way Ellie smelled. He could give Bear a run for his money in the sniffing department.

"I haven't removed anything in her home," John said.

While they were talking, the light in the kitchen flickered on.

"What the . . . ," Bouchard didn't finish his question. He jumped up and ran to the kitchen. "Who turned on this light?"

"We're the only ones here, René," Harmon said.

Steele thought Harmon was handling things fairly well, even though he had paled a bit.

When Bouchard returned to his seat, he saw a heart bracelet lying on the cushion. He picked it up and examined it closely. It was one of Ellie's designs, just like the one at his home. He glared at the three men. "Who put this here?"

"What are you talking about? We haven't moved?" Harmon said.

"This is not funny, Rob." Bouchard handed the bracelet to him. "This is Ellie's. Did you put that on the sofa?"

Rob looked at the bracelet. "No, I swear I didn't put it there. I told you we didn't move. I don't know where it came from."

Rob tried to hand the bracelet back to Bouchard, but Bouchard backed away and sat down. "This is crazy."

"Would you like me to go get a bottle of wine or perhaps some bourbon?" Steele asked.

"Ellie used to keep some bourbon for me," John said as he stood. "I know where she kept it." He walked to the kitchen, opened the cabinet, and pulled out the bottle of Kentucky Bluegrass Bourbon that Steele had placed there earlier in the day. He poured two shots into each glass.

John was carrying two glasses to the living room when he saw a bust of Nero floating across the room. It landed softly on the coffee table right in front of Bouchard.

Bouchard's eyes widened, and he jumped to his feet. "What's going on here?" His gaze slid to Rob, then Steele, then to John. "That looks like my bust!"

Harmon looked at John and said, "Did Ellie have this in her home? It's just like one in René's home."

John shook his head. "No, I've never seen that before."

Steele looked at Bouchard and asked, "Are you saying that statue is yours?"

"I don't know if it's mine, but I have one just like it."

Steele noticed Bouchard's hands were shaking. "Why would Ellie have your busts?"

Bouchard leaned over, trying to see if the head of Nero could be turned. It could. It was his statue. He tossed back his bourbon.

Edward appeared carrying the bottle and refilled Bouchard's glass. To everyone in the room, it looked like the bottle was floating through the room. At the same time, Ace carried Ellie's portfolio to the living room. He placed it on the table, sat beside Bouchard, and started flipping through her drawings.

Bouchard nearly jumped over the sofa in his effort to put some distance between him and the moving portfolio, and the floating bottle of bourbon. "Rob, we need to get out of here! Now!"

"I'm scared too, but I've never seen anything like this before," Rob replied. "I've never thought ghosts were real. We need to find out what she wants." He looked around the room as if he thought Ellie would appear. "Ellie, if you're here, do you want us to have a séance?"

Steele looked at Ellie, and she rolled her eyes.

"If you do, tap three times on the table," Rob said.

Steele nodded at Ellie, and she knocked on the table.

CHAPTER SIXTY-FIVE

Protect the Woman You Love

In the middle of the night, Steele awoke and felt Ellie's hand on his chest. He placed his hand on top of hers and gently squeezed. "Hi."

Ellie snuggled against his side. "I can't tell you how many times I walked on the beach thinking how much I wanted to go to sleep at night with my hand on the beating heart of my love. I thought that dream was lost to me."

Moonlight lit the bedroom through the patio doors, and Steele could see Ellie's eyes. "You can do it every night now. My mom used to say that life was full of surprises."

Ellie smiled. "Your mother was right. I love to feel your heartbeat. It's so strong and steady, and your skin is so warm."

"Can I ask you something?" Steele brought her hand to his lips and kissed her fingers.

"Of course."

"What did you normally wear to bed?" Steele noticed that she was dressed every morning when he woke.

Ellie smiled at him. "A tee shirt or sometimes something short and silky."

"Wouldn't you be more comfortable in something like that? You can bring some clothes here if you'd like. I don't own anything short and silky, but you can wear one of my tee shirts."

Ellie knew she could change her outfit easily, but the thought of him asking her to wear something of his was meaningful. She loved the openness and the intimacy between them. She'd never experienced that in previous relationships.

Steele's eyes followed her as she crossed the room to his dresser. "Top drawer on the right. Pick out the one you want."

Ellie opened the drawer and pulled out a blue tee shirt. "Is this one okay?"

Steele nodded and said softly, "Ellie, I want to watch you put it on."

Ellie unbuttoned her dress and let it slide to the floor.

"Did you know séances and mediums were quite popular in my era?" Edward asked as they sat around Steele's dining table.

"I had no idea." Steele ate his breakfast which consisted of hot cinnamon rolls and scrambled eggs. The spirits watched him with envy each time he took a bite of the cinnamon roll.

"It was a bunch of table-knocking fakeries, but mediums were popular with the ladies," Edward said.

Steele laughed. "You mean only women went to see the mediums?"

"Yes. I imagine they wanted the mediums to tell them about their husbands' mistresses." Edward looked at Ellie and said, "Mistresses were very common in my day."

Ellie arched her brow at him. "Did the women have lovers?"

Edward nodded. "Quite often."

"Did you ever attend a séance, Edward?" Steele asked.

"Never."

"In my day, everyone visited Granny Woodcock and asked her to get in touch with their dead folks," Ace said.

"Who was Granny Woodcock?" Steele asked.

"She was an old woman who lived in Apalachicola on the beach. Some called her a soothsayer. My mother said Granny Woodcock had *the gift*. I don't know what she had, but folks believed she talked to the dead. They came from all over the country to see her."

"Did you ever seek her talents?" Edward asked.

"No, but I know people who did."

"Maybe we should have a séance, as Rob suggested. If he thinks I'm haunting them, and if he sold my designs to Bouchard, he might confess," Ellie said.

Steele laughed. "It might be a good way to get Rob to start talking and tell us why he did it. Was it for money, or did they plan your murder together? We could have Mae act as the medium. I'll ask Morgan and Tom if they would like to join us."

"Bouchard probably won't come if we have a séance. I think we scared the devil out of him last night. He forgot to take his Nero bust with him," Ace said.

"He might be scared, but he'll want to know if Ellie's ghosts will continue to haunt him now," Edward replied. "That man is evil to the core to have murdered Ellie."

"It wasn't his actual bust, I just thought of one that looked like it, and it appeared," Ellie said. "So when he got home, his bust was right where it was supposed to be. That probably freaked him out more."

"I don't mind scaring the hell out of Bouchard since I can't do what I want to do to him." Steele looked at everyone around the table and said, "I want each of you to think about what would happen if we change history. What would be the repercussions if I shoot Bouchard before he shoots Ellie? I want to hear various perspectives. It lessens the chance that I will miss something."

"We'll think about it, Steele," Edward promised.

"Steele, I want to know what's in that room that Bouchard is hiding," Ace said.

Nodding, Steele said, "I was thinking the same thing. We need to plan a visit to his place."

"We need a safe cracker if you won't let me blow it open," Ace replied.

Ellie reached over and squeezed Steele's hand. "Steele, I don't want you to commit murder."

"My job is to protect the woman I love. I would be defending you."

"You've got me, Steele. I wouldn't mind shooting that varmint," Ace said.

CHAPTER SIXTY-SIX

Almost the Perfect Murder

"Do you two want to come to a séance?"

"What?" Morgan and Tom asked at the same time. They had Steele's call on speaker so they could both hear what he had to say.

"Have you gone over the deep end? Do we need to remind you that you not only speak to dead people, but you can also see them?" Tom said.

Chuckling, Steele said, "The séance is not for me. And you better not let Ellie, Edward, or Ace hear you call them dead."

"They aren't listening, are they?" Morgan asked.

"No, I'm alone."

"Then why a séance?" Tom asked.

Steele told them about Bouchard and Harmon coming to Ellie's haunted house last night. "You should have seen the expression on Bouchard's face when he saw the Nero bust floating through the air. It was difficult not to burst out laughing. Harmon mentioned having a séance, and the more we thought about it, we liked the idea."

After they stopped laughing, Morgan asked, "Why are you messing with that SOB Bouchard? You already know he killed Ellie?"

"I want to know why he killed her. I think Ellie needs to know."

"Makes sense. If someone killed me, I'd want to know why," Tom said.

"She didn't know Bouchard well, did she?" Morgan asked.

"No. He was friends with Harmon. Ellie called Bouchard *creepy.* She told me she tried to avoid him when he visited her studio."

"What do you think of him?"

"He thinks he's smarter than everyone else. I have to agree with Ellie. There's something about him that's not quite right. I wouldn't say *creepy*, but . . . I don't know what it is."

"Do you think Bouchard will come to the séance?" Morgan asked.

"I think he will. After last night, I think he'll want to try to make sense out of what he saw."

"He might think he's going crazy," Tom said.

"He is crazy—he committed murder," Steele replied.

"There is that."

"Will Ellie's uncle come for the show?" Morgan asked.

"He wouldn't miss it. And I'm going to ask Mae to be our medium."

"That's perfect. We'll be there," Morgan said.

"There's something else I wanted to tell you." Steele told them about the impenetrable room in Bouchard's home.

"Why would a man need a steel wall with a combination lock?" Tom asked.

"I thought it might be a panic room, but why the combination lock? That doesn't seem very convenient," Steele said. "Not only that, but Ellie drew the layout of his home, and there are more convenient areas for a panic room. We thought he might be hiding valuables, like artwork."

"Stolen?"

"I don't know. But my question is, how can I open that lock without the combination? Ace wants to dynamite it open."

"Ace is a man after my own heart," Tom said. "I'd pay to see that."

"I may know a guy who can help with the combination lock," Morgan said.

"There is one additional problem. I'm going to have to sneak into Bouchard's home. That's no problem with Ace's and Edward's help, but I can't involve anyone else."

"Why can't Edward or Ace just walk through the wall and take a peek in that room?" Tom asked.

"They tried, but they can't get through. Ellie can't get through it either, and she can usually appear wherever she wants."

"Steele, who cares what Bouchard has in there?" Morgan said.

"I guess it doesn't matter. But if I can't shoot Bouchard before he kills Ellie, I'd like to find some dirt on him. If nothing else, I can have him arrested for other crimes."

"Speaking of shooting, I have the parts for Ace's Colt," Morgan said. "I'll bring them with me."

"It might be better to let a ghost kill Bouchard instead of you," Tom said.

Steele lowered his voice, "I hope you two don't have an audience for this conversation."

"We're alone in here right now," Morgan said. "But we've been thinking about Ace shooting Bouchard. That's the smartest thing to do. No weapon will be left behind, no one will see Ace do it, and no fingerprints on anything. The tide can take Bouchard out. Think about it—it's almost like the perfect murder."

"How will we explain Ellie being alive?" Steele said.

"Tom and I thought about that. She would be introduced as a distant cousin or a half-sister. Her uncle could say his *relative* not only looks like Ellie, but she is also a designer and was working in France. Ellie could go back to her design business, just use a different name. We will get her new identification."

Steele liked their idea. "That's not a bad plan. And Ace is itching to shoot Bouchard. He could wait until Bouchard pulls his weapon and then shoot him. That way, he wouldn't be committing murder. I don't want him whisked away to hell."

"Do you think that would happen?" Tom asked.

"I have no idea. But now that I've seen spirits, I don't want to take chances with anyone's soul."

Everyone grew silent, and Steele said, "I'll call Mae and call you back to let you know the time of the séance."

CHAPTER SIXTY-SEVEN

Hocus Pocus

"Steele, will you make sure that I sit beside Bouchard tonight?" Mae asked. "I want to hold his hand during the séance, and maybe I can connect with him."

"Sure, no problem."

"You can do that? Connect with someone by holding their hand?" John Marlowe asked.

"Sometimes. I hope it works with Bouchard," Mae replied.

Steele handed John a glass of bourbon. "I'm glad you came early, John. We wanted to let you know what to expect tonight."

"I can't wait to hear what you're planning."

Steele handed Morgan and Tom their bourbon and a glass of iced tea to Mae. He sat down across from John and said, "Tonight, Mae will talk to the dead—meaning she'll speak to Ellie, Edward and Ace. At some point in the séance, Mae will tell us that Ellie says something that incriminates Bouchard."

"What do you think Bouchard will do?" John asked.

"He'll deny it and say it is all hocus pocus," Morgan said.

"I agree, but I think we can get Harmon to confess to selling Ellie's designs to Bouchard." Steele looked at John, and said, "It will be up to you to decide what you want to do with Harmon. You may want to file charges or work out a deal with him."

Steele looked at Ellie and said, "Can Mae wear your bracelet tonight?"

"Of course." Ellie removed her bracelet and handed it to Mae.

"I'm sure Bouchard will notice it." Steele looked at John and added, "If Bouchard asks Mae where she got it, would you say you found it on Ellie's coffee table today? He'll know it's the same one that was left at his house."

"Of course."

"Good." Steele then said, "Mae, I want you to mention the room with the steel door in Bouchard's home. We don't know what's in that room, but we want to see his reaction."

"I want to know what he's hiding there. Mae, you should tell him I'm going to blow a hole in that wall," Ace said.

Steele and Mae laughed, and Steele repeated what Ace said to the others.

"I can't see or hear you, Ace, but if you blow a hole in that wall, please do it when Bouchard is standing there," John said.

"Steele, tell John I'd be happy to," Ace replied.

Steele grinned and repeated Ace's response. "Ace, we've been talking about a scenario where you could shoot Bouchard." He explained Morgan's and Tom's idea to have Ace shoot Bouchard before he shoots Ellie.

Ace smiled wide. "I like this plan!"

Steele looked at John and added, "We thought you could introduce your other *niece* as a designer who has been living in France, and she can take over the business."

John's eyes lit up hearing their tentative plan. Evelyn was my grandmother's name. We could keep the same initials on Ellie's designs. Nothing would change other than the fact I would have to remember to call my niece Evelyn."

"Are you sure you can get Ellie new identification?" John asked.

"Trust me, that is the one thing I know we can do," Tom said.

John smiled. "Steele, you mentioned there could be consequences if you change history. Do you see any negatives in this plan?"

"No one can see Ace, so if anyone is on the beach that night, all they would see is a man dropping to the ground. They won't even see Ellie, at least not at first. There are a few things that trouble me about the idea. If Ace shoots Bouchard, and Ellie isn't shot, does she come back alive at that moment? Will she be on the beach with a dead Bouchard? Or will she disappear and go somewhere else? I don't know how that will work."

Silence filled the room as they thought about Steele's question.

"I guess that's why you're the brains of this outfit, Steele. I didn't think about that." Morgan glanced at Tom and asked, "Did you think about that?"

Tom shook his head. "No. We'd better hope no one is on the beach when we do this."

"A rainy night might be best," John suggested.

Steele said, "We might need to do it on the same day and time as the night she was killed. Let's think about it."

"It's supposed to storm tonight," Mae said. "Let's see what the beach is like tonight."

"A storm tonight will add to the theatrics of our séance," Edward said, smiling at the thought. "Can Ace and I add some drama?"

Steele smiled at him. "I think some drama would be appropriate. I'll leave it up to your imagination, Edward."

Edward elbowed Ace. "I think we might lose the electricity tonight."

A glance at his watch reminded Steele that Bouchard and Harmon would arrive in an hour. "Let's go to Ellie's and get everything ready. We want it to be dark and spooky."

"I like Edward's idea of the power being out, and we'll have candles burning," Mae said. "I'm wearing all black, so I'll look the part."

"I agree, Mae. But we can't forget we'll need to end the séance before midnight," Steele reminded them. They understood that Ellie would have to be on the beach at midnight.

Mae said, "I'll make sure we wrap it up before then."

Just then, the wind picked up, and dark clouds rolled in. The lights in the house flickered and then went out.

"Looks like Mother Nature is going to help us out," Steele said.

CHAPTER SIXTY-EIGHT

Spin the Colt .45

Steele handed everyone a flashlight to see their way to Ellie's home. He couldn't have organized a more appropriate setting for a séance if he tried. It was a dark and stormy evening, and the wind was blowing sand against the patio doors, sounding more like pebbles hitting the glass. The electricity was out, so they lit candles throughout Ellie's house. It was an eerie atmosphere with the howling wind and the flickering candles casting spooky shadows in every nook and cranny.

"Ellie, don't forget to tell Bear to bark occasionally," Steele said.

"Why don't you tell him to take a nice chunk out of Bouchard's derrière?" Edward suggested.

"Why not have Bear go for his throat?" Ace asked.

Steele chuckled at their comments. He couldn't wait to see what Edward and Ace had planned for the night.

Everyone waited for Bouchard to take his seat at the table. They'd been instructed to make sure Bouchard sat beside Mae so she could touch him.

Mae sat beside Bouchard and held her hand out to him. "We will all hold hands." She didn't know if it was her imagination, but she felt like she has grasped the hand of the evil one when Bouchard linked his hand with hers.

Bouchard glanced down at Mae's hand and noticed the bracelet on her wrist. "Where did you get that bracelet?"

"That's one of Ellie's designs," Harmon said.

"I found it on the coffee table today. I gave it to Mae to wear because it helps her to connect if she has something that belonged to the deceased," John said.

Steele thought John sounded very convincing, and he noticed Bouchard didn't take his eyes off of the bracelet.

Mae looked around the table at everyone. "We want to call Ellie's spirit now. Before I begin the session, does anyone want to ask her a question? If so, tell me now because I will need complete silence once we begin."

Steele waited to see what Bouchard or Harmon would say.

Harmon spoke up first. "I want to know if Ellie saw the person who murdered her." He looked at Bouchard and said, "René, don't you want to ask Ellie something? You were so frightened the other night, so I thought you might want to know if she's a ghost."

René nodded. "Yes, that's what I would like to know. But I don't believe in ghosts."

Morgan said, "Ask her what we can do for her?"

"I want to know if she would come back if she could," Tom said.

John said, "I want you to tell her that we'll find out who did this to her."

Mae looked at Steele and asked, "Is there anything you would like to ask Ellie?"

Steele hadn't thought of a question since he could ask her anything he wanted at any time. But for some reason, he said, "I want to know what she did the entire day she was killed."

Ellie was standing behind Steele with her hand on his shoulder. "You know I can't remember that."

Mae glanced at everyone and said, "Please be very quiet, and I will try to contact Ellie. No matter what happens, don't break our circle and don't speak." Mae closed her eyes and then appeared to go into a faux trance-like state. "Ellie, we are here to ask you to come to us. We know you are a spirit, and we want to connect with you."

Suddenly, the table raised slightly, and Steele heard Edward and Ace laughing. They were beneath the table, trying to lift it off the floor. Under the candlelight, Steele could see Bouchard's and Harmon's eyes were huge.

"Ellie, are you here?" Mae asked. "If you are, touch my bracelet."

Ellie leaned over and turned Mae's bracelet on her arm. Everyone around the table heard the heart charms jingling. Mae felt Bouchard try to jerk his hand away, but she held on and would not let him go.

"Ellie, we have questions for you. Steele is now your next-door neighbor, and he's trying to solve your murder. Morgan and Tom are his friends, and they're detectives. Steele wants to know what you did the entire day of your murder. If you speak to me, I will hear you and relay your response."

The room was silent, and a few minutes passed before Mae said, "Ellie says she was at the shopping mall." Mae grew quiet again, then said, "Mr. Bouchard wants to know if you're a ghost."

No one said a word. Edward and Ace opened the patio doors, and the wind extinguished the candles in the room.

Bouchard and Harmon gasped when the doors closed without assistance. Then, Ellie struck a match and relit the candles. Mae could feel Bouchard's entire body shaking as he saw the match float from candle to candle.

At Ellie's command, Bear jumped from his pillow on the floor and started barking at the patio doors.

Mae waited for Harmon and Bouchard to collect themselves before she continued. "Ellie said she prefers you call her a spirit—not a ghost. Ellie, Morgan wanted me to ask if we can do anything for you."

Edward and Ace were now at the front door, opening it and slamming it closed several times.

"Ellie said she's not alone. Other spirits are with her. She said they saw her murder, and they are going to make the murderer pay. She said to tell Morgan she wants someone to find a way to bring her back."

Edward and Ace picked up two candles and carried them around the table.

"Ellie, do you want to have your life back? That is Tom's question."

"Yes, I do," Mae repeated. Mae took a deep breath and said, "Your uncle John said he will find out who killed you, no matter how long it takes."

Bear started barking again as Ace and Edward blew out the candles they were carrying.

Mae straightened and said, "Ellie, I'm not sure I understand what you mean. Would you repeat that?"

Steele thought Mae was doing an excellent job creating drama.

"Ellie, did you say that you know what's in the locked room in Mr. Bouchard's home? What does that mean?" The silence was intense, and Mae said, "No, please don't go yet. Rob wants to know if you recognized the person who killed you."

All eyes were on Mae. Mae cocked her head as if she was listening intently to Ellie's response. "Ellie, would you repeat that?"

Ace took his Colt from his holster and placed it in the middle of the table. He spun it around like he was playing spin the bottle. The barrel was pointing directly at Bouchard when it stopped—with Ace's help.

Mae opened her eyes. She looked at Harmon and said, "Ellie said Rob should ask Mr. Bouchard that question."

Bouchard jerked his hand from Mae's. "Why should Rob ask me?" He stared at the Colt on the table and leaned back in his chair. "Who put that gun there? Why is it pointed at me? And what does she know about my home? She's never been there!"

Mae turned to Bouchard and said, "You've broken the connection."

Bear moved to Bouchard's side and growled menacingly.

"I don't think that dog likes you," Rob said to Bouchard.

Bouchard stared at the growling dog. "I don't care for dogs."

Rob looked at Mae and asked. "Are you sure Ellie said I should ask René who killed her? That doesn't make sense."

CHAPTER SIXTY-NINE

She Talks to the Dead

Bouchard jumped up and shouted, "Anyone who believes in this nonsense should see a shrink, not a psychic!" He pulled open the patio door and ran out into the tropical storm.

Rob sat in stunned silence, looking at the open patio door. After a few seconds, he turned to look at everyone around the table. "Wow, this was an interesting evening. I think René is frightened. I'm sorry to leave so soon, but we came in my car."

Suddenly the patio door closed, and Rob couldn't see that Ace had closed the door. His eyes widened, and he whispered, "She's really here, isn't she? She's a ghost."

"Before you go, I'm curious to know what Bouchard keeps in that locked room Mae mentioned. I can't understand why he became so angry," Steele said.

"He told me he has a panic room, but I've never seen it." Rob stood and started to leave, but Mae stopped him. "There was something else that Ellie said that didn't make sense. She said to ask you why Bouchard had her designs. Do you know the answer to her question?" Mae asked.

Rob stared at her and mumbled, "I . . . I don't know what that means."

Steele almost laughed. Harmon was a terrible liar, and he knew if pressed hard, he'd cave in seconds.

Rob headed for the open patio door, and without looking at anyone, he said, "Thanks again for a most entertaining evening." He then ran out the door into the torrential downpour to his car. After he slid into the driver's seat, he saw Bouchard shivering in the passenger seat. He started the car and turned on the heater, hoping to dry their clothes. "René, what on earth is wrong with you? Why did you leave so suddenly? And why were you angry?"

"I wasn't going to sit there and let them think I was falling for their scam."

Harmon turned on his windshield wipers. "It's raining too hard to drive. Do you want to go back inside?"

"No, I don't want to go in there. I can't imagine why Ellie's uncle is involved with those charlatans."

"I don't think it's a scam. I believe that lady can talk to the dead," Harmon said.

Bouchard looked at him and shook his head. "If that's true, why did Ellie say you should ask me who killed her?"

"I don't know. Maybe Ellie thought you knew her killer or—something like that. Or maybe that psychic misunderstood what Ellie was saying." He shrugged and said, "Do you know anyone who would commit murder?"

Bouchard sighed loudly and shook his head back and forth. "Of course not."

"What do you think Ellie meant when she said she knew what you had in that room in your home?"

"There's nothing in there other than things one would keep in a panic room; a phone, a small refrigerator, things needed in an emergency."

"That medium didn't know you, so how did she know about that room? I'm telling you, she can talk to the dead."

"Rob, Ellie was never at my home. How would she know I had a panic room? Unless you told her."

"I never said anything about a panic room to her or anyone. It's not a topic that ever came up in conversations," Harmon said.

Bouchard looked out the window and said, "The rain has slowed, let's go." He looked down at his shaking hands and clutched them together. He couldn't make sense of what just happened in that house. *Even if Harmon told Ellie about the room, how did that medium know what I did—unless . . . she could talk to the dead? No, that's impossible. It must be a con. But what did they want? And how are those two detectives from Miami involved?*

Rob started the car and pulled out of Steele's driveway onto the street. "What about the noises, the doors opening and closing with no one there, the table lifting off the floor, and the candles floating around the table? And what about Ellie's portfolio? You must admit, some strange things are going on in that house."

"Nothing happened that they couldn't have set up beforehand. I'm telling you that woman is a charlatan, and I don't know if they are planning on extorting us for some reason, but we need to stay away from them."

"After you left, the psychic said Ellie asked why you had some of her designs. How do you explain that?"

Bouchard's head snapped around. "What did you say?"

"I said I had no idea what that meant. René, you know only the two of us to know about Ellie's designs."

Bouchard stared at him. "Are you conspiring with these people to extort me?"

Harmon slammed on his brakes and faced René. "What are you saying? Do you hear how irrational you sound? Why would I conspire to do anything with these people? I hardly know them."

"All I know is that after that investigator talked to you, he visited my office. I didn't even know Ellie that well. Now, two detectives just happen to be involved in the séance. You're right, something strange is going on, and you are the only one who could have led them to me."

"I don't care what you say. That psychic can talk to the dead! And she's talking to Ellie!"

CHAPTER SEVENTY

An Intern Angel?

"In the middle of the night, I thought of another question," Steele said as he poured coffee for Morgan and Tom.

Morgan looked around the room and asked, "Are we alone this morning?"

"Yes, Mae's still sleeping. John had to leave early for a meeting, and Ellie had something to do at home." Once the cups were filled, Steele said, "Let's go out on the patio." He grabbed a bone for Bear, and everyone walked outside and sat down.

"What's the question you thought of in the night?" Tom asked.

"If Ace shoots Bouchard just before he shoots Ellie, does Bouchard need to be at the beach? Mae and I couldn't see Bouchard when he shot Ellie, but Edward and Ace see him."

Morgan said, "I see what you mean. If we can't coerce Bouchard to the beach, can Ace kill the Bouchard he sees at that moment?"

Steele nodded. "Does Bouchard need to be here when we change history?"

"I don't see how things could change if he's not here," Morgan replied.

"I don't know," Tom said. "Do you think Bouchard is supposed to be the one who is dead? Maybe you were meant to change the outcome."

Steele stared at him a moment. "Are you suggesting that the higher powers made a mistake and someone was supposed to kill Bouchard before he killed Ellie?"

Tom chuckled. "Maybe someone made a rookie mistake. Possibly a new angel?"

"An intern angel?" Morgan quipped.

They laughed, and Tom said, "If Steele can see ghosts, I can't think of anything that would be out of the realm of possibility."

"There is that," Morgan agreed.

"I agree with Morgan. It seems logical that Bouchard has to be here," Steele said.

"Yeah, we don't want a live Bouchard version somewhere else and a dead Bouchard version on the beach," Tom said.

"That's two too many Bouchards for my tastes. It's all I can do not to strangle the guy when I see him," Steele said.

Morgan sat his empty cup on the table. "He's a piece of work, and guilty as hell. I wanted to beat the crap out of him last night."

"Me too. And I really want to know what's in that room. Why did he get so bent out of shape over that? He reminds me of the kind of guy who would buy stolen artwork and show it off when he wanted to impress the right people," Tom said.

Morgan held up his hand and said, "Hey, I have an idea."

"What's that?" Steele asked.

"Why don't we have a trial run without Bouchard at the beach? I can repair Ace's Colt today, and then we can see what happens tonight."

No one spoke for a few minutes, then Steele said, "If Ace shoots Bouchard when he sees him, then we don't know what will happen. I think we have to wait until we get him to the beach at midnight."

Tom leaned forward and stared at Steele. "There's something I've wanted to ask you, Steele. How do you know that Ellie was the first ghost you ever saw? You thought she was alive, and it wasn't until we couldn't see her that you knew the truth."

Steele looked out at the surf. "After seeing Edward and Ace, I've wondered the same thing. Of course, I knew something was odd about Edward and Ace by the way they were dressed. After they told me how many ghosts are on this stretch of beach, I believe I've seen others without being aware."

"I guess the only way we would know is if we walk down the beach with you and tell you the people we see." Morgan pointed to people collecting shells a few feet from the shore and asked, "How many people are on the beach right now, Steele?"

Looking up and down the beach, Steele said, "There are four people. Two picking up shells and two strolling along the shoreline."

Tom turned his gaze to the beach, stood, and looked both ways. He turned back to Morgan, and said, "I see two people."

"That's what I see."

They both looked at Steele, and he stood and pointed, "There are two people right there filling a bucket with shells." He pointed thirty yards farther down the beach and said, "There are two people walking side by side."

"It's two more ghosts," Morgan replied.

"Are you two messing with me? You don't see the two people walking?"

Morgan and Tom shook their heads from side to side.

"No one is there—at least two of them are not living, breathing people," Morgan said.

"It's weird knowing there are so many spirits running around that can't move on to their destination—wherever that may be," Tom said.

Morgan nodded his agreement. "There's probably a lot of them who are thankful they're not moving on. Maybe they're getting a second chance to make things right."

"I wish Bear could tell me what he sees," Steele said and leaned down to scratch Bear's back. "Back to the original question. What do you think?"

Before Steele or Tom could respond, Mae walked through the door clutching a cup of coffee. "What are you guys talking about?"

Morgan pulled her onto his lap. "How many people do you see on the beach?"

Mae gave him a quizzical look, then looked toward the beach. "Four."

CHAPTER SEVENTY-ONE

Spirits are Everywhere–Not Just at the Beach

"Steele saw four people. Tom and I see two," Morgan said.

"Two are spirits," Mae replied.

"I wish we could see them. Anyway, before you joined us, we were discussing a trial run at the beach tonight. Do you think Bouchard needs to be at the beach, or can Ace shoot the one he sees at midnight?" Morgan asked.

"How much coffee have you guys had?"

"Just one cup. Why?" Morgan asked.

"Go get the coffee pot. You obviously need more. "Of course, Bouchard needs to be at the beach. And Ace needs to be the one to shoot him just before he shoots Ellie. We need to lure him to the beach somehow. You three are smart enough to come up with a plan to get him here at the appointed time."

Morgan walked inside and grabbed the coffee pot. When he returned and filled their cups, he said, "Okay, Mae, what would you suggest?"

"I think if you continue to leave Bouchard notes and make him think Ellie is watching him, he'll be too frazzled not to come. Even if he doesn't believe in ghosts, he'll come to make sure she's dead. Ellie can leave a note for him, telling him she wants to meet him on the beach at midnight."

The men looked at each other and nodded their agreement.

"That's a good plan," Steele said.

"But after the way Bouchard ran out last night, I can't see him coming back anytime soon," Tom replied.

"Yeah. He must think one of two things—that we're onto him, or that we're on a fishing expedition," Morgan replied.

Steele chuckled. "There is a third option. He thinks we're all nuts. Sometimes I feel like I'm going crazy. But I think he had to conclude that we have some information that would incriminate him. Maybe he suspects Harmon said too much when I interviewed him."

"Did Harmon mention Bouchard's safe room to you?" Tom asked.

"No, he didn't say much about Bouchard. But I bet after last night, Bouchard asked Harmon what he said to me in that interview."

"He probably interrogated Harmon when they left. When I touched Bouchard's hand last night, all I felt was evil." Mae shivered at the thought. "He has a frightening mind."

"I think he suspects we know something, but he can't figure out how we know. I'd bet Steele is right. He'll blame Harmon for giving Steele too much information," Tom said.

"Let's give him a couple of days to think about what he heard last night. I'll ask Edward and Ace to keep an eye on him," Steele said.

Everyone agreed to wait a few days, and then Mae asked, "Why did you ask how many people I saw on the beach?"

Morgan explained that Steele saw two more ghosts, and Mae's eyes lit up. "Steele, that gives me an idea. We might try a different approach on Amy's case."

Steele's eyes widened. "I'm listening."

Mae saw the hopeful look on Steele's face, and said, "I don't want to get your hopes up, but it's something we haven't tried."

"Mae, I'm willing to listen to anything at this point on Amy's case."

"We both see ghosts, but we don't know that they're ghosts unless we're with someone who can't see them. What if we take Morgan and Tom to the shopping mall with us? Perhaps we can find a new person, or spirit to talk to. If we see a spirit there, then it's likely that they are there frequently. We know someone saw something. All we need to do is find that person. Since we haven't found an alive person who witnessed the incident, maybe we can find a spirit. Spirits are everywhere, not just at the beach."

Steele stood and smiled at Mae. "Mae, I think it's a brilliant idea. If a spirit saw someone, who would they tell? I guess it's a long shot, but I've only hit dead ends. This is the only thing I've heard that has the potential to produce a result. I'm game if you are." He opened the patio door. "Let's get ready to go to the mall."

CHAPTER SEVENTY-TWO

Whacked Over the Head

Reaching the mall, Steele said they should walk through *Infinities* first, hoping to find a spirit. "This is the largest store, and more people shop in here than in the other stores."

He glanced at Morgan and Tom, and said, "I guess the best way to handle this is to ask you how many people you see." It was a slow, arduous process since people were coming and going, making it difficult to keep track of everyone they saw.

They were inside the store nearly an hour before they saw an older woman whom Morgan and Tom couldn't see. When she left the store, they followed her.

"It might be best if you approach her alone, Mae. We don't want to frighten her," Steele said.

"I agree." Mae caught up with the woman on the sidewalk. She spoke to her for several moments before she motioned for the men to join them.

"Steele, this is Mrs. Violet Watson. I told her you were a private investigator, and you're investigating the disappearance of Amy Carson."

Mae then introduced Morgan and Tom. "They can't see or hear you."

Violet looked at Steele, and said, "Mae told me she's a psychic. Are you one as well, young man?"

"No, ma'am, and I can't explain why I can see you. I haven't figured that out yet. But I would very much appreciate it if you would talk with us."

Violet gave him a wide smile. "Mr. Harper, I can't tell you how nice it is to talk to you. You're the only people who have been able to see me. I just knew it was going to be a wonderful day."

Steele smiled at the older woman, wondering why such a sweet lady was still roaming the earth as a ghost. He was curious how long she'd been deceased. "Mrs. Watson, how long have you been . . ."

"Dead?" She returned Steele's smile and patted his hand. "It's okay, dearie, to ask me that question. It doesn't offend me. And please call me Violet. I've been dead for three years. And since you're a private investigator, maybe you could help me. The coroner said I died of natural causes after a fall. I didn't fall. Someone whacked me in the head with a candlestick." She patted Steele's hand again. "Did anyone ever tell you that you're a handsome devil?"

Steele grinned at her. "No one as lovely as you, and thank you, Violet."

Tom and Morgan rolled their eyes.

"Oh, I'm sure all of the ladies are after you and your friends." She pointed to Morgan and Tom, and added, "You can tell them I said they are quite handsome, too."

Steele repeated what Violet said to Morgan and Tom.

Tom inclined his head toward Steele and Morgan and said, "They're taken, but would you like to go to dinner with me?"

Violet chuckled, "If I were forty years younger, I would accept your offer, young man."

Tom chuckled when Steele told him how Violet responded.

Steele wanted to know more about her murder. "You said you were murdered."

She nodded. "I know my nephew, the greedy young rake, did me in."

"I'm sorry to hear that." Steele could see him adding another case to his growing list, after Edward's and Ace's.

Violet pursed her lips. "That's a story for another time. "She pointed to Mae and said, "This lovely woman told me about that adorable young girl that was taken from this mall. I've seen her picture everywhere. I didn't see the incident, but I have a friend who did."

Steele couldn't believe their luck. "You're positive your friend saw someone kidnap Amy?"

"Indeed, I am. She tried to get help for the girl."

"Can you give me your friend's name, phone number, or address?"

"Not really, dearie. She's dead—like me. We just roam around."

Steele and Mae exchanged a glance.

Violet continued, "You see, my friend worked for *Infinities* for several years, and I was her best customer. She worked in the make-up department, and she was such a talented woman who could make anyone look better."

Steele's first instinct was to interrupt Violet and get back to the information he wanted. But the poor woman hadn't talked to living people in such a long time, he let her ramble.

Violet didn't draw a breath. "Anyway, she left the store late one night and was killed by some miscreants who tried to rob her. I heard everyone talking about it in the store. It was such a sad day. She was so well-liked and a good worker. She was killed a few months before that young girl was kidnapped."

"And you see this woman frequently?" Mae asked.

"Yes, she likes to go into *Infinities* and see what's new in make-up. I thought she might be here today. She said the kidnapper was a well-dressed man and he forced the little girl into a black car. She told me she yelled for help, but no one could see her or hear her. Another woman, not a ghost, also saw the man, and she tried to help the girl, but she fell and hit her head."

"Would you tell me what your friend looks like so I can talk to her if we see her?" Steele asked.

"Of course." Violet gave him a detailed description. "Her name is Helen McCray. You can tell her you spoke with me."

"Do you ever go to the beach?" Mae asked.

"Not often. Why do you ask?"

"We have some friends that you might like to meet. One gentleman is older, and I'm sure he would like to become acquainted with you."

"You mean they're ghosts?" Violet asked.

"They are, and they are helping us on another case." Steele gave Violet his address.

Violet promised she would visit. "If I see Helen, I will bring her with me." She walked away, and before she reached another store, she disappeared.

Steele looked at Mae and grinned. "Matchmaker."

"Violet is perfect for Edward."

CHAPTER SEVENTY-THREE

Dead as a Doornail

Steele, Mae, Morgan, and Tom remained at the mall for a few hours hoping to see Violet's friend, Helen.

"How many times have you been in these stores, Steele? People in every store know you by name," Morgan said.

"I've been here several times and spoken to everyone. I hope we see Helen because this is the only lead I've had in weeks."

"I think Violet will bring her to your home," Mae said.

"Yeah, she's the kind of woman who would keep her word." Glancing at his watch, Steele said, "It's getting late. Let's go home."

Ellie, Edward, and Ace were waiting for them when they arrived home. Steele told them about meeting Violet, and the information she gave them about her friend.

"All of us can help you look for her," Ellie said.

"Thank you. I will take you up on that offer."

Morgan pointed to the box on the counter. "That's the parts we ordered for Ace's Colt. If Ace will hand you his gun, I'll start working on it."

Ace handed Steele his pistol. "Tell Morgan I appreciate this. It'll be nice to know my weapon is useful again. Am I going to shoot Bouchard tonight?"

Steele explained to Ace and Edward the dilemma over Bouchard being in two places if Ace shot him.

"That is an interesting quandary," Edward said. "But it seems logical that Bouchard would need to be on the beach when Ace shoots him. What I can't figure out is why Ace and I see Bouchard when you can't?"

Steele shrugged. "I don't know."

"I just want him dead as a doornail," Ace said.

Steele smiled at Ace. "I think we can all agree on that."

"Touché." Edward glanced at Mae, and said, "Now tell me all about this lovely woman you met, Mae."

"Violet is such a sweet woman. I think you and Ace would enjoy her company. Maybe you could spend time with her on the beach."

"We certainly will. It will be nice to have some feminine company," Edward said. "And you say she thought she was murdered?"

"That's what she told us. She said her nephew killed her with a candlestick three years ago."

"I shall look forward to making her acquaintance."

"Ellie, you might have some competition. Violet said Steele was a *handsome devil,*" Mae said.

"Well, she has good eyesight," Ellie replied.

Ellie was sitting on the arm of Steele's chair, and he pulled her onto his lap. "So, you think I'm a *handsome devil*?"

She leaned to his ear and whispered, "The most handsome and the sexiest man in the world, but not a devil."

Steele winked at her. "Sexy, huh? I kinda like the sound of that. Can we have this discussion later?"

Tom grabbed his laptop off the coffee table and opened it. "All this mushy stuff is getting to me. I'm going to see what I can find out about Violet Watson's murder."

"Steele, I think your list of clients will be growing," Morgan teased.

"I thought the same thing."

"You're going to be a busy man. I hope you can afford it," Ellie said.

"All may not be for naught, Steele. There is one thing I have not shared with you," Edward said."

"What do you mean, Edward?"

"I know there is no way for spirits to pay your fee for your assistance, but I may have a solution." Edward glanced at Ace and said, "I think it's time we told him."

Ace grinned. "Yeah. I think it's time they had some good news."

"I told you I had sailed from England to New York. I didn't tell you I had buried some money at my New York estate before I was waylaid. After Ellie instructed us on how we could transport our bodies to different locations, Ace and I have been practicing going farther and farther away each day. Today we visited New York. I remember where I buried the money, and we appeared in the exact spot. There's only one problem."

Steele arched his brow. "And that is?"

"We will need help bringing the money back here."

"That was a long time ago. What you buried has probably turned to dust by now." Morgan said.

"What did you bury the money in?" Tom asked.

"A trunk. I doubt that gold and coins turned to dust. That trunk held a fortune in gold and exquisite jewels." Seeing the men exchange a look, Edward added, "Rest easy; it is not stolen property. I was very wealthy in my day. You might be able to help Ace and me find out who murdered us, but if not, I want you to use my fortune to help others."

CHAPTER SEVENTY-FOUR

Buried Treasure

Steele looked at Ellie and asked, "Can you bring the trunk here using your—whatever you call your talent of making objects appear?"

"I don't think my powers extend to something like that," Ellie replied.

Tom asked Edward for the address of his estate in New York, "I can look at the place on Google Earth."

"What is Google Earth?" Edward asked.

"Tom will show you," Steele said.

Edward recited the address and added, "One of my descendants owns the place now."

When Steele repeated the address for Tom, he tapped the keys and said, "Tell Edward to look at my computer screen."

Edward looked over Tom's shoulder and said, "That's the place! How magnificent that you can see it on your little screen. What an amazing invention!"

"Your family has rights to that trunk," Morgan said as he continued to work on Ace's pistol.

"It's my property, and I'm giving it to Steele. No one in my family knew about the trunk. My valet, my butler, and I buried it. I paid them handsomely for their discretion. They were loyal to me," Edward replied adamantly.

"How do we remove it without being seen?" Tom asked.

Edward tapped the computer screen, and said, "It's in a hidden area at the back of the property right here. Several large trees and shrubbery provide excellent coverage. No one will see us."

Steele repeated what Edward said, and Morgan said, "Easy for him to say. Tom and I aren't spirits. People can see us."

Ace said, "Edward and I could be your lookouts."

Tom shrugged and glanced at Morgan. "We have some vacation time coming. Why don't we drive to New York and see what we can do?"

"Edward, how much do you think the trunk weighs?" Morgan asked.

"You two better start lifting your weights because Edward says he thinks the trunk weighs about five hundred pounds," Steele replied.

"You said there were gold coins," Tom said.

"American gold coins, and many, many jewels," Edward replied.

Steele whistled and repeated, "American gold coins and jewels. Edward, you could be talking about a fortune."

"My dear man, I am well aware of the value. In today's market, that trunk will be worth millions. And I want to give most of it to you so you can help the other spirits in need. It's mine to do with as I please, is it not?"

Steele said, "If Morgan and Tom get caught taking the trunk from the property, a court of law might not see it that way. Your family could file charges against them."

"I understand the problem, but the fact is, no one has a right to my property. I did not include that trunk in my Will and believe me, I left my family a fortune. Tell Morgan and Tom I will make it worth their while to retrieve my buried treasures."

Steele told Morgan and Tom what Edward said.

Morgan said, "Ed, we're doing this to help you; we don't need payment to do you a favor."

"You three are the most honorable men I've met besides Ace. I feel quite fortunate, and I am most appreciative. I've never had such friends I could count on before. If you decide to move here and help Steele, I will buy you both a house. That way, I know the spirits will have three good men working on their behalf."

"We're equally as fortunate to have met you and Ace," Steele said.

"It's settled then. Ace and I will ensure that Morgan and Tom will not get caught," Edward said.

Morgan reassembled Ace's Colt and handed it to Steele. "Every piece is clean, and there are new cartridges. I think it will work now."

Steele handed Ace the pistol to inspect. "See what you think."

Ace removed the cartridges, spun the cylinder, checked the hammer, and pulled the trigger. "It's like a new pistol. I wish I could use it on that low-down dirty skunk tonight."

Steele repeated Ace's words, and everyone chuckled.

"Steele, I think you have a guest," Ellie said.

"I didn't hear the doorbell," Steele said.

"No, she's at the patio door."

Steele looked at the patio door, and he saw Violet. He hurried to let her in. "Hello, Violet."

"I hope you don't mind that I came so soon, but when you mentioned I could meet more spirits, I couldn't resist. And I rarely get to the beach. The last time I was here, I was a bit intimidated by how many spirits were walking around, and I didn't know anyone."

"I'm glad you're here. Let me introduce you to everyone. You know Mae, Morgan, and Tom." He then introduced her to Ellie, Ace, and Edward.

Edward stood, took Violet's hand in his, and bowed politely. He then lightly kissed her hand. "It is a pleasure to make your acquaintance."

"Thank you," Violet said softly.

Ace tipped his Stetson. "Howdy, ma'am. Pleasure."

"Hello, it's so nice to meet you," Violet replied. Her eyes met Ellie's, and she said, "And you are the beautiful young woman who was killed on the beach. My friend, Helen, told me she saw you in *Infinities* many times. She so admired your clothing line."

"It's nice to meet you, and thank you for helping Steele."

"I didn't see Helen today, but as soon as I do, I will bring her here. Everyone wants to know what happened to that sweet child."

"Madam, could I tempt you with a stroll on the beach?" Edward asked.

Violet blushed. "I would love it!"

CHAPTER SEVENTY-FIVE

Blushing Ghosts

"I didn't know a ghost could blush. Did you guys see Violet blush?" Mae said.

Steele laughed. "You mean a *spirit* blushed."

Grimacing, Mae said, "Right. Sorry, Ellie. I think Violet is already smitten with Edward."

"Edward seemed equally taken by Violet. She seems like such a sweet woman," Ellie added.

"I told Mae she would win the matchmaker of the year award," Steele teased.

"My hunch worked, Steele, and I will gladly accept that award."

"I think it's wonderful that Violet has new friends. I know how lonely it can be when you don't know anyone," Ellie said.

Steele clutched her hand. "You'll never be lonely again."

"Now that they're gone, what do you think about getting Edward's trunk from New York?" Morgan asked.

"We can't double-cross Edward and tell his descendants about it. Edward would never forgive us," Ellie said.

"I agree. We should honor his wishes," Mae added.

"Do you two want to go after the trunk?" Steele asked Morgan and Tom.

"I do," Tom said.

"I do, too. And look at it this way, Steele, when Tom and I join you in the private eye business, we'll need some money to support us while we solve the murders of every spirit in this town."

Steele grinned. "True. I can see I'm going to have a full client roster, albeit not a lucrative one. Do you think you guys will eventually join me in this venture?"

"We were going to tell you this weekend that we've decided to give our notice next week," Morgan said.

Steele glanced at Tom. "Both of you? Are you serious?"

Tom nodded. "We're serious. We both like it here, and we like what you're doing. The three of us can take on a lot more cases."

"It's a bonus for me since Mae lives here. I can see her more often," Morgan said.

Mae smiled at him. "I'll like that, too."

"This is great news, and it calls for a celebration." Steele left the room and grabbed a bottle of bourbon and four glasses. "I don't have champagne, Mae. How about drinking some bourbon with us?"

"Of course."

He leaned over and kissed Ellie on the cheek. "I wish you could join us."

Ellie smiled at him. "That's okay, I don't like bourbon."

Once everyone had a glass, Steele held his in the air and said, "To our successful business relationship."

As they drank bourbon, Steele said, "Have you found someone to help me with that combination lock in Bouchard's home?"

"I have, and he's willing to accompany us and open the lock himself. He said it would take too long for us to open it since we don't know what we're doing," Tom said.

"What happens if we get caught?" Steele was willing to take a chance to find out what was in that room, but he didn't know if he could knowingly involve someone else in an illegal activity.

"I told him it's illegal. He owes me a favor, and he's not against breaking the law if he thinks the cause is just."

"I don't know how just it is, but for some reason, I need to see what Bouchard is hiding. I don't buy the story that it's a panic room," Steele replied.

"Bouchard's reaction the other night says it's not a panic room," Tom agreed.

"After seeing Edward's and Ace's theatrics during our séance, I think we can rely on them to create a distraction at the guardhouse while we search Bouchard's home," Morgan said.

"All we have to do is find out when Bouchard will be away for a few hours one evening. We'll have a better chance of getting inside his home unobserved at night," Steele said.

"Maybe Uncle John can help us with that. He could invite Bouchard and Rob to dinner," Ellie said.

"Great idea," Steele repeated what Ellie said. "Morgan, find out what day your friend will be available, and we'll contact John. I want to do this as soon as possible."

"After we get that done, Tom and I both have a lot of vacation time, and we'll take a few days off and fly to New York. We'll drive back with the trunk," Morgan said. "With both of us driving, it won't take long."

Steele smile. "Sounds like a plan. But it might take longer than you think with Ace and Edward along. They'll be like two kids in a candy shop seeing all the sights."

CHAPTER SEVENTY-SIX

There are no Coincidences

"I don't want to join you for dinner," Bouchard said.

"John said he wanted to apologize for the disastrous séance evening," Rob replied. "I think he feels terrible about the way the night ended. He didn't know the medium personally."

"Rob, do you think John knows about our agreement?"

"No, and there's no way he knew about all of Ellie's designs. He wasn't involved in the business until after Ellie died. Why are you asking?"

"Before Ellie was killed, she called me and said she wanted to meet," Bouchard replied.

"You've never told me that before. Ellie never mentioned speaking with you."

"We didn't speak; she left me a message. I didn't have a chance to call her back. I just remembered her call the other night. I was wondering if she discovered what we were doing and if that was the reason for her call." Bouchard hesitated a moment, then said, "Of course, you were just selling her jewelry designs then."

"René, you can relax. No one knows about our arrangement. I don't know why Ellie called, but there was no way she knew what we were doing. Go to dinner with us, and you will see how little John knows about the business now."

"René hesitated, then said, "Okay. What night?"

Steele ended his call with John, and said to Morgan and Tom, "John set up a dinner with Harmon and Bouchard for Thursday night. Tom, can you call your friend and tell him it's a go on Thursday night?"

"Sure, I'll call right now."

While Tom made the call, Steele said, "John is making reservations at a restaurant between Palm Beach and Miami, so that should allow us ample time to get into that room. He's going to call me when they leave the restaurant."

"Good. Let's pray Edward and Ace can keep the security guards busy while we're breaking into Bouchard's home."

Steele walked to the patio doors and watched the storm clouds rolling in from the ocean. He was about to ask Morgan and Tom if they wanted to walk down to the restaurant on the beach for lunch, but he saw Edward, Ace, Violet, and another woman walking toward his house. He wondered if Ace found himself a spirit girlfriend.

As they neared his patio, Steele opened the doors.

"I'm delighted you're home, Steele. Violet has a surprise for you," Edward said.

Steele said hello to everyone, and he looked at the woman standing beside Ace. He remembered Violet's description of Helen. "You must be Helen."

The woman smiled at him. "Yes, I am. Violet told me that you were trying to find Amy."

"Please come in and meet my friends." Once he introduced Helen to Tom and Morgan, he said, "They can't see you, Helen. I'm sorry that Ellie and Mae aren't here. They just left to go to the grocery."

Everyone sat down, and Steele said, "Helen, I appreciate you coming here to tell what you know about Amy's kidnapping. Violet said you tried to stop the man. Did you get a good look at him?"

"Not really, I was trying to pull the little girl away from him, but my fingers kept going through her arms. I remember that he had dark hair and he was tall. I also remember thinking he didn't look like the type of man who would take a child. That poor little girl was terrified."

"Ted Bundy didn't look like a serial killer," Tom said.

"Who's Ted Bundy?" Edward asked.

"Another criminal," Steele replied. "Go on, Helen."

"I was screaming, but no one heard me. I thought no one saw what was happening, and no one was coming to help. But a woman appeared—I don't know where she came from. She hit the man, but he didn't lose his grip on the child. He hit the woman with his fist, and she fell. She hit her head so hard on the concrete that I thought he'd killed her. But she opened her eyes and reached out for the little girl as the man was shoving her into his car. She clasped Amy's wrist and tried to pull the child away. The man was stronger. He jerked Amy's wrist from the woman's hand, then slammed the car door and pulled away. The woman scrambled to her feet and tried to run after his car. He sped away and was out of the parking lot in seconds. The poor woman dropped to her knees, and I could tell she was hurt, but she didn't know I was there, and I couldn't help her."

Steele thought he had another lead if he could find the woman. "Can you describe the woman?"

"Of course, but I know her name. I didn't recognize her until I tried to help her up. It was Eleanor Marlowe. You may not have heard of her, but *Infinites* carries her clothing line, and I had met her before in the store. I worked there for ten years, and that's how I met Violet. I heard about Miss Marlowe's death from the conversations I picked up in *Infinites*. I still go there quite often. I miss all of the wonderful friends I made." Helen noticed everyone was staring at her, but no one was saying a word. "Did I say something wrong?"

Steele shook his head. "No, I'm sorry, but you did say Ellie . . . Eleanor Marlowe was the lady who tried to help Amy?"

"Yes, it was her. Do you know her?"

"Yes, I'm trying to find her murderer." Steele looked at Morgan and Tom, and said, "She must have been injured that day. That's why she can't remember."

"Did anyone come to help Miss Marlowe that day?" Steele asked.

"No, I ran into *Infinities* and tried my best to get someone to see or hear me. But I was of no help. When I ran back outside, Miss Marlowe was gone."

"Her uncle said they found her car in the shopping center parking lot," Steele said.

"That's some coincidence," Edward said.

Steele, Morgan, and Tom said at the same time, "There are no coincidences."

CHAPTER SEVENTY-SEVEN

Why Did You Kill Me?

Steele and Bear were home alone, and they fell asleep on the patio while waiting for Ellie to return. Bear lifted his head and let out a contented groan. The sound woke Steele, and without opening his eyes, he knew Ellie was petting him.

She leaned over and kissed him gently on the lips. "How are my two favorite guys?"

Steele opened his eyes, sat erect, and pulled her onto his lap. "We're good, and we have news for you." He told her about meeting Helen and repeated the story about the day Amy was kidnapped.

Ellie was momentarily speechless. "She was positive it was me?"

"She met you several times when you were in *Infinities* before her death."

"Why can't I remember any of this?"

"Helen said you hit your head hard on the concrete when you fell. Maybe you had a concussion. You wrote in your diary that you had a large bump on your head and a gash."

"Would a concussion affect my memory?"

"I imagine it's possible."

Ellie leaned back against his shoulder. "I wish I remembered. Did Helen see him? Can she describe him?"

"She said he was tall and had dark hair, but she didn't get a good look at his face. I'm afraid that's not a useful description. She didn't know the make of the car, other than it was black."

"I saw him, and I can't even help you. I'm so sorry."

In a comforting gesture, Steele ran his hand over her hair. "It's not your fault. It's no one's fault other than the pervert who took Amy."

"It's just frustrating to know I was there, and couldn't do anything to stop him. I guess that explains why my uncle found my car at the mall. Did Helen know how I got home?"

"No, she tried to find someone who could see her, and when she returned to the parking lot, you were gone."

Steele could see she was upset, so he said, "Something will turn up." He wasn't as confident as he sounded. But he refused to give up. At the moment, he didn't know his next move, but he vowed he wouldn't stop.

Steele told Ellie about John's planned dinner with Bouchard and Harmon.

"Please don't get caught. I'm not sure I could break you out of jail."

"You could always bring me a file in a big brownie. Although I would have my face in the brownie and forget all about escaping," Steele teased.

She laughed. "I did think of something we could do that might goad Bouchard into meeting me on the beach. What if I start leaving notes at his house and sign my name? I would dare him to meet me, and then Ace could be waiting."

Steele smiled at her. "I was thinking about the same thing. Do you think Bouchard would show the note to Harmon and see if it was your signature?"

"I think he would, and Rob would recognize my writing. After our séance, I think Rob is already a believer in spirits. What do you think about leaving Rob a note that says something like, *why are you selling my designs*?"

"That would scare him to death. His fear would probably send him to the confessional. But I don't want him confessing his misdeeds until after we deal with Bouchard."

"You're probably right about that." Ellie stood and reached for his hand. "Let's go write some notes for Bouchard."

Giving her a mischievous grin, Steele said, "I'm going to have some fun."

They sat at Steele's desk, and he gave Ellie a pen and paper. "Here's the first note: *René, why didn't you believe I was at the séance with you?*"

"Oh, that's good," Ellie said as she started writing. "What about this one: *I want to know why you murdered me.*"

"Good." Steele thought for a minute and said, "*I'm watching you.*"

Ellie finished writing, and Steele knew what the last note should be. *"Meet me tomorrow night at midnight on the beach."*

Steele leaned over and kissed her neck. "Now, it's time for the fun I was talking about."

Ellie stood and started to unbutton his shirt. "I thought you'd never ask."

Swooping her up in his arms, Steele said, "I'm a lucky man."

CHAPTER SEVENTY-EIGHT

Low-Down Dirty Skunks are Predictable

Bouchard spotted the errant piece of paper on his immaculate coffee table as soon as he walked in the door. The only item that was to grace that table was an expensive Baccarat crystal sculpture of a panther. The cleaning lady wasn't scheduled on Tuesdays, so how did the piece of paper get there?

Ace elbowed Edward in the ribs. "He didn't see it!"

"Calm yourself, Ace. He saw it. He's going to check that room," Edward assured him.

Just as Edward said, Bouchard hurried to his office and twisted the bust of Nero, and the wall slid behind the bookcase. The steel wall was intact and the combination lock was still secure. After he turned the Nero bust again, the wall slid back into place.

"Dang, I wish he'd opened that combination lock," Ace said.

"I know, but I'd hate for us to get locked in there," Edward replied.

Walking back to the living room, Bouchard grabbed the piece of paper from the table and crumpled it in his fist.

Edward screamed, "Read it, man!"

Bouchard started to toss the paper in the garbage, but he noticed the beautiful script. He sat on the sofa and smoothed the note on the table. *René, why didn't you believe I was at the séance with you? Eleanor Marlowe.*

"I wonder what that sniveling varmint is thinking now," Ace said.

"After his behavior at the séance, I wouldn't be surprised if he soiled himself," Edward replied.

Ace chuckled. "Now that you mention it, I think I smell something."

Bouchard read the note again. "What the devil?" He ran through the house and checked all of the rooms, including the windows. Windows were all locked, and there was nothing out of place.

He grabbed his phone and called the security guard at the gate. "This is René Bouchard. I'd like to know who came to my home today."

"Hold one moment, Mr. Bouchard. Let me check the log."

"Maybe we should tell Ellie to sign the guard's log the next time she's here," Edward said.

"Can she do that without the guard noticing?" Ace asked.

"I should think so. She has amazing talents."

Seconds later, the guard said, "Mr. Bouchard, no one was at your address today."

"Are you sure? Someone left something inside my home."

"We don't have a record of anyone going to your home. Have you checked your security camera? Shall I call the police?"

"No, no, it's probably something I hadn't noticed before." Bouchard hung up and returned to his office to look at Ellie's drawings. He'd seen her initials, and he was confident the *EM* on the note was the same. He held the note and compared it to the initials on the drawing. It was a match. If someone was trying to scare him, they were doing a damn good job. *Rob Harmon? He was the only one who knew how nervous I was at the séance. But why would Rob want to scare me? I'm paying him handsomely for Ellie's designs. And how would he get inside my home?*

Bouchard stood in the middle of the room as he thought about his next move. He'd call Rob but decided he wouldn't mention the note.

Ace watched Bouchard with a snarl on his lips. "He's just standing there. He ain't exactly a man of action."

"He's trying to figure out his next move," Edward said. "How can he tell anyone about the note without them thinking he has lost his mind?"

Ace pulled his pistol and twirled it around. "I'll like to help him on his way to hell."

Edward put his hand on Ace's arm. "Hold on, Ace, you cannot dispatch him yet. We have to get him to the right place at the right time."

Bouchard sat back down on the sofa and called Rob Harmon. "Rob, it's me."

Harmon asked a question, and Bouchard said, "I'm fine. Yes, dinner is still on. I have a question for you. Has anything strange happened to you since the séance?"

Bouchard listened for a moment, then said, "I don't know, I've just felt like someone is watching me. Sometimes I feel like someone has been in my home."

While Bouchard listened to Rob, he thought of a way he could get Ellie's full signature. When Rob stopped talking, Bouchard said, "Well, you're probably right, and it's my imagination. By the way, I was thinking of designing a scarf in honor of Ellie. It's been a year since her death. I thought if you have something with her full signature on it, we could do white scarves with her signature covering the surface.

We could design it with her signature in several colors. I think it would be a nice tribute, and we could get it in the stores right away."

"Oh, he's smooth—he wants to honor the woman he killed," Edward said.

Ace narrowed his eyes at Bouchard. "Yeah, most low-down dirty skunks are predictable."

CHAPTER SEVENTY-NINE

Below Snakes

The next night was a repeat of the prior night. Bouchard read the note left in the same spot on his coffee table.

Why did you murder me? Eleanor Marlowe.

He slumped to the sofa and read the note over and over.

"I hope he's scared to death," Edward said.

"I can't wait until he's below snakes," Ace replied.

"What do you mean, Ace?"

"Dead."

"Yes, well, I think death might be visiting him soon."

Bouchard called Harmon. "Is dinner still on with John Marlowe?"

Rob responded, and Bouchard said, "Good. I want to talk to him about Ellie. Did you find her signature?"

After listening to Rob's response, he said, "Bring it to dinner, will you?"

The next night, the message said, *I'm watching you. Eleanor Marlowe.*

Bouchard poured himself a whiskey and sat down. *Am I going crazy? What if Ellie's ghost is watching me?* He looked around the room. *I can't see ghosts. Could that medium see and speak to Ellie's ghost?*

This is crazy thinking.

There are no ghosts.

He crumpled the note in his fists and threw it across the room. "You're dead, Eleanor Marlowe! I killed you!"

Edward and Ace looked at each other in disbelief upon hearing Bouchard confess to Eve's murder. Edward picked up the note and carried it back to the table.

Wide-eyed, Bouchard watched the note move through the air and land on the table. Gulping his whiskey, he stood and ran out the door.

Edward and Ace returned to Steele's home and told him about Bouchard's reaction tonight.

"He's a nervous wreck. He called Harmon to make sure they were still planning dinner with Mr. Marlowe," Edward said.

"Good."

Steele's phone rang, and seeing it was Mae, he answered.

"Steele, I connected with Amy again. She is so sad, almost like she's giving up. She's still clutching something in her hand, and I feel like I should recognize what it is, but it's not clear. For some reason, I think if I saw what was in her hand, it would help solve the case."

"I still have nothing new to go on," Steele said. "Helen saw the abduction, but she can't identify the perp."

Steele met Morgan, Tom, and the locksmith near Bouchard's home. Morgan introduced the short, white-haired man carrying what looked like a doctor's medical bag. "Steele, this is Red Hart. He's going to open that lock for us."

"Nice to meet you, Red." The men shook hands. "I want you to know we could be in real trouble if we get caught."

"I'm not worried. I'm seventy years old. I'll act like I have dementia and say I wandered into the wrong place if the police show up."

Steele chuckled. "I imagine that would work as well as any excuse. Or we could say we senior-napped you."

After John called and told Steele that Bouchard and Harmon entered the restaurant, Steele turned to the men and said, "It's a go." He whistled loudly, sending a message to Ace and Edward.

Steele pointed to a pathway near the guardhouse where they could enter Bourchard's home unobserved. Steele turned to Red and said, "We'll wait here until the guards are distracted."

Red looked at Morgan and asked, "Who's going to distract them?"

"It's hard to explain."

Suddenly, the door to the guardhouse opened, and papers started flying out. The two guards on duty ran outside and tried to collect the papers floating through the air.

Steele, Morgan, and Tom grinned at each other when they heard one guard yell, "How the hell did that happen?"

"That's our signal." Steele led the way through the neighborhood to Bouchard's home. Reaching the back door, he said, "Edward left the door unlocked for us."

"Well, they can't get us for breaking and entering," Tom replied.

They slipped inside the house, and thanks to Eve's description of the home's layout, they walked directly to Bouchard's office.

Steele pointed to the bust of Nero and said to Morgan, "Turn Nero's head."

Morgan twisted the statue's head, and the wall slid behind the bookcases.

Red set his black bag on the table. "Neat trick. Maybe one day you'll explain what happened in that guard house."

CHAPTER EIGHTY
Stairway To?

Red went to work on the lock while Steele, Morgan, and Tom disarmed the cameras.

As soon as Steele walked to the living room, Ellie appeared. "What are you doing here?" Steele asked.

"I thought I would come to see if anyone needed my help. I checked on Ace and Edward. They're doing a great job keeping the guards occupied."

Steele chuckled. "Those guards don't stand a chance."

Morgan joined Steele and Ellie in the living room. "Has anyone been upstairs?"

"Morgan, Ellie's here."

"Hi, Ellie. Did you check on Edward and Ace?"

"Ellie said they are keeping the guards busy," Steele replied.

Morgan grinned. "Good, I don't want to go to jail today. Steele, have you seen a staircase leading to the upstairs?"

"No, I haven't." It was a large two-story home, and he hadn't seen one visible staircase.

"There's also something weird about the layout in the kitchen."

Steele and Ellie followed Morgan to the kitchen, and he pointed to one wall. "It looks like a staircase was on that wall, but it's now enclosed."

Steele knocked on the walls and then stood back and looked at the row of custom cabinets. "You're right, Morgan. This kitchen is weird."

"I have a friend who has a home very similar to this one, and there are two staircases to the upstairs. One is in the kitchen and another staircase is near their office. Do you think a staircase could be behind that wall with the lock?" Tom asked.

"Why would anyone close up staircases to the second floor?" Morgan asked.

Steele started opening the cabinet doors. "Good question, Morgan." When he opened one door, he said, "This is interesting."

Morgan and Tom moved beside Steele to see what was inside the cabinet.

"A dumb waiter?" Morgan asked.

"Yeah." Steele pulled a small flashlight from his back pocket and held the light above the box. He saw cables leading to a second floor. He pointed to the control panel on the side and said, "You unlock it here, then push this button, and it takes you to the second floor."

They looked at each other, and Tom said, "It's only big enough for a tray. We're too big to fit in that box to see what's up there."

"There's not enough room to climb above the box. And we can't tear out the wall because we couldn't repair it before Bouchard returns," Morgan added.

"I can fit in there," Ellie said.

Steele looked at her and said, "Yeah, you'd fit." He told Morgan and Tom what she said.

"Give her your gun," Tom said.

Ellie laughed. "Remind Tom that no one can see me."

Steele laughed with her and told Tom what she said.

"What if spirits are up there?" Tom asked.

"Then they're already dead, and a gun won't help," Morgan replied.

Steele reached for Ellie and lifted her into the dumb waiter. "I'll control the buttons. Tell me what you see as soon as you open the door on the other end. There'll probably be a latch you'll have to open to get out."

Steele pushed the buttons, and the dumb waiter lifted slowly to the second floor. Ellie yelled to him when it came to a stop, "Steele, you were right. There's a latch to open the door."

"Open it, peek inside, and tell me what you see."

Ellie unlatched the door and inched it open. She didn't know what she expected to see, but the small door opened to a beautifully decorated sitting room. "It's just a small sitting room with four skylights," she said to Steele. "I see a doorway. I'm going to see what's in that room."

"Keep talking to me." Though he knew she was a spirit, and as illogical as it sounded, he was concerned about her safety.

Ellie crawled out of the dumb waiter and walked across the thick, lush white carpet to the doorway. The door led to a huge bathroom and, beyond that, another door. She walked across the bathroom and stopped by the next door. The room was so dark that she couldn't see anything. She thought it odd that no windows were visible in the room. "Steele, I walked through a bathroom to another room, but it's so dark that I can't see anything. Should I turn on a light?"

"I've got the lock open," Red yelled from the library.

Steele yelled up to Ellie, "Hang on a minute. Red has the door open."

CHAPTER EIGHTY-ONE

I Want to go Home

Steele, Morgan, and Tom ran into the library, where Red stood beside the opened steel door.

"It's a stairway," Red said.

"Stay here, Red." Steele pulled his gun, flipped on a light, and took the steps two at a time with Morgan and Tom right behind him. When he reached the top, he walked down a wide hallway and stopped at a padlocked door. Steele used the butt of his pistol to knock it off. He turned the doorknob and slowly pushed the door open. The room was dark, and when he slipped inside, the first thing he saw was Ellie's silhouette in a doorway on the other side of the room. He found a light switch and flipped it on, but the room was empty.

Morgan and Tom followed him into the room.

Steele hurried to Ellie's side. "Ellie, did you see anything?"

"No. But look at this room; it's decorated with hearts."

Steele turned around and looked at the entire room. Hearts were everywhere. His eyes landed on a big heart pillow on the bed. Mae told him that when she connected with Amy, she saw a big heart pillow. He glanced at the wallpaper . . . pale pink hearts. *It couldn't be. Could it?*

"Amy," he said.

He listened but heard nothing. Morgan and Tom stared at him, and Steele placed his forefinger to his lips.

"Amy, my name is Steele Harper. Your mom and dad hired me to find you. If you're here, come out. I promise you'll be safe. I have two policemen with me."

Nothing.

Ellie turned to Steele and she handed him her bracelet. "She loves hearts, so give her my bracelet. She's under the bed."

Morgan and Tom couldn't see Ellie, but they saw her bracelet as soon as Steele held it in his hand.

Steele crossed the room, sat on the bed, and held the bracelet down so Amy could see it. "Amy, your mom told me you love hearts. This bracelet belongs to my friend and she told me to give it to you. She tried to help you that day. I promise you that we are here to help you. You don't have to be afraid. I'll have the two officers show you their badges."

Morgan and Tom walked to the bed and held their badges for Amy to see. No one looked at her, allowing her time to feel comfortable.

Everyone was quiet while they waited. Steele saw a small fist stick out from beneath the bed. Amy opened her palm beside the bracelet Steele was holding, and he saw the other half of the heart that had broken off Ellie's bracelet.

That was the talisman that Mae saw Amy holding when she connected with her. Amy had held onto that broken heart for a year.

Steele knew Amy recognized the bracelet, and he choked up thinking about her year-long ordeal. He remembered that Mae thought the poor little girl was on the verge of giving up. It broke his heart to think about how hopeless she must have felt. He wished he had an hour alone with Bouchard. "Aw, sweetheart, please come out."

Amy crawled out from beneath the bed and looked at Steele with frightened eyes. "The lady tried to help me. That man broke her heart bracelet in the car door." She launched herself into Steele's arms. "I want to go home."

By this time, Red had joined them in the room, and everyone had tears in their eyes.

"Steele, have her parents meet you at your home. We can't let anyone know we were here," Morgan said.

"Yeah. Let's get out of here." Steele held Amy in his arms and ran down the stairs.

Once downstairs, they put everything back exactly like it was. The only thing missing when Bouchard came home would be Amy.

Steele wasn't about to let go of Amy. He threw Tom his keys. "Tom, you drive." He glanced at Red, and added, "Red, you're invited to my home as well. You deserve an explanation."

"I wouldn't miss this for anything," Red said.

Steele glanced at Ellie and said, "Tell Edward and Ace that we're done here, and come to the house."

She smiled and nodded.

"Morgan, don't forget to call Mae and tell her what happened. Tell her about the broken heart."

On the way home, Steele called Amy's parents. "Mrs. Carson, I can't explain now, but I want you and your husband to come to my house. Bring an overnight bag. Now, I have someone here who wants to talk to you." He held the phone to Amy's ear and said, "Talk to your parents."

Listening to their conversation, Steele could hardly contain his emotions, and he blinked back tears. *Some tough guy you are.*

Amy held the phone to Steele and said, "My mom wants your address."

Steele told Mrs. Carson his address, and he said, "Don't tell anyone where you are or that we found Amy. Let's just say I didn't do it the legal way."

CHAPTER EIGHTY-TWO

Connected by Hearts

They made it back to Steele's home in record time, and Ellie, Edward, and Ace were waiting for them.

"Steele, why don't you let Amy and her parents stay here, and everyone else can stay at my house," Ellie said.

"Thanks, Ellie. I think that would be good for them."

Amy hadn't looked up from Steele's shoulder until he sat down with her in his lap.

"Thank you for helping me," she whispered.

Steele smiled at her. "I like to help pretty ladies."

Amy pointed to Ellie. "She's the lady who tried to help me that day."

Steele and Ellie looked at each other, and Steele said, "Yes, she is."

Amy pointed to Morgan and Tom and said, "They're the policemen."

"That's right." Steele pointed to Red and told Amy his name. "He opened the lock to the door where you were."

Amy pointed to Edward and Ace. "Who are they?"

The room grew silent, but Steele answered without showing surprise, "The man in the tall hat is Edward, and the cowboy is Ace."

"You have a lot of friends," Amy said.

"I'm a lucky man. They're your friends, too. They helped to find you."

She looked at every person in the room. "Thank you." She held Ellie's bracelet out to Ellie. "Here's your bracelet. It's too big for me. But can I keep this one?" She held out half of the broken heart.

"Yes, you can keep it, and I will keep my half to show we are friends forever. Steele will get you a bracelet that will fit you. It will have smaller hearts and you can add your half-heart to it," Ellie said.

Amy turned her light blue eyes on Steele. "Will you really get me a heart bracelet?"

"Yes, I will. That's a promise."

Ellie touched Steele's shoulder, and said, "I think we should go to my house while you wait for the Carsons. We don't want to overwhelm them."

Steele agreed. He didn't think it would be a good idea to tell the Carsons that their daughter could see ghosts. They had enough to deal with, and he could break that news at a later date. "I'll be over later."

Amy's reunion with her parents was very emotional. Steele gave them time alone to reconnect and allow Amy to tell her story at her own pace. Once Amy fell asleep in her father's arms, Steele sat with them and explained how he'd found her.

"So you're saying while you were investigating a man who murdered the designer, you found out he killed her because she saw him kidnap our daughter?" Mr. Carson asked.

"That's right. I had no idea Bouchard kidnapped Amy. Miss Marlowe was injured trying to save Amy from Bouchard, and she lost her memory. That's why she didn't go to the police that day."

"And then, Bouchard killed her. That poor woman," Mrs. Carson said tearfully. "That man has caused so much pain for so many people."

"Of course, we will take Amy to a child psychologist. She'll need to talk to someone." Mrs. Carson's lips started to tremble, and she buried her head in her hands.

"Mrs. Carson, I agree that she will need professional help, but if it eases your mind, I don't think Amy was physically abused."

Mr. Carson reached over and rubbed his wife's back. "Let's not jump to any conclusions, honey."

"I haven't figured out how to tell the police about Amy. I can't say we entered Bouchard's home illegally because I have friends to protect," Steele said.

"Why don't we say Amy escaped and called me? I won't allow anyone to speak with her. My wife and I discussed going to my sister's for a few weeks. She lives in Tennessee, and I doubt the police would come that far to speak with us," Mr. Carson said.

"Let's sleep on it and then make a decision tomorrow," Steele replied. "You're welcome to stay here as long as you want. I'll be staying next door if you need me."

"Steele, I can't tell you how much we appreciate what you've done for us. No one will ever know what you did to find Amy. That'll be between us forever." Mrs. Carson hugged him before he left for Ellie's.

Ellie handed Steele a bourbon when he walked in. "Thank you. I needed this. It's been an emotional day."

"An unexpected day," Morgan said. "How are the parents doing?"

"Great. They're wonderful people, and they know how to help their daughter. Amy told them that Bouchard was nice to her, and he didn't hurt her in any way."

"He was grooming her," Morgan said.

Steele nodded. "Yeah, that's what I thought." After he told them about his discussion with Mr. Carson, he said, "I think Mr. Carson's plan is a good idea. We'll say Amy escaped. Let's all think about it tonight." He glanced at Red and said, "Red, have you concluded that we're all nuts?"

Red chuckled. "You mean because of the ghosts?"

Steele's eyes widened. "You can see them?"

"Not exactly. I guess you could say I *feel* ghosts," Red replied.

"Red wants to talk to us about his son. Joe was a Marine, and he's been visiting Red in his dreams. Joe was murdered, and it's another unsolved case," Morgan said.

Steele owed Red for his help tonight. "We'll do what we can to help you."

"We were just telling Red that if you hadn't met Ellie, you might not have found Amy," Morgan said.

Steele smiled at Morgan and said, "I was thinking the same thing on the way over here."

"That's some coincidence," Red said.

"There are no coincidences," Steele, Morgan, and Tom said in unison.

"It was a God-incidence," Ellie said.

Steele reached for Ellie's hand and kissed it. "I think you're right. It seems hearts connected everything. And now, everything is about to come full circle."

"What do you mean?" Ellie asked.

He tossed back his bourbon and said, "I know how we will get Bouchard to the beach."

CHAPTER EIGHTY-THREE

Won't be Enough Left to Snore

"Ace and I are going back to Bouchard's to see what he does when he finds Amy is no longer upstairs," Edward said.

Steele couldn't help but smile at them. "I'll be interested to hear about that."

Once Edward and Ace left, Steele said, "Red, do you want to tell me about your son?"

"Yes, thank you for asking."

Steele, Morgan, Tom, and Ellie gathered in Ellie's living room and listened intently to what Red had to say.

"I told you Joe was a Marine. And believe me, he was Marine through and through. Joe was the toughest man I know—knew. I'm so proud of him as a man and everything he's accomplished."

Steele noticed how Red would slip and refer to his son as if he were still alive. Then reality smacked him in the face, and he corrected himself. He understood how Red felt.

"Joe's in the elite Marine Raider Unit, and he'd survived Afghanistan and Iraq. Who would ever believe that after everything he'd been through, he'd be murdered when he came home?"

"It's a damn shame. Where was Joe killed?" Steele asked.

Red pointed to the beach. "Right here on this beach. He was vacationing here with his girlfriend. The police never solved his murder. He was shot from the back. Someone didn't even have the guts to face him."

"Did he mention having problems with anyone?"

"No, he didn't. But knowing Joe, he wouldn't have wanted to worry me about anything."

Steele thought that sounded like a Marine. "Was he alone at the time of his murder?"

"No, his girlfriend was with him, but she wasn't hurt."

"It wasn't a robbery?" Morgan asked.

"According to Joe's girlfriend, someone shot him and took off running. It was dark, and she was concerned about helping Joe, so she didn't get a good look at the man. She said he didn't take anything from either of them."

"Did the police clear the girlfriend?" Steele asked.

"They said she wasn't involved. I didn't know her well, but she seemed like a nice person. They'd only been dating for a few months."

"Do you know where he met her?"

Red thought about his question for a few seconds. "No, I don't think Joe ever mentioned where they met."

Steele pulled out his notepad and asked for the girlfriend's name and number. "You said he was visiting you in dreams."

"Yeah. He's talked to me several times. I always ask him if he has any idea who murdered him, and he said he didn't know. Then I wake up."

"I'll look into his case and see what I can find out."

Red tried to contain his emotions, but his voice broke when he said, "I appreciate your help. I think the police have just written it off as a cold case."

"Steele has an excellent success rate. Of course, he has Tom and me to help him out," Morgan teased.

Red smiled, appreciating a moment of levity. "I didn't doubt that for a minute."

Edward and Ace returned, and everyone was anxiously waiting to hear about Bouchard's reaction.

"He went crazy," Ace said.

Edward said, "Everything was how he left it when he left for dinner, so he had no clue that anything was missing. He opened the steel door, walked upstairs, and looked for Amy in every room. When he couldn't find her, well, as Ace said, he went crazy. He destroyed every room upstairs."

Ace laughed. "Yeah, then he came downstairs and looked everywhere for her like he thought she would hang around if she escaped her upstairs prison." Ace shook his head and said, "He's plumb loco. You should see his home now. It's a total mess. He even threw . . ." Ace looked at Edward, "Who was that statue?"

"Nero," Edward answered.

"Yeah, Bouchard threw Nero against the wall and smashed him to smithereens. Now, when do I get to blow that jackass to smithereens?"

"Ace, don't insult jackasses," Edward said.

"Yeah, I don't want to insult those fine animals. When I'm done with Bouchard, there won't be enough left of him to snore," Ace said.

CHAPTER EIGHTY-FOUR

Dispatch to Hell

Considering Red's talents, Steele was curious about his background. "Red, Morgan told me that you are retired. Do you mind if I ask about your prior profession?"

"I was in counterintelligence and paid by the government. I might be able to help you guys out from time to time."

"I appreciate that." Steele looked at Morgan and Tom and said, "I guess we need to tell Red what's going on. He's one of us now."

"Agreed," Morgan and Tom replied.

"If you're going to tell me there are ghosts around here, I already feel them. Besides, you've been talking to them in front of me. I know Ellie is in the room right now. And I don't think it would be a wild conclusion to say that she is very special to you, Steele."

Steele arched his brow at him. "How did you know Ellie was here?"

Red smiled. "It's obvious by the tone of your voice when you talk to her. And your hard-as-nail facial features soften when you look at her. Something tells me you don't look at everyone that way. The only piece of advice I would give you is not to play poker when she's around."

Steele groaned. He hadn't realized he was so transparent. "I can see why you were in counterintelligence." He glanced at Ellie and laughed. "You're going to be the death of me."

Ellie punched him in the arm. "Don't even tease about that."

Steele rubbed his arm. "You don't hit like a girl spirit."

"You felt that?" Ellie asked.

Steele just winked at her. He turned back to Red and said, "There are some things we need to tell you." He told him about Ellie's murder and their plan to try to change the past, hoping they could save Ellie's life.

Red didn't speak for a few minutes, and Morgan said, "So, now do you think we're all nuts?"

Shaking his head from side to side, Red said, "Before my son visited me in my dreams, I might have thought you were all crazy. But now, it doesn't sound so far-fetched. Steele, were you always able to see ghosts?"

"Tell Red we prefer spirits over ghosts," Ellie said.

"Ellie said to call them spirits. As far as I know, Ellie was my first encounter. But it seems that I can now see a lot of them."

"After we get things worked out with Ellie, I'll work on Edward's, Ace's, and your son's cases. As Morgan told you, they are joining forces with me. With three of us working together, we'll be able to devote more time and resources to each case."

"But how will you get paid if you're working for ghosts . . . I mean spirits?" Red asked.

Edward said, "You can share the information about my fortune, Steele."

Steele told Red about Edward's fortune and how he was supporting their endeavors. "Of course, we will take on other cases, particularly missing children."

"After tonight, I can see why you want to continue those cases."

"Red, I don't want to mislead you. We intend to eliminate Bouchard," Steele said.

"I'll be dispatching Bouchard to hell," Ace said. "We know Bouchard will be armed and ready, but I'll be faster, and I won't miss."

Steele repeated what Ace said to Red.

"I'd love to meet this cowboy and the English gentleman. After what Bouchard did to that little girl, he needs to go to hell."

"That's the plan," Steele replied.

"I can get Ellie a new background with all the documents she'll need," Red said.

"That would be great. We want to keep the initials EM because of her business. Her uncle said he had some family in France, so we thought that would be a good cover story."

"No problem. What name does she want to use?"

"My uncle's grandmother's name was Evelyn, so I'd like Evelyn Marlowe," Ellie replied.

After Steele repeated what Ellie said, Red said, "No problem. I'll get it done right away."

"Red, you're a good man to know," Steele said.

"I'd like to help you guys if I can. I'm retired, and I need something to do. I have some contacts that could be helpful."

"Thanks, Red, and we'll take you up on that offer," Steele replied. "We're going to try to get Bouchard to the beach as soon as Amy and her parents leave town."

"I'd like to be there when Ace dispatches him to Hell."

CHAPTER EIGHTY-FIVE

You're Dead, You Son-of-a-Bitch

Steele glanced at the group sitting in Ellie's living room and said, "I think tonight would be a good night for Ace to practice on the beach."

"You mean he gets to practice shooting that reprobate? I'm envious. I wish I had been wearing my sabre when I was murdered. I could run him through after Ace shoots him," Edward said.

Steele chuckled at Edward's comment and repeated it for everyone in the room. He glanced at Red and thought he should tell him what they were planning. After explaining the nightly events on the beach, he said, "I never see Bouchard shoot Ellie. But Ace and Edward can see him. They described him to a sketch artist, and that's how Ellie identified her murderer."

"I see why you need Bouchard to come to the beach at that specific time. So, the plan is for Ace to shoot Bouchard before he shoots Ellie," Red replied.

"Yes, that's what we're going to try. They can't arrest Ace, and they won't find a murder weapon. After it's over, we'll report a body on the beach," Steele said.

Red smiled and arched his brow at Steele. "I've got a boat. I could take him out to the deep blue."

"I like this guy," Ace said.

"I've thought about that, but if we spend too much time on the beach, someone might be out for a midnight stroll and call the police. We want this to be done in under a minute," Steele said.

Red nodded his agreement. "But I can call some guys I know who can make his body disappear no matter where he is."

"If the police don't buy our story, we may need them." Steele glanced at his watch. "Ace, don't forget to remove your cartridges." He smiled at him and added, "You might get trigger-happy when you see that low-down varmint. But you get to practice your draw on him tonight. Tomorrow, we'll take you to a place you can practice drawing and pulling the trigger with live rounds."

"Bouchard gets my dander up. That's a fact," Ace replied.

"I think we should leave a note in the same place for Bouchard. This one will say, *I have Amy. Meet me on the beach at midnight. Eleanor Marlowe*. After I speak with the Carsons, we'll put the plan in motion." Steele noticed Ellie's pensive expression, and he knew what she was thinking—it was time to go to the beach. "Let's go."

Ace emptied the cartridges from his Colt and tossed them on the table. "I'm ready, Steele."

Seeing the cartridges appear on the table, Red's eyes widened. "How did that happen?"

"We can't explain it. But when I touch Ace's Colt, you can see it." Ace handed Steele his Colt.

Steele held the gun out for Red to see. "This is what Ace uses. He was killed in 1888."

Red took the weapon and looked it over. "This is a beauty." He handed it back to Steele. Steel gave it to Ace, and once again, the Colt disappeared.

"Damn, I would never believe this if I didn't see it," Red said.

They reached the beach, and Steele pulled Ellie to his side. "I hope we stop doing this soon."

Ellie leaned into his body and took comfort in his strength. "I do too, but if it doesn't work out that way, I want you to know how much I appreciate what you've done for me."

"If this doesn't work, I'll find another way. That's a promise." Steele was confident that Ace could shoot Bouchard. What he didn't know was what worried him. *Would Ellie disappear forever? Would she go to Heaven? How will I find her?*

Ellie kissed his cheek and stepped away from him.

The scene played out as it did every night. This time, Ace was standing next to Ellie, and while she was looking at the ocean, Ace was facing the opposite direction. Next to Ace, Steele and the other men were facing the spot where Bouchard would be standing when he murdered Ellie.

Ace's arms were at his side, his gaze intent. He knew he had to draw his Colt just as Ellie turned around. It would all happen in a split second, and he couldn't lose focus. He couldn't look at her, but the light from the moon was bright enough for him to see her movements in his peripheral vision.

Bouchard appeared, and he walked toward Ellie. When he was standing directly behind her, he called her name.

Ace was ready. He took a deep breath and released it slowly. He saw movement out of the corner of his eye. *One, two* . . . he drew his Colt and fired his non-existent round.

"You're dead, you son-of-a-bitch."

CHAPTER EIGHTY-SIX

Make One Perfect Shot

Steele told the men how fast Ace drew his Colt, and his confidence in Ace tripled. Their plan would work. "Were you always that fast, Ace?"

"Yep."

They laughed when Steele repeated Ace's response.

"Look whom I found on the beach when I was swimming this morning," Morgan said and pulled Mae into the kitchen.

"Good morning, Mae," Steele said.

"Hi, Steele. I'm so excited that you found Amy. I bet you slept better than you have in a long time."

Steele nodded and said, "I slept pretty soundly. We couldn't have done it without your help. Did Morgan tell you that the room where Amy was imprisoned had heart wallpaper? And there was a huge heart pillow on her bed. It was just like you described when you connected with her."

"He did, and he told me what she was holding in her hand. That half a heart is what got her through her ordeal. She knew someone out there saw what happened to her."

Red walked into the kitchen, and Morgan introduced him to Mae.

"Morgan told me about you," Red said.

"He told me about losing your son. I'm sorry. I'll be happy to help if I can," Mae replied.

"Thank you. Morgan said that I should talk to you."

Steele stood and said, "I'm going to talk to Mr. and Mrs. Carson this morning. When I get back, we can take Ace to the shooting range. I don't think he needs practice, but he's looking forward to it."

"Where is the dynamic duo?" Mae asked.

"Walking on the beach with Ellie. I think they're looking for Red's son, Joe."

"I showed them a picture of Joe." Red opened his wallet and removed the photograph of his son.

Mae looked at the handsome man in his military dress uniform. "He looks like you, Red."

"I'll take that as a compliment, but Joe is about ten times my size."

"Mae, you and Ellie are welcome to go to the shooting range with us," Morgan said.

Mae laughed. "Let me see, shopping or the shooting range. Hmm . . . such a tough decision."

Steele was grinning on his way out the door. "Yeah, I guess the shooting range doesn't have a chance. I just don't understand why that doesn't appeal to you, Mae."

Everyone was waiting for Steele when he returned from speaking with Mr. and Mrs. Carson. "They're leaving town in the morning. Once they're out of town, they'll call the police and tell them that Amy escaped and called them. They plan to be away for several months, so they should be able to avoid putting Amy through the trauma of answering a lot of questions."

"How is Amy this morning?" Ellie asked.

"I thought she looked good. Mrs. Carson told me she ate a big plate of pancakes."

"I'm so happy for them," Ellie said.

"Okay. Now about our plan. I think we should set Bouchard up for the day after tomorrow. Is that good with you guys?" Everyone in the room nodded their agreement.

Before Steele left for the shooting range, he gave Ellie his credit card. Will you buy that bracelet for Amy while you're shopping? We can give it to her before they leave in the morning."

She smiled at him. "I'll have to give your card to Mae. I don't want the salesperson to have a heart attack."

Steele laughed. "Yeah, I tend to forget that no one else can see you."

Ace pulled cartridges from his holster and reloaded his Colt. "Wow, this is easier than shooting bottles off a wall."

Steele pushed the button, and the paper target returned to the stand. "All six shots are dead center in the chest."

Ace shrugged. "That target wasn't very far away."

"Let's take it out to one hundred yards." Steele put up a new target, pushed the button, and sent it one hundred yards away.

"Where do you want them this time?" Ace asked.

"To the head," Morgan said.

Ace drilled six shots to the head. "I don't know if I would be as accurate with a moving target. This is pretty easy."

"You're one heck of a shot, Ace," Steele said.

"I've never seen anyone who could shoot like that," Morgan said.

"I just want to make *one* perfect shot."

"You will."

CHAPTER EIGHTY-SEVEN

Could it be the Last Terrible Night?

The next afternoon, Ace and Edward returned to Steele's home, where everyone had gathered to wait for them.

"We left Ellie's note on Bouchard's coffee table in the same place as the others," Edward said.

Ace sat down across from Steele and Ellie. "A lady was there cleaning the place, and she had everything back to normal. The door to the upstairs was open, so we decided to take a look. Workers were changing the wallpaper, and there wasn't one piece of furniture in the rooms. Before we left, delivery men arrived with new furniture.

Morgan laughed. "Sounds like Bouchard's been busy."

"I think Ellie's note will scare him to death," Mae said.

Ace frowned. "I hope not. I don't want to waste all of that practice."

Steele told them what Ace said, and they laughed, breaking the tension in the room. They were all thinking about tomorrow night. It would be their only opportunity to see if the past could be changed. No one wanted to discuss what could happen—Ellie might continue to remain a ghost, or she could move on to . . . wherever.

Steele wanted her alive, but he would settle for a spirit if that was the only way she could be in his life. He didn't want to think about her moving on without him. No one knew their destiny, and all he could do was think about making the most of the moments they had together.

"Do you think Bouchard will believe Ellie has Amy?" Tom asked.

"I don't know, but I think he'd do anything to get Amy back. Ellie's note will be like waving a flag in front of a bull. He's that intent on having Amy for himself," Steele said.

"Yeah, it's a sickness with men like Bouchard. If he can't have Amy, he'll soon be on the lookout for another victim. He wants to groom a young girl for what he thinks will be the perfect mate," Morgan said.

"If tomorrow night doesn't work out, will you turn him over to the police?" Red asked.

"Even if Bouchard is charged and went to trial, his lawyers will get him off on a technicality," Tom said. "Everything we did was illegal."

Steele glanced at Ace. The set of his square jaw indicated he was a man on a mission. "Ace, what's on your mind?"

"I'm not worried about what I'm going to do if that's what you're thinking. I know what will happen to Bouchard—he'll be dead. I'm just worried about . . ." he glanced at Ellie and finished what he was going to say, "I'm worried about Ellie. I don't know what will happen to her."

Steele released a breath. What everyone was afraid to say was now out in the open.

Mae said softly, "Ellie, are you worried?"

"Yes, a little. I think fear of the unknown is always troubling."

Steele noticed the tears in her eyes and took her hand in his. "Honey, we don't have to do this. We can leave things the way they are."

Ellie smiled at him. "I know. But if there's a chance I could have a life with you that's normal, I want to try."

"I hope you can see us if you are no longer a spirit, Ellie," Ace said. "In case you can't see or hear us, just know Edward and I appreciate all you've done for us."

"I couldn't have said the words better, Ace," Edward said.

Ellie smiled at them. "Let's think the best." She couldn't say what she wanted to say without crying, so she'd wait until tomorrow night to say what was in her heart.

"We're going to return to Bouchard's tonight to see his reaction when he finds the note. We heard his housekeeper tell the workers that they had to be done by 5:00 p.m. since Bouchard would be home with a guest," Edward said.

"It'll be interesting to see how he reacts if he sees the note in front of his guest," Morgan said.

Mae thought they needed to get their minds off tomorrow night, and she had the perfect suggestion. "I think we all need to go for a long walk on the beach."

Morgan stood and said, "Mae's right. We need to clear our minds of all the *what-ifs*. A walk will do us good."

Edward and Ace were at Bouchard's a 4:45 p.m. and waited for his arrival. They were sitting on his sofa when Bouchard came home with his guest.

"He's got a woman with him," Ace said.

Edward leaned over to get a good look at the woman. "This should be interesting."

Bouchard led the woman to the living room and said, "Lorna, would you like a glass of wine?"

"Yes, thank you." She walked to the sofa and sat down while Bouchard pulled a bottle of wine out of the bar cooler. Ace quickly moved, or Lorna would have sat on his lap.

"René, there's a note on your table." Lorna picked up Ellie's note.

Before she could finish reading it, Bouchard hurried to the sofa and jerked the note from her hand. "It's probably from my maid. She should stop leaving notes lying around everywhere. She knows I dislike clutter."

Lorna looked around the perfectly organized room. "It looks like she does a great job."

Bouchard didn't hear Lorna. He was staring at the note in his hand. *She has Amy. How is that possible?* His hands shook as he shoved the message into his pocket. He walked back to the bar and opened the bottle of wine. He poured a glass for Lorna, but he opened a whiskey bottle and filled a glass for himself.

After he downed half of the whiskey, he took a deep breath and glanced at Lorna. He couldn't think about the note right now. He had to pretend that nothing was wrong. He walked to the sofa, sat beside Lorna, and handed her the glass of wine. "Tell me about your daughter."

Edward and Ace returned to Steele's home and told him what happened when Bouchard found the note.

"His hands started shaking after he read it. Before we left, we heard him ask Lorna about her daughter," Edward said.

"Looks like we'll save another young woman from him," Morgan said.

Everyone, including Red, planned to stay at Steele's home for a few more nights. They were together at midnight for what they hoped would be Ellie's last terrible ordeal on the beach.

After Ellie disappeared, they retired for the evening, but Steele remained awake until Ellie returned almost two hours later. They held each other and talked most of the night about everything—everything but what could happen the next night.

CHAPTER EIGHTY-EIGHT

A Fresh New Start

"I just spoke with John. He'll be here tonight," Steele said to Ellie.

"I was hoping he wouldn't come."

"Why?"

"Because we don't know what will happen to me. Uncle John has heart problems, and I don't want him to get upset if . . . well, I don't want him to go through losing me twice."

Steele took a deep breath, trying to keep his emotions in check when he responded. "I don't think we could keep him away."

"You're right." Ellie hesitated a moment, then said, "Steele, if I disappear forever, promise me you'll look after him."

Steele pulled her into his arms and kissed her forehead. "You know I will." Taking her hand in his, he said, "Everyone is giving us some time together, so why don't we go for a walk with Bear."

She laced her fingers through his. "I'd love that."

They strolled along the shoreline, and Steele threw Bear's ball in the water for him to retrieve. They walked on the beach for an hour, talking and entertaining Bear. When they returned home, Morgan and Tom were grilling hamburgers.

"Hope you've worked up an appetite," Morgan said.

Steele wasn't hungry, but he wouldn't disappoint them since they were nice enough to cook. "It smells great."

After dinner, Edward and Ace appeared on the patio.

"What did you two do today?" Steele asked.

"We escorted Helen and Violet for a walk on the beach," Edward replied.

Ellie smiled at them. "That's nice of you. I'm sure they welcome your friendship."

Ace jabbed Edward in the ribs. "Edward's sweet on Violet."

"And why not, my good man? She is a lovely woman," Edward replied.

Ace jabbed him again. "I think she's sweet on you, too."

Edward's chest puffed out a bit. "You do?"

"She's always smiling at you and agrees with everything you say."

Edward elbowed Ace. "That just proves she's an intelligent woman."

Steele was repeating the conversation for those who couldn't hear Edward's and Ace's banter. It was a brief light moment that everyone appreciated.

When they grew quiet, Steele glanced at his watch and said, "Ellie and I are going to spend some time alone for a while at her house. You guys stay here as long as you want. We'll be back before we go to the beach."

They reached Ellie's house, and without discussing what they intended to do, they walked into her bedroom. Exhausted from the day's activities, Bear plopped down on his bed and closed his eyes.

Steele stripped out of his clothes, walked to Ellie, and looked into her eyes as he unbuttoned her top. Ellie slid her skirt off before Steele removed her blouse. He stood back and looked at her. "You're beautiful."

"You're partial."

"Yes, I am." He picked her up and carried her to bed. "When you're old and gray you will be beautiful to me. I love you, Ellie."

"I love you, Steele. No matter what happens, never forget that."

Later that night, Steele and Ellie walked in silence to his house. Being together that afternoon, they'd said everything they needed to say without words.

Once they entered Steele's house, Ellie wanted to tell all of them what they meant to her just in case they didn't see her again.

She hugged Edward and Ace and thanked them for all they had done for her.

"Ellie, I'm not going to miss," Ace said confidently.

"I know. I believe in you, but we don't know what will happen to me."

Ace pulled his Stetson off and gave her another hug. "One way or the other, we'll see you again."

Edward wiped tears from his eyes. "Yes, we will."

Ace whispered in Edward's ear, "Cowboy up. Don't make her cry."

Ellie turned to Mae and hugged her. "Mae, thank you for everything, and for being my friend."

Mae was so emotional that she could hardly speak. After a moment, she managed to say, "I wish I knew what was going to happen."

Ellie turned to Steele and asked him to thank Morgan, Tom, and Red for her.

The men told Steele they wished they could see her so they could hug her.

Bear walked to Ellie and nudged her hand. Ellie kneeled and put her arms around his neck. She whispered in Bear's ear. "I love you, Bear. If I go somewhere else, I want you two to take care of each other."

Bear smothered her face with sloppy licks.

Just then, her uncle tapped on the patio door. Steele pulled the door open, and when he put his arm on John's shoulder, he felt him shaking.

Ellie kissed her uncle on the cheek. John couldn't see her, but he put his hand on his cheek and looked at Steele. "Did Ellie just kiss me?"

"Yes."

John smiled. "I felt that, Ellie. I want you to know I love you, honey."

"Tell him I love him too, Steele."

Steele repeated what she said to John before checking his watch again. "We have to go. Ellie, Ace, and Edward will be with you, but the rest of us will stay behind that big log on the beach. It's dark there, and Bouchard won't see us."

"What if he doesn't come?" John asked.

"He'll come," Steele said. "Let's go."

Ace pulled his revolver and checked his cartridges one last time.

Steele shook hands with him. "Good luck, Ace. I appreciate what you're doing."

Ace nodded. "I'm happy to do it."

Steele hugged Ellie one last time. He didn't want to let her go, but he had no choice. He kissed her and said, "I love you."

Ellie didn't want to leave him, and she couldn't stop her tears. "I love you."

After pulling away from her, Steele hurried to hide with the others in the darkest area on the beach. They were about twenty-five feet from where Ellie would be standing.

"Did Ellie tell you she has been working on becoming visible?" Mae whispered.

Steele didn't take his eyes off Ellie, but he answered, "No, she didn't tell me."

"It's only worked for a few seconds, but she wanted Bouchard to see her so he would think she's alive."

"Shh. Here he comes," Morgan whispered.

Ellie was standing between Edward and Ace, facing the ocean. Edward and Ace were facing Bouchard as he walked toward the shore.

Steele saw Bouchard's head swiveling from side to side. He didn't see Ellie, but he walked to the spot where he'd shot her.

Suddenly, Ellie became visible, and Morgan whispered, "It worked, I can see her."

For the first time, John, Morgan, Tom, and Red saw her.

Bouchard saw her too. He took a halting step like he was surprised he didn't see her until that moment. He called her name.

"He's going to ask her about Amy. I should have thought of that," Steele said. "Ace can't shoot him too soon."

"Where's Amy?" Bouchard said from behind Ellie.

Ellie turned and said, "She's safe with her family. You'll never get her."

"I killed you. How can you be here?"

"Haven't you ever heard of ghosts?"

Ace knew this wasn't an exact replay of the night Ellie was killed. *Patience*, he told himself as he drew a bracing breath.

"I don't believe in ghosts. But this time, I'll make sure you're dead." Bouchard pulled his pistol from his pocket.

Ace watched Bouchard's eyes. He knew the moment Bouchard was going to fire. He drew his Colt and fired.

Suddenly, everyone started moving as several things happened at once.

Bouchard dropped to the ground with a bullet in his forehead.

Ellie fell to the ground, and Steele raced to her side. Ace was already kneeling beside her, shaking her and yelling her name. He looked at Steele, and said, "Bouchard didn't get a shot off! What happened to her?"

"I don't know." Steele placed his palm on her cheek. "Ellie! Ellie!" When she didn't respond, he looked for blood on her white dress.

There was no blood.

Edward and Red approached Bouchard to make sure he was dead.

Steele leaned and whispered into Ellie's ear. "Don't leave me, my love. Please open your eyes. Bear and I will be lost without you."

Ellie's eyes fluttered open. "Steele?"

Steele clutched her to his chest. "Thank God!"

Everyone was standing around them, and suddenly sand started swirling as if a tornado hit the beach. A hole opened in the earth, and two creatures with long, narrow pitted red faces, dressed in dark hooded robes crawled from the earth. They screeched an ear-splitting, other-worldly sound as they clawed at Bouchard's body. Once they latched onto his corpse, they disappeared into the dark hole and the earth closed behind them. The air cleared, and the hole was covered by sand.

Everyone stared at the non-existent hole that was present a moment before.

"What was that?" Morgan asked.

"I don't think we want to know. That was straight out of a horror flick," Tom replied.

"We don't have to worry about getting rid of a body now," Red said.

Steele helped Ellie to her feet. He didn't know if she was alive or still a spirit. She didn't look different to him.

"Ellie, I can see you," John said and hugged her.

Morgan reached out and touched Ellie's arm. "We can see her, too."

Steele and Ellie looked at each other, and Steele wrapped his arms around her. They embraced for several moments, unable to voice their emotions.

Once they collected themselves, they both turned to Ace, and Ellie said, "Ace, I don't know how to thank you."

Ace grinned. "No thanks needed. I'm just glad you can still see me."

She hugged Ace and Edward. "I can still see both of you."

Steele slapped Ace on the back. "Ace, you didn't practice that shot. That was one hell of a shot. Thank you for changing the past. We couldn't have done it without you."

Edward put his hand on Ace's arm. "It was right in the center of his forehead. Well done, Ace!" He looked at Ellie and Steele and said, "You two have a fresh new start. You have a wonderful life in front of you."

Looking at the two men, Steele couldn't wait to see if he could help them live again if it was possible. Edward and Ace were important to him, and he would do what he could to solve their murders.

Suddenly a deep voice behind them said, "Dad?"

Steele, Ellie, Mae, and the spirits turned around and saw a tall, well-muscled blonde man wearing red swimming trunks.

"Oh, my. I think Thor is here," Mae said as she stared at the man with chiseled facial features and a Greek god physique.

"That's not Thor. That's the Marine." Steele knew he had another spirit to help.

CHAPTER EIGHTY-NINE

May the Angels Protect Us and Heaven Accept Us

Steele told Red that his son, Joe, was beside him. "I've invited him to go home with us."

"I can't believe it," Red said. "Hello, son."

Joe put his arm around his dad's shoulders, and Mae answered the questions between father and his son as they walked to the house.

Steele asked Morgan and Tom to listen to what Joe had to say in case there was something significant they could use to find his murderer. "I'm going to put Ellie to bed so she can rest."

Once Steele put Ellie in his bed, he and John sat down beside her.

Ellie whispered, "Steele, what do you think those things were who took Bouchard? I have never seen them on the beach before."

"I can't say for sure, but I think they were the Devil's disciples escorting Bouchard to the Lake of Fire."

"I think Steele's right," John said. "That's something you'll never have to worry about. I sure as heck never want to see them again."

Ellie's eyes filled with tears as she looked at Steele and her uncle. "I can't believe I'm really here. I'm not sure I allowed myself to think this could happen."

"This is what I prayed would happen, but we couldn't be sure it would. Thank God for Ace's accuracy," Steele said.

"I don't think many men could have made that shot." John stood and said, "I think we could all use a drink. I'll be back in a minute."

When John left the room, Steele leaned over and kissed Ellie. "I'm so happy that you're here with me."

Ellie wrapped her arms around his neck. "I feel the same. I want a lifetime with you."

"You are never getting rid of me. I can't imagine my life without you in it." Steele noticed she was still trembling, so he covered her with a blanket. "Do you remember everything that happened before your murder?"

Ellie thought for a couple of minutes before she said, "Yes. I saw Bouchard trying to get Amy in his car that day. I tried to take her away from him, and he punched me with his fist. I hit the concrete, and I think I was unconscious for a moment. He knew I recognized him."

"I'm sure that's the reason he killed you. It didn't have anything to do with stealing your designs," Steele replied.

John returned, carrying three glasses and a bottle of bourbon. He filled the glasses and said, "I want to propose a toast, and then Ellie should get some rest." He held his glass in the air and said, *"May the angels protect us, and Heaven accept us."*

They clinked their glasses together, and John said, "Both of you get some rest." He kissed Ellie on the cheek and left the room.

Red sat in the chair next to the one where Mae said Joe was sitting. "Son, I'm so glad to know you're with us, even if you are a spirit. Can you tell me who murdered you? The police haven't solved your case."

Mae repeated Joe's response to his father. "Red, he said he can't think of a reason why anyone would murder him."

"Ace and I have never seen Joe on the beach. How did he know where we were?" Edward asked.

After Joe's explanation, Mae repeated his response, "He heard from several spirits that a man in a tall beaver hat and a cowboy were looking for him. They told him where he could find Edward and Ace. From a distance, he saw us on the beach." She looked at Joe and added, "Joe, I haven't even introduced you to Ace and Edward."

"Welcome to our little spirit and human club," Edward said, tipping his hat to Joe.

Ace touched the brim of his Stetson. "I'm glad you found us."

Mae explained to Joe that she could see spirits as well as Steele. "No one else can see you." They explained what happened to Ellie and the reason they were on the beach tonight.

Joe shivered. "I saw those creatures take that body away. That's the first time I saw something like that."

"Ace and I have never seen anything like that either," Edward replied.

Mae repeated their conversation for John, Morgan, Tom, and Red so they would know what was being discussed.

Joe said to Mae, "Tell them I've seen angels come down and escort people to Heaven. It's a beautiful sight to see."

"We didn't know what was going to happen to Ellie. We thought she might go to Heaven," Ace said.

"Do you think it means there was some sort of mix-up, and she was supposed to be alive?" Joe asked.

After Mae asked Joe's question aloud, everyone shrugged.

"We don't know," Edward replied.

Red walked over to stand beside his son's chair. "I knew Morgan and Tom, and they asked me to help Steele on a case. When they told me about Steele's ability to see spirits and how he was helping Ellie, I asked if he could help me find out what happened to you."

Morgan said, "Joe, tell us about the night of your murder. What you did that day, until the last thing you remember."

"I want to ask a question first," Joe replied.

"What is it?" Mae asked.

"Why does everyone say *spirits* instead of *ghosts?*"

CHAPTER NINETY

The Greek God

Life had changed for Eleanor Marlowe.

By the next afternoon, Red provided Ellie with her new identity.

Evelyn Marlowe.

Ellie was now Eve.

A delivery driver knocked on Steele's door with a special delivery for Red Hart. After Red opened the large manila envelope and looked over the materials, he handed them to Ellie.

Ellie sat down on Steele's sofa and studied the newly minted identification cards, including a new social security number with a new birth date and a passport.

Steele leaned over her shoulder and read the information on her ID. "Wow, I'm dating an older woman."

Eve glanced at the date and rolled her eyes. "One day older." She narrowed her eyes at Red. "Did you do that on purpose?"

Red shook his head from side to side. "I didn't know Steele's birthday. It's a coincidence."

Steele, Morgan, and Tom looked at each other and said in unison, "There are no coincidences."

Red shrugged. "Then chalk it up to unseen forces because all I told my contact was a birth year, and I guessed at that."

Steele slapped Red on the back. "Thanks for getting these so quickly. They look great."

John sat next to his niece and said, "Now, all I need to do is dismiss Rob, and send out an email informing the staff that my niece, who has been working in France, will be returning to Florida to run the company. When would you like to come back to the company?"

"I want to move the office nearer to me when I return." She glanced at Steele. "I think I need a week or two to adjust to the new me. What do you think?"

Steele grinned at her. "I think you need two weeks. We have some catching up to do. And you can help us on these cases while you're adjusting to being Eve."

"No problem. I'll take care of it," John said.

"Morgan and I are leaving in the morning to go to Edward's home in New York," Tom said.

"Do you need some help?" Mae asked.

"I don't want you to get into trouble if we get arrested," Morgan replied.

Tom held up his hand. "Wait a minute, Morgan. Mae has to go or we won't be able to communicate with Ace and Edward."

Morgan looked at her and said, "I forgot we couldn't talk to them. We'd love for you to come with us."

"It's settled then. Mae will go with you. I think we need to see if we can get Joe into some clothing," Steele said.

They all turned to look at the Greek god in their midst.

Ellie, aka Eve, and Mae exchanged a smile, and Mae arched her brows, silently telegraphing that Joe Hart was a magnificent male specimen.

Joe looked down at his red swimming trunks. "Well, this is the beach. And as far as I know, this is the first time anyone alive has seen me."

"Ellie, I mean Eve, taught us how to change clothing," Edward said. "We'll work with you today and show you how."

"It would be nice to wear my fatigues again." Joe pointed to his swimming trunks and said, "This is what I was wearing when I was murdered."

"Joe, your dad said you were with your girlfriend that night. Were you two alone on the beach?" Steele asked.

"Yes, I had two weeks before I was deploying again."

"Your girlfriend's name was Emma Lake, correct?" Steele asked.

"Right."

"Where did you meet?"

"We met in Jacksonville about three months before my death."

Steele thought about Joe being shot from behind. "Do you think Emma Lake could be involved with your murder?"

Joe shook his head. "I have no reason to think she would. But then, I don't know why I was murdered."

Steele thought that was the one thing the spirits had in common—they didn't know why they were murdered. He wondered if Bouchard felt the same way—wherever he was now. Then he thought about Violet. She thought her nephew murdered her for money, but she didn't actually see him commit the crime.

"Joe, where were you being deployed?" Steele asked.

Joe was silent for a few seconds, then looked Steele in the eye. "I almost said that was confidential. But the truth is, I can't remember where I was assigned."

"Your dad said your deployments generally involve highly-dangerous missions; special reconnaissance, counterterrorism, or intelligence gathering."

"That's right, but we never discussed where we were being deployed or what we were doing." He glanced at his dad and added, "When I returned home, I could tell dad where I had been. He knew I was in Iraq, Afghanistan, and a few other unsavory places."

"I'm aware of your training, and it seems logical that the killer was also aware of your skills. He picked the most opportune time to sneak up on you. It's difficult to hear someone walking behind you on the beach. It was much like Ellie's—Eve's murder."

"True, and Emma and I shared a bottle of wine with dinner, so if I heard anything, my reflexes would have been slower. And it's not like I could carry a weapon in swimming trunks."

"Even if your reflexes were slower, if you heard your murderer, he would be the one dead," Red said.

CHAPTER NINETY-ONE

You're my Spirit

"Morgan, would you and Tom mind if Joe and I go with you to New York?" Red asked.

Morgan smiled, "Mae will be busy repeating conversations, but you're welcome to join us."

"Well, my SUV seats eight, so we're good," Tom said.

Morgan laughed. "This should be an interesting road trip."

"It'll be good for Steele and Ellie . . . I mean Eve, to have some time alone," Edward said.

Eve smiled at him. "That's thoughtful, and we're very appreciative."

"Yes, it's very thoughtful. Thank you, Edward." The thought of spending time alone with Eve excited Steele. They'd been alone during the night and talking in bed each morning, but he wanted to spend time with her doing *normal* things. They could have dinner and walk down the beach, and everyone could see her. He could have his arm around her and kiss her when he wanted without looking like he'd lost his marbles by hugging someone who wasn't there.

Edward winked at Steele. "Anytime, old chap."

John spoke up, "I'm going back to Palm Beach tonight. I have some early morning meetings, and I'll get everything prepared for Eve's arrival."

"Come back anytime you want, John," Steele said.

"You know you can always use my house, Uncle John," Eve said. She turned her attention to Joe, and said, "Since you're going to New York, you'll definitely need to change your wardrobe."

"I second that motion," Morgan said. He didn't want Mae riding all the way to New York eyeing the Greek god, or she might think he didn't measure up.

Mae smiled and leaned close to his ear, "You don't have anything to worry about."

"Damn psychics," Morgan muttered.

The next morning, everyone left for New York, and Steele and Eve took Bear to the beach for an early morning swim.

"Bear said he was happy I'm alive again," Eve said when they sat down on their towels.

"Really?" Steele said. "Did he say why?"

"Yes, he said you needed me."

Bear crawled on Steele's lap, and Steele dried his furry body. "You're right, Bear. I need both of you." He looked at Eve and added, "I'm happy you can still talk to Bear. I like knowing what he's thinking."

Bear licked his face. "I understand that in any language.

For the first time, Steele could take Eve out to dinner. He chose a restaurant on the beach, and they decided to sit on the beachside patio. Steele ordered champagne to toast their first date as a normal couple. Every time he looked at Eve, his heart nearly burst with pride. He was a goner, and he knew it. He loved it. He couldn't have been happier unless Eve was his wife. But he didn't intend to rush anything. He wanted her to have time to adjust to her new life.

Since he hadn't given her a gift on Valentine's Day, he bought her a present to give to her tonight. It was in his pocket, but now he questioned if he'd made the right choice since she designed jewelry. He reminded himself it was the thought that counted.

The waiter returned with their champagne, and Steele made a toast. "To the most beautiful woman to enter my life. I hope she stays forever."

Tears filled Eve's eyes. "I plan to," she whispered before she sipped her champagne.

Steele pulled a black velvet box from his pocket and handed it to her. "Happy Valentine's Day."

She opened the *Infinities* box, and he said, "I know you probably have a lot of jewelry, but I liked this."

Twinkling in the box was a sapphire and diamond heart necklace.

"Oh, Steele, it's beautiful. I saw this necklace the last time Mae and I were shopping in *Infinities,* and I told Mae I wanted to meet the designer." She leaned over and kissed him. "Thank you. I'll cherish it forever."

"Turn it over," Steele said.

Inscribe on the back of the necklace were the words; *You are my spirit. I love you. S.*

"This is the loveliest gift I have ever received." She removed the necklace from the box and put it around her neck.

Steele was thrilled that she liked his gift. "It looks beautiful on you."

Opening her purse, she said, "I have a gift for you."

She handed him a box with her initials on top. "I know you don't wear jewelry, only a watch, so . . ."

Steele opened the box and saw a diver's watch with all of the bells and whistles. Engraved on the back of the watch case were the words, *To the man who saved me, and the love of my life. E.*

"We hired a Swiss company to make them for us before my . . . well, before." She didn't want to bring up the past and ruin the evening.

Steele reached over and placed his hand on the back of her neck, urging her closer. He kissed her, an unabashedly intimate kiss in front of everyone sitting on the patio. The thought crossed his mind to pick her up and carry her home, but he told himself to be patient since it was their first date. He ended the kiss, and said, "I love the watch, and I'll wear it every day."

"I heard you tell Edward that you enjoyed scuba diving, and since you swim every morning, I thought you might like it," Eve said.

Steele removed his watch and replaced it with the new one. "Perfect."

As they ate, Steele saw several people walking down the beach toward them. They stopped by the patio and stared at Eve. Before long, ten people were standing near the patio watching them. Steele noticed Eve wouldn't look at them. He glanced from the people to Eve, and said, "I wonder why they are staring at us?"

"They're spirits, and they recognize me. They know I'm alive, and they want to know how it happened. I didn't want them to know I could still see them."

Steele glanced at them, and then he started to hear their conversations. "Geez, no."

"What is it?" Eve asked.

"I can hear them."

"Steele, they want your help."

An exciting preview of

THE GHOST ON THE BEACH

BOOK TWO

MURDERS, MILLIONS, AND MARRIAGE

CHAPTER ONE

The Original G. I. Joe

"Why do I feel like a plundering Viking invader?" Morgan mumbled as he slammed his shovel into the hardened earth.

Tom laughed. "We're not actually invading."

"I'm not a Viking either, but that distinction would be lost on the local police if we're caught trespassing."

"If we are caught, the cops will think we're burying a dead body," Red said.

Morgan grunted. "We'll just tell them we already have enough of those to go around."

"Something tells me if we're caught digging a hole on a twenty million dollar estate, no explanation is going to work," Tom said.

Morgan stopped shoveling and looked at him. "You mean we couldn't tell the police that Edward, the former owner of the property, will explain that we're not trespassing? I can hear that conversation now. *I'm sorry, officer, but you can't see or hear Edward, so Mae, the psychic, will have to translate for him.*"

Tom snorted with laughter, "Keep digging, Huckleberry."

The Bedford House in upstate New York was a stunning example of architectural opulence from an era long past. But the men working at the outer reaches of the grounds after midnight weren't there to admire the magnificent manor or the flora and fauna. Edward Hamilton, the Duke of Bedford, insisted they weren't really trespassing since they were there at his request to lay claim to his property. But legally, the Bedford House was no longer an asset that Edward Hamilton could declare.

He was dead.

He was a ghost.

In the summer of 1835, Edward sailed from his home in England to Bedford House. He planned to remain in New York for a year, but before that year ended, his plans changed.

Edward was murdered.

Months before Edward's untimely passing, he'd buried a chest at the back of his Bedford estate with the assistance of his butler and valet. Edward was the only person who knew the chest held silver coins, jewels, and gold bars worth a fortune at that time. Considering today's market, the jewels alone were worth millions. Edward had not included the valuables in his Will and presumably, the chest was never unearthed.

This night, almost two centuries later, Edward was on a mission to recover his property, and his six friends were there to assist in this endeavor. Edward's friends included three live men; Morgan Armstrong, Tom Grayson, and Red Hart; two ghosts, Ace Barton and Joe Hart; and one live female, Mae Rogers. Mae was a psychic who could see and hear ghosts—or *spirits,* as they liked to be called. She was also the interpreter between the live men and the spirits.

Morgan, Tom, and Red stopped digging and leaned against their shovels. They stared at the three-foot-deep hole, and Morgan whispered to Mae, "Ask Edward how deep we need to dig."

She grinned at Morgan. "Did you forget that Edward can hear your question?"

"Yeah." Morgan arched his brow at her. "Well, what's the answer?"

Mae looked at Edward, listened to his reply, and said, "He said to go two more feet. He buried it in 1835, and he can't remember the exact depth."

"Edward, how can you be certain the chest is still here?" Morgan looked at Mae, waiting for Edward's response.

After Edward finished talking, Mae repeated his reply. "My good man, if you are questioning if my butler and valet would have betrayed my trust, the answer is no. They were men of the highest integrity, and they swore an oath to carry my secret to their graves. And the grounds are the same as they were in 1835. Since you and Tom have joined Steele in his private investigation business, the contents of my chest will help finance your work with other spirits. We need to dig until we find it."

Edward was referring to Steele Harper, Morgan and Tom's best friend. The three men were detectives in Miami until Steele left the department a year prior. He moved from Miami to Siesta Key and became a private investigator. His clientele grew rapidly, and he'd asked Morgan and Tom to join him in the business.

Like Mae, Steele could see and hear spirits. He wasn't aware that he had that particular gift until he started renovating his beach home. Every night, he would see a beautiful woman walking along the shore. When he discovered she was his next-door neighbor, Eleanor Marlowe, he thought he was one lucky man. There was only one problem. Eleanor had been dead for a year. She was a spirit.

From the moment Steele met Ellie, he was smitten. Once he learned that she had been killed on the beach and it was an unsolved crime, he decided to investigate. Ellie didn't know who murdered her or why. Without answers to those questions, she remained in a constant state of confusion. She couldn't move on to whatever destination awaited.

As Steele's investigation progressed, he and Ellie fell in love. They befriended Edward and Ace and quickly formed a close bond with the two spirits. Through a series of unusual events, and with the help of his friends and the spirits, Steele found a way to bring Ellie back to life while solving her murder. With Ellie's new identity as Eve Marlowe, she was given a second chance at life with the man she loved.

Ace Barton removed his Stetson and tossed it in the grass. "I can help you dig." Ace, a true-life cowboy, was murdered on Siesta Key beach in 1888. He was Edward's best friend, and they'd walked the beach for years, never expecting to find someone to help them discover the truth behind their murders.

Mae repeated what Ace said to the men shoveling.

Red chuckled. "Tell Ace that he and Joe can take over if we have to go much deeper." Red was Joe Hart's father, and he'd enlisted Steele's help to find his son's murderer. Joe was a Marine before he was killed on the beach. Like the other spirits, he had no idea why he was murdered.

Steele called him GI Joe, and it was the perfect moniker. Joe was an impressive man, though some might say intimidating. At six-feet-two, two hundred pounds of solid muscle, Joe's perfect posture telegraphed he was all Marine. He wasn't the type of man who would start a fight, but he was the man who would finish one. He'd accompanied his dad and friends on this mission to ensure their safety.

Tom scooped up another shovel full of dirt and tossed it aside. "Let's get busy. It's our goal not to get caught trespassing, so let's get this done."

"Yeah, I don't want to go to the hoosegow," Ace said, and Mae repeated his comment.

Red whispered, "Ace is right. I don't want to spend my twilight years in prison."

The men started digging with renewed vigor, and a few minutes later, Edward said, "Maybe another foot deeper."

Mae chuckled softly and whispered, "Edward said another foot."

Suddenly, floodlights lit up the grounds like a football field hosting a Friday night game. Everyone froze in place, standing as still as the concrete statues dotting the property.

"Bet they didn't have those lights in 1835," Morgan whispered.

They heard a dog barking in the distance. Within a few heartbeats, the ferocious sound drew closer.

"Oh, crap. It sounds big. It's probably a Rottweiler," Tom whispered.

"And it sounds like he's coming this way. If he continues to bark, someone will come out to investigate," Red said.

"If he reaches us, he might think Mae is a snack," Morgan said.

Joe turned toward the sound of the barking dog. "I'll take care of it."

Mae whispered, "I don't want you to hurt a dog." She turned to Morgan and said, "Joe wants to take care of the dog."

"We have to do something. I don't want to shoot it if he starts munching on you, Mae. A gunshot would draw a lot of attention."

Joe said, "Mae, I'm good with dogs. I won't hurt him."

Mae watched Joe run toward the barking dog. In seconds, he was out of sight, and soon after, the barking came to a halt.

While they waited to see if someone would turn off the lights, Morgan admired the perfectly groomed landscape of the estate. "Edward, this is a beautiful place."

"It was a wonderful place to host grand parties. Many a morning, I awoke in my cups, lying on the terrace with dew covering me," Edward said wistfully.

When Mae repeated Edward's comment, the men smiled at the mental image of the proper Duke of Bedford inebriated and lying prostrate on his terrace.

Mae pointed to Joe running toward them. "Here comes Joe."

The lights dimmed, and the men went back to work under the beams of their flashlights. After removing another foot of dirt, their shovels clinked against a hard object.

Edward clapped his hands together. "You've found it!"

They scraped dirt from the top of the chest, and Morgan said, "Let's see if we can lift it out, so we can get the hell out of Dodge."

"This ain't Dodge," Ace said.

Mae giggled. "That's just a figure of speech, Ace."

The men struggled to lift the heavy trunk, and Tom said, "Where's the muscleman when we need him?"

Joe appeared behind them. "Mae, did someone say they needed some muscle?"

"They need help lifting the chest out. But what did you do to the dog?"

"I used my belt to tie him to a statue on the terrace. I think it was Hercules, the statue, not the dog." He arched a brow at her. "I'll let you guess what part of his anatomy I used to secure the dog."

Mae couldn't help but laugh.

Leaning over the hole, Joe said, "Mae, tell them to move out of the way."

The men moved away when she told them, but Morgan asked, "How can he lift it out alone?"

At that moment, the chest floated from the earth and landed at Morgan's feet. "Guess that answers my question. Mae, ask him if he can carry it to the car alone."

Joe nodded at Mae. "No problem." He picked up the trunk and balanced it on his shoulder. "Let's go."

"I can't tell you how happy I am that Joe came with us," Tom joked as they refilled the hole.

"He must be stronger than he looks," Morgan said.

Tom burst out laughing. "Good one, Morgan."

Joe said, "Your girlfriend can see me, and she likes my muscles." He looked at Mae, waiting for her to repeat his comment to Morgan. When he saw her shake her head at him, he winked at her. "Are you afraid to tell him how good I look? Think he'll be jealous?"

"10-4."

"Coward." Joe took off at a jog with the trunk on his shoulder.

Morgan cocked his head at Mae. "Did you just say 10-4?"

"I was answering Joe's question."

The men quickly filled the hole in the ground, and ran across the lawn, following the levitating trunk. By the time they reached the alleyway at the side of the property, Joe was loading the chest in the back of their SUV. Once they all jumped inside, Tom started the vehicle and sped down the alleyway.

Within minutes they were on the freeway, headed to Florida. Morgan pulled out his cell and punched Steele's number. When Steele answered, Morgan, said, "We got it."

"How long did it take?"

"About forty minutes. And thank goodness for Joe. He lifted the chest by himself and carried it to the car. The man is a beast."

"Morgan, tell G.I. Joe that we're lucky to have him on our side."

Morgan laughed. "That nickname is gonna stick. It's perfect—he's the original G.I. Joe."

COMING 2023

About the Author

Scarlett Dunn is the acclaimed author of several historical romance novels, including the McBride Brothers trilogy and the Langtry Sisters series. She has also written mysteries set in Kentucky's beautiful bourbon country.

Scarlett loves to transport readers to different eras and settings and enjoys writing in various genres. When she is not writing, she enjoys many outdoor activities as she plots her novels. The Mark Twain quote, "Find a job you enjoy doing, and you will never have to work a day in your life," resonates with her. "I can spend hours with my laptop, lost in my stories, and time goes by way too quickly."

Visit her website: www.scarlettdunn.com

Made in the USA
Columbia, SC
24 February 2023

12804188R00221